ALSO BY LOLITA FILES

*Scenes from a Sistah*
*Getting to the Good Part*
*Blind Ambitions*
*Child of God*

# Tastes
# Like
# Chicken

---

*A Novel*

# LOLITA
# FILES

SIMON & SCHUSTER PAPERBACKS
NEW YORK   LONDON   TORONTO   SYDNEY

SIMON & SCHUSTER PAPERBACKS
Rockefeller Center
1230 Avenue of the Americas
New York, NY 10020

First Simon & Schuster paperback edition 2005

SIMON & SCHUSTER PAPERBACKS and colophon are registered trademarks of Simon & Schuster, Inc.

Designed by Jan Pisciotta

For information regarding special discounts for bulk purchases, please contact Simon & Schuster Special Sales at 1-800-456-6798 or business@simonandschuster.com

Manufactured in the United States of America

10  9  8  7  6  5  4  3  2  1

The Library of Congress has cataloged the hardcover edition as follows:
Files, Lolita.
    Tastes like chicken : a novel / Lolita Files.
        p. cm.
      1. African American women—Fiction. 2. Los Angeles (Calif.)—
Fiction. 3. Female friendship—Fiction. I. Title.

PS3556.I4257T37 2003
813'.54—dc22                                    2003058986

ISBN 0-7432-4525-3
      0-7432-4526-1 (Pbk.)

This book is dedicated to my wonderful,
magnificent, splendiferous mother
—Lillie Belle Files—
the most beautiful woman
in the whole wide world.

# ACKNOWLEDGMENTS

To God for everything. To my family. To all my friends. To the fans who waited. To anyone who has ever supported me and to anyone who ever will. To my agent, editors, publisher, and all the bookstores. Thanks for everything. Have a wing and a smile.

Additional note: No chickens were harmed during the writing of this book, although many were consumed in their posthumous state.

# CONTENTS

**chicken** (chi•kᵊn) (origin, Middle English *chiken,* from Old English *cicen* young chicken; akin to Old English *cocc* cock)

*n* 1 a : the common domestic fowl (*Gallus gallus*) kept for its eggs or meat, especially a young one b: any of various similar or related birds or their young c: meat from such a bird 2 *slang* a : COWARD b : any of various contests in which the participants risk personal safety in order to see which one will give up first 3 *slang* : a young woman 4 [short for CHICKENSHIT] *vulgar slang* : petty details 5 : a young gay male, especially as sought by an older man 6 [short for CHICKENHEAD] *vulgar slang* (origin, hip-hop) a : a woman who seeks men for their money; GOLDDIGGER b : a promiscuous woman or girl c : a crack addict who performs oral sex for crack or money d : a young woman e: a female who is a talkative nuisance, seeming to "cluck" too much and wander about without purpose, like a chicken f : GROUPIE

*adj* 1 a : AFRAID b : TIMID; COWARDLY 2 *slang* a : insistent on petty details of duty or discipline b : PETTY; UNIMPORTANT

*intransitive verb* 1 [usually used with OUT] *slang* : to act in a cowardly manner; lose one's nerve

# PART 1

---

## *Cluct*

# Photo Finish

"Is it bad luck to be eaten the night before you get married?"

A uniform gasp cut through the room.

"Reesy," Misty said as she rose from the velvet sofa—one of three in the bridal chamber. "That's way too much information for you to be sharing."

She smoothed the front of her eggshell-colored dress and checked for wrinkles on the short train that trailed behind. She looked over at her best friend, Reesy, sitting at a small cherry-wood desk, wearing an elaborate ivory wedding gown, getting a manicure.

"It's bad enough you're going out of your way to do every-thing bass-ackwards," said Reesy's mother, who was uptight because she couldn't dictate the structure of the occasion. "Do you have to defy every convention? You're the only one who's supposed to be in any kind of white. This is your day. A bride should be the centerpiece of everything at her wedding."

Reesy glanced up at her mother, their eyes meeting in a brief standoff. Tyrene Snowden's severe gaze remained fixed upon her daughter. After a moment, Reesy laughed and looked down at her hands.

"Please, Tyrene. We all know it ain't no virgins in this room, but isn't it nice we get to pretend? Be happy and let everybody fake the funk for a minute. When was the last time you got to wear white?"

Tyrene tossed her turbaned head and walked to the window, the hem of her bone-hued African gown making a shuffling sound as her tiny heels clickety-clacked across the floor. The fact that Reesy never addressed her as "Mother" never seemed much more than one of several annoying traits of an insolent only child. Tyrene found herself resenting it now.

"I hope motherhood will finally make you grow up," she said, her back to everyone. "Everything in life is not a joke. Some situations warrant a level of respect."

"Who's laughing?" Reesy asked. "I'm not about to lie to anybody by walking down that aisle like I'm some sort of saint. How stupid is that anyway, wearing white when you're pregnant?"

She wished Tyrene would shut up. The last thing Reesy wanted today was the typical heaping plate of antagonism her mother dished out.

"You're only three and a half months," Tyrene replied. "It's not like your stomach is huge."

Tyrene was right. Reesy wouldn't appear pregnant to someone who didn't know. She was still all long limbs and taut muscle, her body not yet giving over to the softness of maternity. Her breasts were lush, but not stuffed, as was her perfect erstwhile stripper's rear. Reesy's tight, graceful dancer's body was still the envy of her friends.

"I'm pregnant, period," she said, "which means I'm not pure, which everybody, including my fiancé, already knows. Please. If I had a dollar for every man who's seen my naked—"

"Reesy." Grandma Tyler's brow was a series of subtle creases. Soft furrows, not the severe folds that come from the familiarity of worry. Her small, delicate frame was tucked in an armchair near the window, enveloped in chiffon. "Don't mess with your mama. Besides the fact that she's been waiting a long time to see

4

this day, she's right. It ain't fit to have everybody dressed like you." She picked an invisible piece of lint from her dress and flicked it away. "You s'posed to stand out. This day is for the bride."

"Bump all that bride business," Reesy answered. "The fact that I'm doing this at all is outrageous enough. And we're not all dressed exactly alike. You've got on ecru, Tyrene's in bone, Misty's in eggshell, they've got on cream." She pointed at Peggy James and Shawnee Warren, bridesmaids who had been in Misty's wedding just four months before. "And I've got on ivory. It's not all the same color. It's more like . . . variations on a theme."

"What's the difference?" Tyrene countered. "It all looks absurd."

"The difference is, I needed a show of solidarity from my girls, alright? Can I at least have that much on my wedding day?"

Reesy looked around the sumptuous chamber filled with towering vases of long-stemmed white lilies, row upon row of white roses, and endless bouquets of baby's breath. Everything white. The pungent floral scent that permeated the space was as overwhelming as the presence of the color itself.

"Look at all this stuff. Shades of white everywhere. Tyrene, your ability to whip up a last-minute extravaganza never ceases to amaze." Reesy's eyes scanned everyone, her yellow cheeks flushed with color. "Don't you feel like a virgin?" she said to Misty. "Don't y'all feel brand-new?"

Peggy and Shawnee gave each other a quick glance.

Tyrene looked back at her daughter with fire in her eyes. She needed to explode at something. The fact that her Reesy was desecrating such an important event and disregarding everything she had to say about it had her building to a rapid boil.

"Sometimes superstition is based in truth," she said.

"Oh my. Now the super-attorney who never tolerates foolish talk wants to scare me with ancient folklore. Ooooooh." Reesy waved her hands. "I ain't got on nothing old, nothing new, nothing borrowed, or nothing blue." She threw her head back and laughed, an over-the-top move that startled them all. She was deliberately taunting her mother now.

"Tyrene, think about how ridiculous you sound," she said. "If my marriage can be doomed because I wasn't the only one wearing a certain color, then it didn't stand a chance to begin with, now did it?"

The other women were quiet. The air was electric with the tension that hung between mother and daughter.

Tyrene didn't respond, but the sound of sucking teeth could be heard clear across the room.

"I'm only doing this wedding for y'all anyway," Reesy said. "If it was up to me, Dandre and I would be in Vegas right now. This Valentine's Day whooptee-woo is definitely not my style."

Tyrene huffed and clickety-clacked her tiny bone heels out of the room.

Reesy ignored her mother as Vixen Ames, the bridesmaid who had been giving her the manicure, grabbed her fingers so she could finish shaping the nails.

"Not too hard, Vix. These aren't acrylic."

Misty, still standing, walked over to Reesy and touched her braids, which were bound on her head in a topknot. Soft tendrils fell around her face.

"You're beautiful," Misty whispered above her.

She understood what Reesy must have been feeling. They'd been friends for more than twenty-five years, since the second grade. In the past few years, Misty had bounced from Fort Lauderdale, to Atlanta, and now New York, in search of the next best things in career and love. Reesy followed wherever she went, trying her hand at everything from exotic dancing, a disastrous turn as Misty's administrative assistant, and starring in a popular off-Broadway production.

The two were always side by side, looking out for each other.

After what felt like a lifetime of borderline-psychotic, drama-filled relationships, Misty had married the man she considered her soul mate in a touching ceremony just a few months before. The wedding had been a heady moment for her—a celebration of life, love, and expanded possibilities. She knew Reesy was just as giddy about Dandre, despite how cool she seemed now.

"I don't know why you're trying to act so hard," said Misty. "You know you're as excited about this as every one of us in here."

Reesy didn't answer. Misty leaned closer.

"If you're scared, say you're scared. I know you, remember? I know how you act when you're nervous about something."

Reesy looked up at her and grinned.

"The only thing that scares me is the thought that I'll never see another dick again."

Misty gave her head a gentle shove and walked away.

"You're never going to change, are you, girl?" Peggy said.

"What for? Just because I'm getting married? It's gonna take more than that to get me to hang up my hat."

The girls all laughed.

"So . . . who was it that ate your pussy last night?"

The question came from a raspy voice across the room. Grandma Tyler sat in the armchair, poker-faced, waiting. Everyone but Reesy was shocked.

"I'll never tell," she said.

"That means Dandre," Misty replied. "Don't let this old dog make y'all think she's got new tricks. That man has her strung out. Otherwise she wouldn't be here right now."

Reesy looked down, trying to hide the delirious joy squishing its way through every pore of her being. In a few more minutes, she would be Mrs. Dandre LeRon Hilliard.

The thought of it made her feel like she could fly.

Tyrene stood in the hall outside the bridal chamber, her lips pressed tight.

"Unfasten your trap, woman," her husband said, coming up behind her. "Today is a happy day. You've got to relax."

"How can I when our daughter never does anything right?" She was so upset, she was shaking.

"That's not fair," Tyrone replied. He leaned back in surprise when he felt the tremors running through her. "What's wrong with you, woman? Why on earth are you shaking so?"

"Because," she said. "That daughter of yours. Teresa is so contrary, always has been. She has to ruin everything, even her own wedding day."

Tyrone gave her a sympathetic smile.

"You're just angry because she didn't do things your way. That doesn't mean she's wrong. Let go, Tyrene. I have. Let her be free to be the woman she is. Sela."

*Sela* was his word for "amen." He'd been saying it for years. He'd never meant it as much as he did now.

Tyrone turned her around so she was facing him. Her eyes were glistening as she looked up at the distinguished, stalwart, confident man who had been by her side for more than forty years. His stout, imposing stature perfectly offset her wiry, diminutive figure.

Her gaze drifted to his beard. She knew every hair of it—the gray ones, the black ones, and the curve of the follicles that housed them. She knew where his bones were buried because they were her bones too.

They'd been revolutionaries, side by side as Black Panthers in the sixties. They'd even changed their names together; her birth name was Agnes Marie, his was Daavid. He was a man she'd made millions with. She'd built a stronghold with him in South Florida that was admired and unrivaled. There were no other law firms like theirs. They'd turned down judgeships and public office to be together to run their empire. And though she would never admit it, her strength came from him. Without Tyrone, Tyrene was but so much sound and fury, signifying nothing.

"Let our daughter go," he said. "That can be our gift to her."

"I don't know how," she said in a small voice. "I'm afraid to."

Tyrone grabbed her in a tight hug, the full beard brushing a familiar spot along the top of her cheek.

"She's got a good man," he said. "I'm as sure of that as I am of my own name. Relax, dear. We can't hold her anyway. Our baby girl broke loose from us a long time ago."

Tyrene leaned into him, her arms wrapped around his thick waist. She took a deep breath, then released it, letting her tense body go limp against her husband.

The door to the bridal chamber opened as Shawnee stepped out in search of the bathroom.

Tyrene's eyes met Reesy's. Both women's lips turned up in the same soft curve of a smile as the door between them inched itself closed.

The bridal party stood together at the front of the room.

The big-faced pastor beamed, his eyes closed, nodding his head in silent appreciation as the beautiful sounds of chamber music washed over everyone, engulfing them all in a big ball of bliss.

Tyrene held Tyrone's hand. Grandma Tyler clutched her palms together, shaking her head with heartfelt joy.

Dandre's father sat on the other side of the aisle, a flaxen-haired, nubile trinket a mere one-third of his sixty-six years attached to his elbow. One would never guess he was in his sixties. George Hilliard, M.D.—Hill to his friends—was a handsome man: six-four, fit, athletic, with a thick mane of salt-and-pepper curls trimmed neat and low and a well-manicured goatee that gave him an air of suave mystique and sophistication. He had thick brows and whimsical eyes that danced like he was on his way to a good time, or had just come from one.

He was going through what he called his white-girl phase. Alyssa, the bauble beside him, was ripped straight from the pages of *Blondes for Dummies* or *Tiger Woods's Women 101:* she had the requisite fake boobs, the perfect golden salon-induced tan, an ass that had been stair-stepped to life, the bluest eyes, the perkiest nose that money could buy, and hair so sun-streaked, it gave off a glare.

Hill had promised his friends in the know that this phase wouldn't last for long. He was a Howard professor, for goodness's sake, and felt an obligation to uphold the virtues of all things black and historical. He didn't dare sport his ofays, as he called them, anywhere near campus or around D.C. It was pure indoor action when he was on his own turf. But this wedding was in New York, a good-enough distance away, and Alyssa was a road-trip kind of girl. He intended to give her up in time, but she was so much fun. Alyssa was agile and willing, and so were some of her friends, so he was finding her a bit difficult to cut loose. At least for the nonce.

His hand was on her golden upper thigh as his head teetered in an awkward balancing act. He was trying to hold it as straight as he could. The struggle came compliments of a Courvoisier stupor gained at the glorious bachelor bash he'd given his only son the night before.

"That party was one for the books," he said to Alyssa, his voice a mix of gravel and stone.

"Ssssh," the pastor admonished, not bothering to investigate the source of the disruption. Tyrene rolled her eyes and harrumphed at Hill and his white girl. The two of them didn't sit well at all with her former revolutionary spirit.

Hill pinched his lips together and slid his hand a little higher up Alyssa's well-toned quads.

The chamber music played on.

It was a somber, sanctified moment, a tiny window of time slated to occur after the bride's arrival at the altar, just before the vows. The sentiment was one of magical intensity and unmitigated love among family and close friends.

Misty and Rick made eyes at each other, remembering their own recent nuptials. Dandre and Reesy stood close, side by side, the minute space between them tingling with the thrill of imminent merger.

"Wow, what's this?" a loud voice declared, piercing the staid atmosphere like a shark's unexpected fin slicing through shallow water.

It came from a slender woman wearing all black and a delicate black veil. She was sitting at the back of the room. She bent and reached under her pew and came up with a brown manila envelope. She made an elaborate display of tearing it open. A plump lady in an electric blue hat and dress sat beside her. She leaned in for a peek.

Reesy turned, annoyed at the interruption. This euphoric and hallowed period of musical silence was the only other thing she'd requested, besides having all the women wear some form of white.

"What's going on?" she asked no one in particular as she glanced back at the crowd.

"Oh . . . my . . . God," the veiled woman screamed, as she dropped a glossy eight-by-ten photo from the envelope into her lap.

The lady in the electric blue hat reached out with her plump little fingers and snatched the picture. She stared, her fat bottom lip hanging open as she turned the photo upside down, left-side-right, cocking her head like a dashboard pup.

"Lawd hammercy," she gasped, showing it to her husband, who was all teeth and grins at what he beheld. The plump lady in electric blue reached beneath her seat and came up with a manila envelope of her own, holding it aloft.

"Does anyone else have one of these?" she shouted.

Heads disappeared and popped up all around the church as everyone went in search of what the screaming woman had seen. Manila envelopes appeared in great number, and the vulgar sound of ripping paper clashed with the pristine melody the oblivious organist continued to play.

Reesy's heart went kerthunkety-plunk as she watched the brouhaha going on around her. She glanced at Dandre, her eyes full of question, but all she saw was confusion and a kind of primal, instinctive fear, something in his face that seemed to border on terror. The energy he gave off was, in an odd way, familiar; it was a feeling she faintly recalled having experienced before. Dandre was uncomfortable under her gaze. He turned to face the crowd behind him, in search of a clue as to what was going on around them.

Tyrene bent with reluctance and felt under the seat, coming up with an envelope of her own. Her narrowed eyes were on Dandre as the well-manicured talon of her right forefinger slid under the flap and sliced it open with an effortless sweep. Dandre's brow was beaded with sweat. He adjusted the tie that now seemed to grip his neck with the boldness of a noose. Tyrene inhaled deep, holding her breath as she removed the glossy photo.

It was her future son-in-law—in full naked regalia—his wet face and eager red tongue preoccupied, pressed front and center between long cocoa brown legs spread an astonishing width, worthy of the best contortions Universoul Circus had to offer. The gaping legs were attached to a cocoa brown woman with big, meaty breasts and an ass so magnificent, so huge, it loomed beneath her like an unnatural bubble. Dandre's penis was also busy, stuffed deep inside the mouth of a petite yellow girl with fiery-red locks and a raging thicket of black pubic hair.

She dropped the photo with both hands in a grand gesture, as if it were a grenade, raising her palms to the heavens in horrified supplication. The organist froze, his fingers immobile above the keys. Reesy now knew for certain that what was happening was something dreadful. She raced from the altar over to her mother and scooped the picture up from the floor.

"No, Reesy," Dandre said, remaining in place. "Put it down."

Reesy knelt holding the photo, her pupils dilating. She couldn't take her eyes off Dandre's dick, deep, deep, deep in the redhead's mouth. She noticed spit on the shaft and her stomach tilted. She was still kneeling when Tyrene, outraged, grabbed her in a hug, further causing her insides to simmer and churn. The place was abuzz with the sounds of raucous chatter as all eyes darted from Dandre to Reesy and back again.

"All men are muthafuckas," a voice proclaimed with ferocious disgust. It was Julian, the choreographer of *Black Barry's Pie*. The show was due to open on Broadway in a few months with Dandre as the primary backer, but the pregnant Reesy wouldn't be starring in it.

Julian was so spellbound by the photos, he couldn't look away. "Better to know he ain't shit now, Miss Thang, than to have to find out about it later."

His lover Tonio sat beside him, nodding in agreement. He pried the pictures from Julian's grip.

Someone in the church was crying, wailing and howling like a dying dog.

"This ain't right," whoever it was moaned. "God knows what this boy is doin' in this pitcha with these gals shonuf ain't right."

"It damn shole look like it feel good, though," mumbled the husband of the lady with the electric blue hat. She jabbed him hard in the stomach with her solid, fleshy elbow.

"Ooof," he said with a cough. He was silent after that, the blow knocked the wind out of him for a good five minutes.

"We can sue him, you know," Tyrene whispered to Reesy. She seemed energized with the satisfaction of knowing, had she been in control, things would have been better, different. These were the moments she lived for, the chance to do self-righteous damage control. Her daughter had been publicly wronged and, dammit, there was going to be hell to pay.

"He won't get away with it," she continued. "I told you all of us wearing white was bad luck. It was wrong to make a mockery of something as sacred as marriage."

Reesy glared at her mother.

"Get off me, you bitch," she said, pushing Tyrene out of the way. "You wanted this to happen." Tyrene fell back on her bone-colored African-gowned butt, her bone heels clickety-clacking first on the floor, then kicking in the air. Reesy stumbled forward up the aisle, her stomach toiling and troubling as she headed for the door.

Misty had been standing at the altar in shock. The sight of Reesy running rattled her from her daze. She rushed after her friend. Dandre made a move, but Rick grabbed him by the arm.

"Just stay put, man," he said, shaking his head. "This is a really bad scene. It can't get no worse than this."

Dandre stopped, his cheek twitching as he looked at Rick's hand on his arm.

"What the fuck just happened?" he asked. "I don't understand."

"This had to be one of your women, man," Rick said. "I would have thought by now you had your house in order."

"I did," Dandre said. "I thought I did."

"I'on know, this is some dumb shit. This is like some kind of urban myth that you hear about, but, you know, that kind of stuff doesn't ever happen for real."

They heard a sick, shrill scream outside.

Dandre broke away from Rick and ran out of the church into the brisk February air, followed by everyone else.

They arrived to see Misty in an awkward squat at the top of the church's front steps. Reesy lay at her feet in a heap of ivory chiffon, silk, and taffeta.

"She fell on the steps," Misty said, her faced streaked with mascara and tears. She looked up at Rick and Dandre. "Call 911. I can't get her to come to."

Rick pulled his cell phone from the pocket of his tux and dialed.

"How could you do this?" Misty asked Dandre in a pleading voice. "How could you do something like this to her . . . today?"

Dandre dropped to his knees, cradling Reesy's head in his arms.

"Get away from my daughter," Tyrone bellowed as he approached. "This is all your fault."

"This isn't my son's fault," a voice behind Tyrone answered. "This is the doing of some crazy bitch who doesn't know how to let go. My son can't control that. How the hell can you expect him to? These chickens are crazy nowadays."

"Oh, you're a fine one to talk," Tyrene said, getting in Hill's face. "We've heard about you, you corrupt son of a—"

"Tyrene."

Tyrone pulled his wife away, her heels clickety-clacking.

Dandre ignored them as he rocked Reesy in his arms with gentle motions. He felt as if he were walking in a fog.

"Lawd Jesus, my baby's bleeding."

It was Grandma Tyler. She pointed at Reesy's waist. The front of the ivory dress was stained with red flecks, and a small pool of blood was gathering beneath it.

Dandre's head was spinning. He could see the hemorrhaging, but it didn't register enough to make sense. The din above him was overpowering as indecipherable words flew around his head, along with random blows and boxes to his ears delivered by anonymous assailants. In the midst of the pandemonium, all he could hear was the clickety-clack of Tyrene's tiny bone shoes as she paced around him.

He focused on her feet as they passed him again, but now they didn't seem so very tiny. And the heels were black. Patent leather. Stiletto. With cocoa brown ankles sprouting out of them. He followed the legs all the way up as they passed.

The woman with the delicate black veil, not Tyrene, was attached to the ankles. His eyes met hers for a brief moment as she looked down at him sitting on the steps, holding the head of his bleeding, unconscious fiancée. Dandre watched the veiled woman as she walked away.

The swaying motion of her magnificent bubble ass was hypnotic.

"Is that who I think it is?" Rick asked as he came up beside him.

Dandre couldn't hear him above the roaring in his head.

# UFO's

All was dark for the first few seconds. Reesy blinked a couple of times and the hue of things changed a little, fading up into a deep boggy gray.

"Wha . . . ?" she said with a struggle and a cough. She tried to lean forward and everything did an instant spin. She fell back, blinking again, looking around for Vanna and Pat. They must be near. She already knew where the wheel was.

"Tweety?"

The raspy voice was a familiar anchor that made her relax a little. The room was still spinning, but it was beginning to slow. Something warm touched her right arm.

"Tweety, baby? We're right here. You hear me? You're gonna be okay."

Reesy blinked again and the bog began to lessen. She could make out a shape in the direction of the voice that spoke to her.

It was real short, whatever it was. A midget. It was a gray midget. A gray midget was next to her, touching her arm and calling her Tweety.

She recalled reading about something like this once, in a book by this writer, some guy, what was his name? Whitley something. She remembered the name of the book. *Commu-*

*nion*. This happened to him too. He woke up in the middle of the night and found gray things, midget things, touching him on the arm just like this. That's what it was. An alien. An alien was standing beside her and, to throw her off, was calling her Tweety like Grandma Tyler did.

Those damn aliens, she thought. That's how they rolled, the deceptive little fuckers.

She was relieved to know where she was, at least. She'd been abducted and this was the mothership, she supposed. That explained everything—the hazy room, her being groggy. She cleared her throat and coughed again.

"I thought the Grays were tall with big slanty eyes and the Blues were short with jumpsuits," she said to the midget. "Where's your jumpsuit? What are you, defective?" She breathed deep, exhausted and frustrated. "That's just my luck. I get abducted by some broke-down, B-team aliens. Just don't stick one of them damn needles in my belly. I'm pregnant. Y'all need to back up off the experiments with me."

"Oh Lawd," the raspy voice choked. "She done gon' crazy, y'all. Somebody, anybody, Lawd Jesus, my lil' Tweety done lost her mind."

A wail went up in the room and Reesy heard the sound of scurrying feet.

"Stop it," she said. "Stop trying to trick me like I'm not in outer space. I know how y'all get down. Quit pretending to be my grandma."

The shadowy midget grew taller and hovered close to Reesy's face.

"Tweety, baby, we ain't no aliens," the now-big midget rasped. "We's your family. You in the hospital, baby. You fell down the stairs at the church and bumped your head real hard." The big midget turned to something behind her. "I wonder if she done lost her mind. Y'all thank maybe she got a percussion or something?"

"Wha . . . ?" Reesy asked. "Fell at church? Bumped my head?

How did . . . ?" She blinked again and things began to come into clearer focus. The face above hers was yellow and, although a bit wizened, it wasn't gray. The eyes, full of tears, were not slanted, but warm and familiar. At the sight of her grandmother, Reesy felt better. She leaned forward to hug her. A sudden pain in her abdomen stopped her midway.

"No, Tweety," Grandma Tyler said, giving her a gentle push back onto the pillows of the hospital bed. "Lay down. You need to give your body a rest."

Reesy looked into her grandmother's face and saw something in it that roused a sense of panic.

"My baby," she said, grabbing Grandma Tyler's arm. "Is my baby okay?"

The sound of several scuffling feet came closer. Somewhere in the scuffle was the sound of clicking heels.

A hand touched Reesy's left arm and another familiar voice spoke to her.

"Reesy, just lay back. The doctor wants you to rest. You had a bad fall, but you're going to be fine."

Reesy looked up into Misty's teary face. She wondered why everyone around her was crying in the midst of trying to reassure her that she was going to be okay.

"I hope he burns in hell for this, doing this to my daughter," a sharp voice uttered in the background. The sound of sharp heels made their way across the floor again.

"Hope who burns in hell?" Reesy asked. "What happened? Is my baby okay?"

She looked to Grandma Tyler for an answer, but the older woman just sank back into the chair she'd been sitting in next to the bed, still clasping her granddaughter's hand.

"Misty?" Reesy asked, turning to her left. "Is my baby okay? Did I have a miscarriage? Will you tell me?"

Misty gazed into her friend's eyes, knowing she would want to hear the truth if she were in her position.

"You lost the baby, Reesy," she said, clutching her hand with both of hers. "It was a pretty bad fall."

"Gotdammit," Grandma Tyler said. "That fuckin' boy needs his ass whooped good."

"Why'd you tell her?" Tyrene screeched.

"Because she wanted to know," Misty said. "You can't hide it from her forever."

Reesy closed her eyes, pushing back salty water that squished out anyway. She took three deep breaths and opened them again. Misty waited for the sobs to commence, but they didn't.

"That bastard's gonna pay for this," Tyrene declared in the background, her hands flying about. "She could have died because of his nonsense. Pictures in the church, that woman in black with that big ol' ass. And what about the girl with the red hair sucking on him? Everybody in there got a good look at his, his . . . his business."

"Big business," Grandma Tyler muttered. "Hung like a horse, he was. Surprised he ain't rip Tweety in half with that."

"Umph," said Julian under his breath. "Rip me in half."

"Who you want to rip you in half?" asked a jealous Tonio. "I thought you said all men were muthafuckas."

"Stop it, all of you," Misty said.

"What kind of person would let himself be photographed doing those kinds of ungodly things?" Tyrene inquired. "A pervert, that's who. A psycho. He did us all a favor. Teresa could have been marrying a rapist, for all we know."

"He's not a rapist," Misty said.

"How do you know?" Tyrene barked. "Family and friends are always the last to find out. I've seen plenty of supposed upstanding men with nasty habits hiding in their closets. Look at that fool you lived with that used to work at our firm. Sucking on your breasts and wetting the bed like a big ol' overgrown baby. How long did it take you to find out that he had that in him? A good three years, if I remember, and you were right there in the house with him."

Misty's jaw fell open and she glanced at Reesy, whose eyes were now closed again.

"Yeah, I knew about it," Tyrene said. "You think we'd want to keep a nut like that on our payroll? It's a good thing he quit before we had a chance to fire him."

Reesy heard something that sounded like her father clearing his throat.

"It's a crazy world out there, Tyrone," his wife continued. "You and I both know, as bad as this situation seems, our daughter was just saved from life with a lunatic-rapist-freaknasty-orgymonger."

Reesy wondered where her mother learned the word "freaknasty."

A door squeaked open.

"Can I see her?" asked a voice that struck an immediate chord. "Is she awake? I just want to know if she's okay." Reesy's skin bristled with an unnatural chill.

"Get him out of here," Tyrene screamed. The sound of her voice resonated throughout the otherwise quiet floor.

A team of nurses rushed into the room to squash the ruckus. Everyone was told to leave. That many people shouldn't have been in the room anyway, they were informed. It was a small space in the emergency section, and it wasn't designed for clutter or a crowd. The doctor had promised Tyrene that Reesy would be moved to a larger room later in the day.

One of the nurses, a buxom woman with intolerant eyes and a Jersey accent, lingered behind to make sure everyone left the room.

"Can these two stay?" Reesy asked, straining to be heard. "Please?"

She clutched Grandma Tyler and Misty's hands.

"You need to rest, Miss Snowden," the nurse said. She motioned toward the door for the two women to go. "You've had people with you all day. The sooner you rest, the quicker you'll be outta here."

"Let my grandma and my girlfriend stay," Reesy said. "Please." She tried to hide her saddened surprise at hearing the woman use her maiden name. She had planned on taking Dandre's surname, Hilliard, with no hyphenations. She was looking forward to doing everything the traditional way. But she was still Teresa Snowden and—from the looks of all the disaster around her, the stone in her heart, and the void in her womb— she was going to stay that way.

"They have to leave," the nurse replied, stoic as she went about escorting the others from the room. "There's been too much disruption in here already."

"Have a heart," Reesy pleaded. "I just lost my baby." The nurse stopped what she was doing, turned, and looked at her. Their eyes met. "Today was supposed to be my wedding day."

The nurse glanced over at the big, fluffy dress stuffed into the tiny closet.

"Fine," she said in a softer tone. "But there better not be any more disturbances in here."

"There won't be," said Misty.

The nurse nodded, pursed her lips, and left the room.

Two hours later, Tyrone and Tyrene were still sitting in the waiting room of the emergency area. Dandre and Rick sat in a far corner, out of harm's way. Mary, Rick's administrative assistant, sat with them. She too had been the recipient of an unwarranted dose of Tyrene's hate-gazes. Her long chestnut brown hair was pulled over her right shoulder and hung way past her elbow. She was a pretty girl with a turned-up nose, a happy face, and a loyal heart. She considered Reesy a dear friend, but Tyrene didn't seem concerned about that.

Julian and Tonio were sitting together, also away from everyone. Tonio was chastising him about something; it was apparent in their body language. Julian's arms were folded, his thoughts adrift. He was worried about Reesy, and the intensity of the day—including that eye-popping photo of a naked Dandre, which he found exquisite—had set off within him a series of convoluted, colliding feelings. Tonio leaned forward in his seat, his lips rapid-fire, his finger a pendulum moving in time to his mouth's beat. Julian rolled his eyes and cocked his legs open so his ubiquitous bulge could breathe. He loved it when they fought. He couldn't wait to get Tonio out of there so he could work out some of his inner conflict.

Hill sat two seats down from Reesy's parents, still struggling with the dregs of his hangover from the bachelor party. The melee at the church had reduced the headache to a dull thump, but it was there nonetheless, threatening to revisit. He was doing his best to avoid Tyrene's unforgiving glare. Alyssa was awaiting his return back at the Hotel Parker Meridien, where all the out-of-town guests—and some of the in-town ones—were staying, compliments of Hill. He didn't think it wise for her to remain at the hospital. Tyrene's venom had proved much too potent for Alyssa to withstand. After an assortment of "white hussy"s and "slutty skank"s had been fired at the girl, Hill had given her cab fare and sent her on her way.

After her exit, he and Tyrene exchanged another round of words, more than he cared to remember. He wasn't quite sure why she was so angry at him. He didn't recall doing anything that would cause her offense, and Reesy's falling at the church was an accident, everyone could see that.

Dandre had told him weeks ago that his soon-to-be mother-in-law was a bit contentious. In retrospect, Hill realized his son had been both generous and kind in his description. Tyrene said some pretty foul things to him. Amid the clamor of all the other people with emergencies crowding into the space, fighting for attention, her shrill bitching superseded everything.

"Your son did this," she said. "What do you have to say about that?"

When Hill didn't respond fast enough, she kept at him.

"I'm glad the wedding was interrupted," said Tyrene, shaking her finger in his face. "You and your son have the morals of eels."

Hill stepped away from her, confused, making a mental note to look into the lifestyles of the slick and slithery.

It took tremendous effort from Tyrone, three hospital administrators, and a threat from security to bar her from the premises to tone her down. Hill was astonished at so much ferocity coming from such a small package. All that volatility, the fireworks. She was a rocket, but nice and compact. Like a little Cocola bottle about to go off.

Too bad she's so evil, he thought. He considered her quite attractive and spunky, for an older bird. She had to be in her late fifties or so, but she was sexy. She was petite with a tight body. A real spinner. And with the way she'd cursed at him, he figured she must be hellfire once you got her in the sack. Hill glanced at her sidelong and found Tyrene still staring at him, her mouth twisted like that of a viper about to spit acid.

He cleared his throat and looked away. Whatever. He could show her some tricks that he bet Big Man sitting next to her didn't know, but oh well. He liked his meat young and tender anyway. Pullets, not hens. They had to be robust, the flush of life and excitement still fresh in their skin, at the peak of health and sexual pliability.

With the exception of one person, Hill had never been with what he considered an older broad, which meant anyone above the age of thirty. He had been thirty-three when his wife died in childbirth. It took him five years to recover from her loss. He'd felt such an overwhelming sense of guilt, as if he had somehow failed her and his son. She had been the love of his life. No one else had come close since, and he knew, at sixty-six, no one else ever would.

They'd been together for twelve years, since his junior year in college, when she died. He married Eileen Merrill—a tall, elegant, pretty brown girl with dimples and a delicate bone structure—a week after they both graduated. They agreed to wait for him to complete medical school and his internship before they had children. Eileen was patient, loving, supportive, the perfect doctor's wife. Hill doted on her, supplying every creature comfort that was within, and sometimes beyond, his means. He insisted that she not work. It wasn't right, he said, for a doctor to have a wife who took care of anything but her family's needs.

Everything in their lives went according to plan, except for one slipup when he was thirty. Eileen became pregnant while he was still an intern. She miscarried. The pregnancy had been ectopic, the egg lodged and grew in Eileen's fallopian tube instead of her uterus. The tube ruptured, sending her to the emergency room in excruciating pain. Her then-doctor said it was a miracle the damage hadn't resulted in the need for a full hysterectomy. There was a great deal of scarring, and since she was left with just one fallopian tube, he doubted she would ever get pregnant again; and if she did, it wouldn't be easy. His prognosis for her ability to carry a child to term was even bleaker.

Three years later, Hill had his own practice and was doctor to his wife. Despite the earlier prediction, she was pregnant again, and they were being careful about everything. He was the attending obstetrician. Eileen had experienced many complications, but she and the baby were fine. Hill had seen her through what he thought was the hump—a rough nine months that included a lot of hand-holding, morning, noon, and night sickness, a battery of rashes, unidentified aches and pains, and an underwhelming appetite. But there in the hospital, his wife yielding before him with their entire future in his hands, he had failed her.

For starters, the cord was wrapped around the baby's throat. Tiny Dandre emerged blue and asphyxiated, and had to be resuscitated back to life. Then Eileen began hemorrhaging, and all the blood-clotting medicines, textbook solutions, and expert assists of Hill's short-lived career couldn't save her. Eileen's death on the birthing bed was as shocking to him as the sight of the newborn in his hands that he'd help bring into the world.

Hill had since committed himself to a lifetime of saving mothers and babies, and making sure his son wanted for nothing. Beyond that he liked two other things: acquiring things and girls, girls, girls. Nothing younger than nineteen, and, for certain, nothing older than thirty. He liked his chicken hot out the grease.

Nope, he hadn't been with another woman anywhere close to Eileen's age since her death. She'd become iconic to him. But just as he had canonized her in memory, her age had become his greatest taboo. Something about her being older than thirty had planted the subtle seed in Hill's mind that she hadn't been sturdy enough. That, past the age of twenty-nine, she couldn't take what nature had to dish out.

Reesy was thirty-two, and she'd fallen down the stairs at church and lost the baby. But he'd seen twenty-somethings take similar falls and lose babies too. In fact, he had tons of statistical data and firsthand experience that proved his over-thirty theory wrong on many counts. But there was that perpetual image of the delicate Eileen, thirty-three, bloody, and dying right in front of him. That vision influenced his thoughts more than any rational statistics could ever hope to. It was the thing that always prevailed.

But this little hen in the bone-colored turban was triggering something randy in him. Made his old woody want to peck her. Perhaps it's the Courvoisier talking, he wondered, or perhaps his white-girl phase was passing. In a fleeting moment of panic, he prayed he wasn't entering an old-broad stage.

Hill could hear her yammering in Dandre's direction now, but he was too exhausted to go to his son's aid. Rick was there.

He'd run interference. Hill checked out the cutie sitting with them, but his loins were not stirred. He smirked. The white-girl phase must be passing indeed.

No old broads, no old broads, he chanted in silence. He cut his eyes at Tyrene and felt his manhood swell.

But she's old, he lamented. And she's evil.

"Pipe down, Tyrene," Tyrone said in a booming voice. "This is a hospital, for God's sake. Screaming at everybody won't solve anything."

And she's married, Hill noted. She's old, she's mean, and she's married.

# I See London,
# I See France

Reesy needed some ice chips.

"I'll go get it," Misty said.

"Thanks, Miss Divine."

Misty smiled. Reesy hadn't called her that in a while. That playground nickname had survived many moments. Just hearing her say it spoke volumes of trust.

Reesy watched Misty take a big plastic cup from the table beside the bed. She was used to being Misty's anchor in times of emotional crisis. It felt strange being on the receiving end.

"Be right back, sweetie," Misty said as she pushed the door open and disappeared down the hall.

"You okay?"

Misty slid into the chair beside her husband. She had just given Tyrone and Tyrene an update.

"Yeah, baby, I'm fine," Rick said, kissing her on the forehead.

"How's Reesy?" Dandre asked, his eyes red, his face desperate. She could tell he was torn up about what had happened, but she didn't know how to help him. Fate had played itself out and his past had caught up with him in the most horrid way.

"She's alright. You know. About as alright as a person can be in the face of something like this."

Dandre dropped his head and began to sob into his hands.

"You need to cry," Tyrene yelled.

Mary rubbed his back.

"It's okay, Dandre," Misty said. "She's alright, really. I came out to get her some ice chips. Her mouth's a little dry."

"Can I take it to her?" he asked, looking up with wet lashes. A five o'clock shadow was beginning a slow crawl across his face.

"No, that won't fly right about now," Misty said. "She doesn't want to see you. You have to understand that. This day was a lot for anybody to swallow. It was extremely hard on her."

He looked like a man who'd just been given a death sentence.

"But I lost a child too," he said. "No one seems to get that. I love Reesy so much. I was looking forward to our life together. I slept with my hand on her stomach every night. Did she tell you that? We made life together. And just like that, it got taken away."

Dandre's sobs were so heavy, Misty got up and went over to him and held him as he cried. Hill watched them from across the room, remembering his own awful moments in the hospital with Eileen. It dawned on him that his son was the same age he had been when she died.

He went over to them. Tyrene watched him as he strode across the room.

"That's his role model," she said to Tyrone. "That's where he learned everything he knows. From Pervert Senior."

"Just stop it, would you?" he said. "Everybody's hurting here. There's no need to point fingers."

"So you're saying those pictures didn't bother you?" she asked. "You're saying it's okay that our daughter marry a man who has orgies with women with red hair and black privates?"

The inside of Tyrone's head felt like it was roaring with the waves of a violent ocean. Tyrene's natter had taken its toll. He stood, planning to stretch his legs and body in an effort to clear his mind.

"What are you doing?" Tyrene asked. "Sit back down here, Tyrone. I'm talking to you."

She yanked at his hand and Tyrone felt something inside himself snap. He pulled away, his eyes stern.

"No, you didn't just snatch your hand from me," she said through gritted teeth, as though reprimanding a child.

"Fuck you, Tyrene," he replied, his voice a loud boom that caught the attention of everyone.

Tyrene uttered a small, strangled cry of surprise. Her mouth remained open as she watched her husband walk away over to the automatic doors and out of the building. He stood a few feet from the doors with his eyes closed, breathing in the chill evening air.

Tyrene couldn't believe he'd left her there. It shut her down cold. It had always been the two of them against everything. Her mouth clamped shut as she tapped her foot against the worn linoleum.

"I need to get back to the room," Misty said. "Dandre, everything's gonna be alright, okay? Just give this some time. Let God work it out."

Dandre nodded as his father stood in front of him. Hill had given him a handkerchief and Dandre was dabbing at fresh tears. Misty watched the two of them, wondering why something like this had to happen. They were both good-looking, compassionate black men. Both had chased way too much tail in their day. Heck, she thought, Dr. Hilliard was still doing it. As for Dandre, Misty knew he loved Reesy with everything in him and that his bed-hopping days were long over.

What she knew more than anything, though, was that as

fucked up as karma could be, karma was real. It always collected, and it didn't give a rat's ass how much you'd cleaned up your act and become a better person.

Tyrone was still outside. Tyrene watched him through the windows as he leaned against the building, frost coming from his lips. He didn't look like he had any plans to come in soon. It offended her to think that he'd rather weather the cold than be inside with her. She'd expected him to be angrier about what had happened to Reesy. This was all Dandre's fault. She figured Tyrone would have cracked his skull open by now, and his irresponsible father's. Instead, he had directed his anger at her.

"It's gonna be okay, son," Hill assured Dandre. "All we can do is just make sure she gets better, and then, if you really love this woman—"

"I do," Dandre said. "I love her more than I ever thought I could love somebody."

"—then if you really love her, you do everything in your power to get her back. You bend over backwards and forwards and upside down. I'd do anything to have your mother back. I lost her because I didn't know enough. I lost her because I thought I knew everything."

"Pops, that was out of your hands."

Hill held his palm up.

"We don't know that. I was green. I had no business being her doctor. But you have a chance to do things different. Fight for Reesy. Don't pressure her. Just bide your time. You can get her back. If she really loves you, you can get her back."

Rick and Mary watched the two of them. Mary leaned her head on Rick's shoulder and began to cry. He patted her head, thanking God that this was not his and Misty's situation.

\* \* \*

Tyrene watched Tyrone bum a cigarette from a scurvy-looking woman outside. He hadn't smoked in fifteen years. Her nerves were fraying. Her foot was tapping in double time.

"Where's my ice?"

"Oh shit," Misty said. "I forgot it. I stopped on my way to check on everybody. Dandre's so torn up, it threw me off. I feel so bad for him."

"Is he more torn up than me?" Reesy asked, her expression cold. "Is his womb ravaged? Was he humiliated? Did he fall down a flight of concrete stairs?"

"Stop it, Reesy. His head is fucked up. Sorry, Grandma Tyler."

"That's okay, baby," Grandma Tyler said. "If I was him, I'd be fucked up too."

Reesy laughed in spite of herself.

"Let me go get your ice," Misty said.

"Do me a favor first."

"What's that?"

"Could you mash that dress into the closet and pull it closed so that I don't have to see it?"

"Sure," said Misty.

Reesy glanced at the ring on her left finger. It sparkled.

This has to come off, she thought. As soon as she got her energy up, the awful reminder had to go.

Tyrene was standing at the window now, rapping at the glass, trying to get Tyrone's attention. He ignored her and bummed another cigarette. No one was talking to her, not even her own husband. She was the pariah while Dandre had a huddle of friends and family around him. She was frightened, although she disguised it with rage.

"I'm going to the vending machine," Hill said. "Anybody want anything? A soda, bottled water, some chips, maybe?"

"I could do with a Coke," Rick said.

"Me too," said Mary.

"Dandre? You want something?"

"Nah, Pops," he said in a sad voice. "I'm straight."

"I'll bring you back something anyhow," Hill said, giving Dandre a pat on the back. "Relax, son. Cut yourself a break."

Hill had just put a dollar in change in the machine. He pressed the button for a Coke, but nothing came out.

"You're a son of a bitch," the voice behind him said. "I rue the day you and your son were ever born."

Hill took a deep breath and kept pressing buttons. He'd never even heard the door to the vending room open. Both buttons for Coke proved empty. Sprite was empty too. He pushed the button for Dr Pepper. Nothing.

"If you think this whole situation is going to go unanswered, you've got the wrong person, buddy. You and your son fucked with the wrong woman when you fucked with me."

Hill was tired. And thirsty. And, good grief, now his dick was hard. He punched the button for Squirt. Nothing. Dasani. Nothing. Every single button was lit up red.

"Fuck. The whole damn machine is dry."

He hit the lever to get his change back. Nothing.

"You better face me and answer these charges. I'm thinking of taking this to court. I'm sure there are civil penalties, if not criminal. My daughter almost died today."

Hill didn't want to turn around. He couldn't. That damn turban. The tight body. Those itty-bitty bony shoes.

Tyrene snatched at his arm, forcing his hand. He was facing her now. More like looking down at her. Her eyes were elsewhere.

"What the . . . ? You nasty muthafucka. What is that in the front of your pants?"

It was obvious what it was. They didn't make tuxes with

34

enough slack to hide what he had going on. His crotch was tented like a Boy Scout camp.

To her horror, Tyrene felt her body flush with excitement. Stunned at the reaction, she kept talking in the hopes that it would pass.

"This is why my daughter's in this situation now," Tyrene ranted. "You and your horny son. Just look at you. You're a fucking disgrace."

Hill tried to get past her, but she pinned him in, her thoughts riveted to his battle of the bulge.

"You're going to jail for this. I swear to God on my mother's soul, if I can help it, I'm going to sue you and your son and your practice, and take you for everything—"

His mouth was on hers before she knew what was happening. Before he knew what was happening, she was kissing him back.

Hill melted into her, scooping her small frame up in his bigness. She felt just as tight and wiry as she looked. Her heels dangled high off the floor.

Tyrene rubbed his head with both hands and twisted her face back and forth as their tongues snaked around each other in outrage, lust, desperation, and unabashed curiosity. There was an oak brown regulation table against the wall. He carried her over to it and sat her down. He stood between her legs, pressing against the African gown, holding her face, kissing her hard, running his hands up and down her shoulders and across her breasts. One of her hands was now wrapped around the tent.

When she followed him into the vending room, it was to do what her husband couldn't. That was her plan. Her senses were already heightened by the loss of a grandchild, maternal worry, misdirected rage, and temporary spousal abandonment that had resulted in inexpressible exasperation. The wedding she had been looking forward to with such excitement had been foiled by the son of the man in front of her. In her mind, there were only two logical things for her to do, one of which involved hitting him.

She hadn't expected to respond to Hill's kiss, but his mouth was hot, his tongue pushy and probing. His dick in her hand was rigid—a rod of granite that exemplified power, passion, and manhood. It was a flash to the days of thunder she'd first experienced with Tyrone, back when he used to exude so much testosterone it seemed beyond his control.

Right now, her husband was somewhere outside the hospital taking secondhand cancer sticks from firsthand losers. Hill was in front of her now, helpless, it seemed, to the power of his own volcanic libido. Tyrene realized that she hadn't chosen the situation. She would never, of her own volition, have initiated an act of infidelity. But she hadn't initiated this—and now that she was in it, she didn't want to push it away.

"Ohmygoh . . . ," she moaned against his tongue.

"Oh . . . my . . . God," Misty cried, the plastic cup dropping to the floor. "What the hell is going on in here?"

Hill stepped back from Tyrene, embarrassed, emboldened, erect. He stammered something and staggered his way past Misty, out the door.

Misty glared at Tyrene, then turned to leave. Tyrene raced like a greyhound to the door and blocked it.

"As God is my witness, Armistice Fine. . . ."

Misty cut her off.

"My last name is Hodges, Mrs. Snowden. I'm married now. Like you are—remember?"

Tyrene pushed her back into the vending room and kicked the door closed with her heel.

"Just hold on a minute, young lady—"

"How could you do this?" Misty asked. "How long have you been doing things like this?"

Tyrene didn't know which hat to put on, the one for a lawyer or the one that fit the hysterical mother. She was on her own. Asking for Tyrone's help was not an option in this situation.

"Oh, what a fix, what a fix, what a fix," she complained, opting to go the lawyer route. "That young man has gotten us all into quite a quandary today."

Misty leaned against the door, annoyed and indignant as she eyed Tyrene. Reesy's mother had always been the bastion of self-righteousness and judgment. Any hint at scandal, overt sexuality, covert sexuality—sexuality, period—had resulted in lectures and lambastings since time immemorial. Tyrene had scolded Misty for things Misty's own mother let pass. To catch her now in the act of something as inconceivable as tongue wrestling and groping Dandre's father was beyond shocking. Misty was uncertain what to do, but she wanted to protect Reesy. The last thing her best friend needed right now was to know that her mother wasn't the puritanical piece of terror they'd imagined her to be all these years.

"This isn't Dandre's fault, Mrs. Snowden," she said. "What did he have to do with you being holed up down here in the clinch with his dad? God, I wish I'd hadn't seen that," she said, shaking her head as if the action would dislodge the memory. "Just when I thought this day couldn't get any worse . . ."

Misty turned her head in disgust. She didn't want to even look at Tyrene. She stooped to get the plastic cup.

"Of course it's his fault," Tyrene said. "If it weren't for him, my daughter wouldn't be in the hospital. She wouldn't have lost the baby. She wouldn't have even been pregnant, if you want to take it to its simplest denominator. That Dandre brought all this on us. I . . . I . . . I was hysterical just now." Her eyes were darting all over the place and her hands were following suit. Misty was surprised that, for all Tyrene's years as an attorney, she didn't make a credible defendant.

"I don't know what came over me," she yammered. "I came looking for coffee. I didn't know he was in here. He grabbed me . . . I don't know . . . like he was trying to console me or some-thing, like I wanted his filthy hands on me. Next thing you know, he copped a feel."

"Oh, c'mon, Tyrene," said Misty, now throwing up her hands. "Give me a break. Please. You were the one with his dick in your hand."

Tyrene slapped her. Misty's face stung a vibrant red, as rare as steak tartare.

"Don't you ever let me hear you utter those words again, young lady." Tyrene's teeth were clenched.

Misty's eyes were glazed over when she grabbed the door-knob and snatched it open. She didn't look back as the door hit the wall with a slam and bounced shut with equal fury. Her stomach did the hula. The thought of everything was making her sick.

"Fuckfuckfuck," Tyrene said. "Fuckshitdamn. Fuckfuckfuck."

She paced in the vending room, her body riddled with panic. She wanted to cry, but the act had become so foreign to her, she didn't know how to do it. She kicked the Coke machine. Hill's change fell out.

Halfway down the hall, Misty realized she'd forgotten to get the ice again.

## Ho-tel, Mo-tel,
## Parker Meridi-en

"I hope they let me go home in the morning."

"Yeah, I'll bet."

Reesy stared at Misty sitting in the chair to her left. Grandma Tyler was asleep in the chair to her right, mouth open, her delicate yellow head tipped back against the cushion like an old canary waiting for its ration of worms.

Misty was staring off into nothing. Reesy ended up asking the nurse for the ice chips after Misty returned with just a stupefied expression and collapsed in the chair.

"So everybody's still in the waiting room?"

"For real," said Misty, her voice empty.

Reesy squinted her eyes. Something was not right with her friend.

"I think I just shat on myself," she said.

"Most definitely," Misty answered, still gazing at the air. "I can do that. No problem."

Reesy leaned forward a little so she could see her face. When she moved, it didn't hurt as bad as it had when she'd first awakened. The last set of painkillers had kicked in, and she was feeling more like a somewhat tired version of her former self than anything else.

Misty's cheek was flushed red. Just one cheek. Like she was breaking out in some sort of asymmetrical rash.

Grandma Tyler snorted and shifted her head. She didn't wake up. She cleared her throat and, within seconds, she was snoring.

"Sure," Misty said in response to the rumbles.

Now Reesy *knew* something was wrong.

Grandma Tyler snored louder. Misty looked up at Reesy.

"Why are you sitting like that?" she scolded. "Lean back before you hurt yourself." She stood and tried to get Reesy to settle back into the pillows.

"I'm fine," Reesy said, pushing her hands away. "I need to try to sit up instead of laying down. If they let me out tomorrow, I'll be moving around more anyway."

"They're letting you out tomorrow?"

Reesy eyed her friend. Misty's thick hair had been pulled back into a sleek bun, but now the bun was sprouting weeds. It could use a good brushing. She was still in her wedding attire, as was Grandma Tyler and everyone else out in the waiting room. There were a few spots of dried blood on the front of her dress. Most of her makeup was askew. What was left of her mascara was smudged raccoon-style. Her blush was splotchy and there was a hint of rose where her lipstick had once been. The natural beauty mark on her left cheek was the only thing that was still intact. She seemed exhausted and perplexed.

"You need to go home," Reesy said.

"What?"

The nurse came in. It wasn't their Jersey buxom buddy, but a pretty, middle-aged black woman with narrow eyes and a face that meant business, *Chez Rattagan, R.N.,* her badge read.

"Visiting hours are almost over," she said with a distinct West Indian accent. "Your guests are going to have to leave by nine o'clock."

"But the other nurse told me these two could stay."

"I don't know anything about that," said the woman. "Your visitors have to go. The doctor says he plans to release you in the morning, first thing."

"Then why won't he just release me now?"

"You need to get more antibiotics into you to make sure you're well enough to be checked out."

Grandma Tyler snorted herself out of sleep.

"Go where?" she grumbled, adjusting herself.

"Visiting hours are over, Grandma," Misty said. "You and I are gonna have to leave."

"You've got fifteen minutes," Nurse Rattagan said in her sharp voice. Grandma Tyler mumbled something under her breath as the nurse walked away.

"What'd you say?" Nurse Rattagan asked, whipping around. Grandma Tyler was silent. Nurse Rattagan made a sucking noise as she talked to herself. "Ev'ry night me haffe deal wit' dis nonsense. Chuh."

A new nurse came in and reminded them that visiting hours were over.

"I'll be okay," Reesy assured them. "Really. The two of you need to get some rest." She turned to Misty, her eyes penetrating. "Especially you. You look like you're the one that should be laying in this bed. You didn't seem this tired earlier. Are you feeling okay?"

"I'm fine," Misty said, avoiding her gaze. "I guess everything's just catching up with me. It was a lot today. Too much. I still think I should ask the doctor if he'll let me stay here tonight with you. I don't feel right leaving you alone."

"Me neither," said Grandma Tyler.

"Both of you, go," Reesy said. "You're both staying at the hotel, right? Misty, you and Rick aren't driving all the way back to Connecticut tonight, are you?"

Misty rubbed the back of her neck, looking off at anything but her friend.

"No. We figured it would be a pretty full day, so we have a room at the Parker Meridien, just like everybody else. Dre's dad . . ."

As she said the words, a vision of Tyrene with her hand around Hill's dick flashed through her head. Her mouth grew salty and began to water. She coughed, tried to clear her throat, then rushed into the bathroom.

Reesy and Grandma Tyler stared in her direction as they listened to her heaving what sounded like thick spurts of water and foam.

"Get her out of here," Reesy said to Grandma Tyler. "She needs to rest as much as I do."

"This hospital is making all-a us sick," kvetched Grandma Tyler. "Who knows what she done caught walking round up in here. That might be that Ebola. They never did cure that, you know. They just stopped talkin' 'bout it, like folks'll forget. Next thing you know, your arm falls off. All them germs colliding up in here, no tellin' what's wrong with that gal."

"She ain't got no Ebola, lady," Reesy said with a laugh. She couldn't believe her grandmother was able to bring that out of her on such a tragic day. "We'd hear her heaving up organs if that was the case. She just needs to go home."

Misty wandered out of the bathroom, too embarrassed to make eye contact with either of them.

"Let's go, Grandma Tyler," Misty said. "Before that woman comes back in here."

"Gimme tum tugar, Tweety," the old lady said, hugging Reesy close and kissing her on the cheek. "This gon' all get better. God'll fix it, fo' sho'. It'll be all over in the morning."

Misty grabbed the old bird's arm and pulled her toward the door.

"You wash your hands?" Grandma Tyler said to Misty, looking sidelong at the fingers that were touching her arm.

"G'night, Reesy," Misty said over her shoulder. "We'll be back first thing in the morning."

Reesy was silent, watching Misty guide Grandma Tyler away. She waited until they were almost out of the room before she spoke again.

"Miss Divine . . . aren't you gonna hug me good-bye?"

Misty's eyes dropped in despair as she stared at the hallway beckoning in front of her.

"Of course."

She put on the best face she could muster as she walked back across the room, the poor facsimile of a smile giving her away.

"G'night, girl," she said, hugging Reesy tight. "This is all gonna pass. We're gonna get through this together, just like we've done with everything else in our lives."

"I know," said Reesy. She kissed Misty on the cheek that was flushed. "I love you."

"I love you too," Misty said with a slight flinch.

Reesy's lips moved over to Misty's hostage ear. This time her words came as a whisper.

"I know there's something else wrong, and you're gonna tell me soon enough. If I find out on my own and it's something really bad that you were tryna keep from me, there's gonna be hell to pay, Miss Divine. I swear to God. I'm not playing."

The nurse's eyes were razor thin as she stood beside Grandma Tyler at the door. Misty darted past them so fast, all they saw was the blur of her eggshell dress.

Hill sat on the edge of his bed at the Parker Meridien, his head in his hands, wondering why Alyssa's fourth attempt at a blow job was still not working.

"I think I'm going downstairs for a drink."

"Would you like me to come with?" asked a naked Alyssa, getting up from the floor.

Hill considered the young woman in front of him. That lilt in her voice seemed annoying now. And her nose. He wanted to flatten it into something more Bantu.

The white-girl phase was over without question. Squashed. Finis. He didn't even get the chance to give it a proper swan song.

"No," he said, standing, reaching for his leather coat. He had traded the monkey suit for some slacks and a sweater once he got to the room. That's when Alyssa began her attack. He was glad she stopped. His dick was linguini. He feared any more attempts might have twisted his cap altogether, given his inexplicable encounter with Tyrene.

"So what am I supposed to do?" she asked, climbing into the bed. "I've been up here by myself for hours."

"Watch a movie," he said, slipping on the coat, grabbing the key, and heading for the door. "Order room service. Raid the minibar."

"I did that already." She wasn't lying. There were scads of empty miniature bottles of Tanqueray, VSOP, and assorted bubbly on the floor. A tray with five drained martini glasses, a half-eaten rack of lamb, and a ramekin with the remains of crème brûlée was on the table by the window.

"Then I don't know what to tell you," he said.

She flip-flopped around as if she was unsure what would happen if she didn't do something with all that energy.

"I took some X," she giggled, rolling onto her back, her perfect, prefab tits aimed skyward.

Hill stopped and turned to her.

"Alyssa." He took a moment to check his anger. He'd lost enough control already that day. "Didn't I tell you that drugs are a no-no? What are you, crazy? What if something happens to you? You want me to lose my license to practice? Forget the fact that I'm a black man."

"Oh, and what a black man you are . . ."

"This isn't funny." He was stern now. Paternal. About as sexual as a spore.

"But Hill . . ." she whimpered.

"But Hill, my ass. Look at all the liquor you drank. I don't know what that stuff can do when you mix it with some man-made shit like Ecstasy. This is bad, Alyssa, real bad."

"Oh no, Hill, no."

Oh yes, he thought, oh yes, yes, yes. The white-girl phase, for him, was deader than those sacs of saline she was packing up front.

He made for the door.

"I know," Alyssa said with a grin. "Can I call some of my girl-friends over? Maybe we can help get you back into the spirit of things."

"I can tell you right now you won't be getting any action out of me tonight," he said. Or ever, he thought. "Call them if you want. What you guys do is your business, but there better not be any drugs in here."

"Hmmm," she said, legs open wide, rubbing herself as she contemplated the ceiling. "I haven't had an all-girl-fest in weeks. Maybe that's not such a bad idea."

Hill stood in the doorway staring between her bare golden legs. Nothing.

"Just have them out of here by two," he said as he left. "And if you think that's going to be a problem, let me know and I'll get another room."

"I'm still waiting for an apology."

Tyrene stared at her husband's broad yellow back. A thicket of hair raged across it like a rampant fire.

"Tyrone," she said. "Tyrone, answer me. This is outrageous." She waited for him to acknowledge her, but he didn't. "Instead of having my back," she said, "you choose to curse me out in a room full of people. How could you do that to me? What were you thinking?"

Tyrene shoved him. He responded with a deep grunt that she recognized as sleep.

"I can't believe this," she said, getting up from the bed. "Here I am losing my mind about Reesy, and he drops right off like it was nothing. You big hairy muthafucka. We will talk about this. You can best believe that."

She walked over to her suitcase, ransacking the contents, throwing things onto the floor until she located what she needed. She grabbed a black cable-knit sweater and pulled it over her head, then slipped into a pair of black slacks. She snatched a pair of black ankle boots from the suitcase and sat on the edge of the bed, still mumbling as she pulled them on.

"Fine. Go to sleep, you fat fuck. You've got to wake up soon enough."

She snatched her coat from the closet, determined to go for a walk. She remembered that she was in New York and that her big fat fuck of a husband wouldn't accompany her. Tyrene knew, as huffy as she was, she wasn't prepared to walk the streets alone. She tossed the coat aside, grabbed the key from the nightstand, and left.

Tyrone waited until he heard her angry stomping grow softer, then disappear. He opened his eyes and stared at the wall. He wondered how his daughter was doing. The fact that he could have lost her rattled him to his core. Why did Tyrene keep bringing it up? His grandchild was dead. Both of these blows had almost felled him. They were enough to make him revisit a habit that had once almost torn him and his wife apart.

He hoped Reesy was sleeping well and that her mind was a little at ease.

He reached up and wiped a tear as it made a perpendicular streak down the side of his face.

"But you're already registered as a guest in one room."

"I know," said a frustrated Hill. "But I'd like to get another one."

The hotel attendant poked at the keyboard and squinted at the computer screen. Hill's temples throbbed. He didn't want to go up later and have to deal with Alyssa's shenanigans. He figured he'd go ahead and get a room now.

"So you want to check out of the one you're in?" she asked.

"No. I want to keep the room I'm in now. In fact, there are about eight rooms that I'm paying for this weekend, and I'd like to keep those too."

"Oh really," the pretty redhead said. She poked and punched some more. "Oh yes, right, there it is right there. George S. Hilliard, M.D." She looked up at him, her green eyes dancing. "So you're a doctor, yes?"

The white-girl phase was toast. Even without the Tyrene episode, they were bringing it upon themselves.

"Yes, I'm a doctor. Do you have an extra room?"

She poked again.

"Smoking or nonsmoking?"

"As long as it's not on fire, I don't care."

She punched and pushed, got a key, put it in a cute little folder, and handed it to him.

"It's on the first floor," she said. "If that's a problem, just let us know."

Hill was halfway to the bar before he realized she was still talking.

Tyrene walked right past Dandre as she exited the elevator on her way to the lobby. He was relieved she didn't see him. He watched her make her way toward the bar.

That must mean Tyrone's alone, he thought. He wanted to try

to talk to Reesy's father. Perhaps he could make him understand that he did love his daughter, and that he planned to do everything in his power to care for her and protect her well-being.

"You do like him, admit it," said Tonio, stepping naked from the shower. "I saw how you kept staring at his dingle."

"Honey, that's not a dingle," Julian said. "That's a dongle."

"See? See? See what I'm saying?" Tonio walked into the room with a towel wrapped around his waist.

"Why the modesty, babe?" Julian said. He and Tonio never shielded their nakedness.

"Because you call mine a dingle."

Julian got up from the bed and slid his nude body into his favorite ruby red silk robe.

"You're silly," he said. "You're just looking to pick a fight. You need to be like me, worried about how my girl's doing over at that hospital all by herself."

"Misty said she was doing okay."

Julian stuck his feet into a pair of fleece slippers. His ankles were ashy. He reached for a container of mango butter and slathered the lotion against his skin.

"She's in the hospital," he said. "How okay can that be?"

"I guess you're right," said Tonio. "So how come mine's not a dongle?"

Julian, still bent over, looked up at him.

"Sweetie, you're gonna have to ask your folks about that." He stood. "I'm going to get some ice. I'll be right back."

He grabbed the bucket and the key and headed out. Tonio undid the towel and glanced at himself.

"I do have a dongle." He reached down and lifted it. "Sorta."

"Give me a scotch on the rocks," Hill said to the bartender. "Single-malt, please, Glenfiddich if you have it."

"Make that two," said a voice sliding into the seat beside him.

Hill's head dropped. No, no, no, he thought. Not now. Not here. He didn't need this.

He had a headache. He had an almost-daughter-in-law laid up in the hospital and a son two hysterics shy of jumping off the roof. He had a white girl upstairs on the verge of an orgiastic Ecstasy crash that would ensure his well-crafted career went down in a glorious blaze of ignominy.

And as if that weren't enough, his now rock-hard dick was thumping something fierce.

Dandre knocked at Tyrone and Tyrene's hotel room door. His rap was gentle at first. It was late, past eleven, and he didn't want to make a fuss.

He rapped a little harder. He put his ear to the door. He thought he heard movement, then the sudden sound of heavy snoring.

He stood, perplexed for a moment, his knuckles raised to knock again.

Go to bed, his better judgment said.

Seeing as ignoring his better judgment in the past was what had gotten him into this jam to begin with, he figured it was time he started to listen.

Tyrone had been pacing the room, smoking an extra cigarette he had gotten from the woman outside the hospital. The knocks at the door startled him. Tyrene must have forgotten her key.

He opened one of the dresser drawers and mashed the cigarette out inside. He waved at the air with frantic motions to kill the scent, then made a perfect Mark Spitz for the bed. The mattress let out an agonizing creak when he landed. His snoring commenced at once. The rapping continued.

Let her go back downstairs and get another key, he thought.

For the first time, his wife had gotten on his nerves so bad, if he could have choked her and gotten away with it, she would have been wearing a palm necklace that night.

Julian's bucket was filled with unnecessary ice when he saw Dandre get off the elevator. He'd been hoping to get another glimpse of him.

It's not like he wanted Reesy's man. He loved her to pieces, and had seen the two of them go through so much over the past few months, even though Dandre might now be a free agent. No, he realized, he wouldn't do that to Reesy. Besides, he loved Tonio, dingle and all.

He was just curious. It was so big in the photo, and that red-headed girl was taking it all. He just had to see it. He wondered if Dandre would show it to him. Everybody always commented to Julian about how much he was packing, which was why he liked to show it off in his tights at work. Maybe he and Dandre could compare notes, sort of *mano a mano*, but different. More like *dongo a dongo*.

He could ask, he thought. What harm would that do?

"And now he's smoking again," she said. "He's gone crazy. It's like I don't even know him anymore."

Hill was on his third scotch. The last two were straight, no rocks. He was hoping the heat from the swill would kill the fire down below. He figured if he didn't look at her, his rise would fall.

Neither tactic had proved effective. There was something about her endless yammering and the shrill pitch of her nonstop voice that challenged him. He wanted to physically shut her up. Shove himself so deep inside that bottomless trap that she wouldn't think of talking for the next ten years.

"I got another room," he said when she paused for a breath.

He sipped his drink with casual effort, not even looking at

her. She was quiet for a moment. She thought of her husband. The first image that came to mind was the look on his face as he'd barked "fuck you" at her.

Tyrene pursed her lips and tried to steel the shaking in her body. She was nervous, and more than a little bit frightened. Nothing had gone the way she planned this weekend. Not her daughter's wedding. Then there was the miscarriage. Tyrone's outburst. And now she was on the verge of committing full-blown adultery. This wouldn't be a blip like the kiss-'n'-grope scene in the vending room. There was no sweeping this king-sized dilemma under anyone's rug.

"Did you hear me?" asked Hill.

Tyrene picked up her drink and hurled it against the back of her throat. She loved her husband, but he'd left her alone one time too many that day.

"Is that white girl still in it?" she asked.

"I said I got another room," Hill replied. "It's on this floor."

Tyrene stood. Hill stood too, making a signing motion at the bartender.

He cashed them out and brought over a receipt. Hill pulled the cute little folder out of his pocket and looked at the room number. He wrote it on the bill, signed his name, then touched Tyrene in the small of her back as he guided her through the lobby, around the corner, and into the privacy of his old bird chamber.

"Hey, Julian. I'm surprised you're still up. I figured almost everybody was knocked out by now."

"Yeah, man, this day was crazy. My adrenaline's high. It's kinda hard to sleep, you know?"

"Yeah, I hear ya," Dandre said, leaning against the wall, his eyes closed. Julian put his hand on Dandre's shoulder.

"It's gonna be alright, man. Really. I mean, those weren't, like, recent pictures or anything . . . were they?"

"Nah, man," Dandre said, leaning toward him. He was relieved to have someone that was considered Reesy's friend believe him. "That shit happened over three years ago. I haven't been with any-body since Reesy. That girl is my heart."

"Mmmm-hmmm," Julian said, rubbing his shoulder. "I un-derstand you, man. I know you love her. I saw what y'all went through, remember? I mean, because of you, we still have a show on Broadway."

"Yeah, well, I'd do anything for her. She makes me rise to my better self, you know what I'm saying?"

"Oh yes," said Julian, the bucket blocking his own self's ris-ing. He tilted his head back and forth a few times, measuring the moment.

"So you doing okay?" he asked. "You need anything?"

The hand that had been rubbing Dandre's shoulder was now making its way down toward his wrist.

"I'm straight, man," Dandre said with a weak smile and a look of gratitude. "I appreciate you asking. I think I just need to unwind, you know?"

"Yeah," Julian said. "Unwinding is probably a good idea."

His hand was now past Dandre's wrist, hovering near his belly.

Dandre had closed his eyes again and was rubbing his temples. He was tired, worried, on edge, oblivious to everything. He wanted to go back to the hospital. The thought of Reesy there alone, because of him, was the most unsettling thing of all.

"You look exhausted," Julian said.

"Yeah," Dandre replied, eyes still closed. "My head feels so tight."

"Mmmm-hmmm," said Julian. "I can imagine. You just need to relax. Let yourself feel good for a minute."

His hand was on Dandre's crotch a few seconds before the

sensation registered. Dandre opened his eyes, confused. He glanced down at Julian's hand clutching his nuts.

"Man, what the—?"

"Mmmmfffhmmmfffummmphhh," Tyrene grunted as she knelt between the legs of a standing Hill, pulling him deep into her mouth. His trousers were around his ankles and his Mandela was free.

"Shut up, you old hen, and take it."

She did. Tyrene grabbed him in both hands and gag-reflexed him in a move he'd only seen done on film. By Janet Jackme maybe, but never by anyone in the flesh.

"Good grief," he cried, falling back on the bed.

She pounced on him with her petiteness and rode him like she was Billy Shoemaker. She stared into his eyes as he gazed up at her, mesmerized.

"I think I could love you, you evil broad," Hill murmured.

"Shut up, you old fool, and fuck me," she said.

Tonio had been watching from the cracked door of their room. He suspected that Julian was up to no good. And considering how freaky Dandre was in those pictures, no telling what he was down for.

"Get off my man," he screamed, running up the hall in just the towel. "Get off him. I knew it. I knew it. I knew this shit was about to go down."

Dandre's attention shifted from Julian to Tonio, who was flying at him like a black banshee. Halfway there, the towel fell off.

"Oh Lawd," Julian said, dropping his head into his hand.

"What the fuck is wrong with y'all?" Dandre said, several feet now between him and Julian. "My girl is in the hospital, and the two of you are out here fucking around with some stupid sex antics. Ain't nobody thinking about no damn sex right now." He glared at Julian, his jaw tight, fists clenched. "You're lucky I don't fuck you up for that shit you just pulled."

Tonio rushed Dandre, pushing him against the wall and clocking him in the right eye.

"What the—?" said Dandre, shoving him off.

"You and your dongle keep away from my man," Tonio screamed. "Go handle your own business. I got this."

Doors opened and heads peeked out. Tyrone heard the scuffle but stayed put for fear of unearthing Tyrene.

"C'mon, babe," Julian said, "before they call security." He led Tonio past the peering faces. "C'mon. Get your towel there. Yeah. Pick it up. We don't want all the nice nosy white folks looking at your dingle."

Tyrene lay entangled in Hill's arms, breathing in the smell of him. It was a sensual, animal scent mixed with a light sesame that made her want to taste him again. When she had gone to the lobby, it was with the hope of finding him again, just to see if what had happened in the hospital vending room had indeed been a fluke. When she came upon him in the hotel bar, she knew it hadn't been. She wanted more. When he took her to his room and rent her ways she hadn't been by Tyrone in years, she felt like the young, fiery Panther she'd once been. In that moment, she was a woman with a purpose. And as Hill mounted her and spanked her fifty-eight-year-old tight yellow ass, she was given a taste of power that she hadn't felt in years.

There was something about the way he talked to her. So vulgar and disrespectful on the surface, but she could tell he was in awe of her in a guarded kind of way.

"What happened to your eye?" the bartender asked.

"I don't want to talk about it."

"You sure?" he said. "That's what they pay me for."

"Nah, man. I just want this day to be over with. Lemme have another scotch."

The bartender poured him his sixth Glenfiddich.

"You're not planning on driving, are you?" he asked, hesitating.

"I'm upstairs. I'm about to call it a night."

The bartender pushed him the drink.

"You want the check?"

"Yeah, man. Gimme the check."

The bartender rung him up and gave him the receipt. Dandre scribbled his room number, wrote in the tip, and signed his name.

"I'm outta here, chief," he said, getting up with care. "Take it easy."

"You too, big guy. Tomorrow's another day. Remember that."

Dandre stopped and looked at him.

"My girl always says that."

"That's because it's true," said the bartender, taking the check. "Sounds like you've got a smart woman. Consider yourself lucky."

Dandre made his way out of the bar before the waterworks could start. He crossed the lobby and pushed the elevator buttons. He waited, dabbing at his face with the handkerchief he'd been clutching since his dad had given it to him. He took a few deep breaths and tried to shake off the anguish. He turned around, for no reason other than he felt like it.

His vision was blurry and one eye was damn near shut. He stared, unsure of what he saw, then dismissed it altogether as the ding of the opening elevator doors stole his attention. He stepped in.

As the doors hung open for a moment, he thought he saw the hazy image of what looked to be his dad—and Tyrene—coming around the corner. They stopped and looked around, then hugged.

That's nice, he thought. At least they had made peace.

The doors dinged, then began to close on Dandre's drunken, cockeyed take of Hill and Tyrene in a passionate lip lock.

He laughed, realizing how bad he needed sleep.

"I must be going crazy," he said.

Rick was out, his arms wrapped tight around his wife. They'd made desperate love that night. Rick's sex drive was high anyway, but he seemed extra pressed after the events of the day. What had happened between Dandre and Reesy had put the fear of losing Misty in him.

He'd already had one major loss in his life and the effect, for him, had been catastrophic. He and his old girlfriend Keisha had been inseparable. Their relationship was challenging, exciting, comfortable, and contentious—things he couldn't appreciate at the time. Keisha had been very much in love. Rick had been unsure and afraid, even though they had been living together for more than two years and dating even longer. He felt tremendous pressure from her to get married. The more she'd pressed, the more resistant he'd become. He did come to see how much he loved her. Unfortunately, it had proved too late for both of them.

He was so grateful for Misty, and the most accessible way he could think of to show it was to mount her the second they were in their hotel room.

He was at peace now, on his fifth dream, far removed from the horror and trauma.

Misty stared at the ceiling, recapping everything that had happened, sick to her stomach from all she had seen. She had been too exhausted for sex when they'd got to the Parker Meridien, but Rick was insistent, and her mother had told her many years before that she should never turn her man away.

"All it takes is a time or two," she'd said. "Then he'll turn to somebody else. Always make sure you take care of home."

Misty had taken those words as her marital credo, so whenever Rick pressed, she accommodated him. She didn't feel like a martyr for it. Making love with him was always an enjoyable, passionate, intense experience.

But the passion had stripped her of any shred of remaining energy. All she had left was nausea and a madcap assortment of thoughts, the most vivid of which was the scene in the hospital vending room.

She could still feel the sting of Tyrene's hand on her cheek.

Dandre was the first person at the hospital the next morning. The doctor told him that Reesy was ready to be released.

"I don't want him to be the one to take me home," Reesy said when the nurse came in and told her she was being checked out.

"It's okay," said Misty, rushing into the room, out of breath. "I'm here. As soon as you're ready, you're leaving with me."

# After the Morning After

"I think we should stay. Who's going to take care of you until you get better?"

"I'm here, Mrs. Snowden," Misty said, staring into her cup of tea. "I'll stay with her as long as she needs me."

Tyrene didn't respond.

The four of them—Tyrone, Tyrene, Reesy, and Misty—were together in the living room of Reesy's Harlem apartment. The wedding party had all dispersed to their various domains. Rick was back at home in Greenwich, Connecticut, and Hill and Alyssa were headed back to D.C. Dandre was at his place, just a phone call away, hoping, praying, that he'd be summoned.

Even though Reesy had been spending most of the past few months at his Upper West Side brownstone, she hadn't give up her Harlem walk-up. She was relieved now that she'd had the instinct not to.

"I'm better now," said Reesy. "It was just a fall."

She was stretched out on the sofa with her head resting in her father's lap. He'd been hovering over her since she got home. She'd never seen him so protective.

"The doctor said that, other than me losing the baby"—she felt Tyrone's thigh flinch beneath her—"I'm perfectly fine. I'm just tired, but that's because of all the chaos from planning the ceremony."

She thought of the photos of Dandre and the two women and her throat felt thick. She reached for her tea on the coffee table, took a sip, and put it back.

"Plus I was laid up in that hospital, being pumped full of antibiotics, so that drained me even more. But I'm in good shape. I take care of myself, so I don't break too easily. Besides, they wouldn't have let me out of the hospital if I wasn't okay."

Tyrone stroked his daughter's head. "Those hospitals don't give a damn about people," he said. "They let you out to make room for someone they can rape for more money. If something happens to you as a result of being released too soon, I'm going to sue them."

Reesy sat up and looked into her father's face. It was riddled with panic and concern.

"I'll be okay, Tyrone," touching his arm.

The thought of what she'd gone through was too much for him. He wanted to take her back to Florida, but he knew that wouldn't happen. Reesy was far too independent. His nerves were jittery. For once, the powerhouse caretaker was at sixes and sevens about how to fix things.

"I'm going outside for a minute," he said, getting up. "Is there a drugstore around here anywhere?"

"There's a Duane Reade on the corner," Reesy said. "You feeling alright?"

"Oh yeah," he said with a forced smile. "I'm just fine, daughter. I figured I'd go get me a paper."

"There's a bodega downstairs if you don't want to go too far."

"No," he said. "I think the cold air will do me some good. Don't get much of this down in Fort Lauderdale, so I kind of appreciate it." He took his coat from the arm of the couch and slipped it on. "When I was a boy in Chicago, I couldn't stand the winter. The damn thing was like my archenemy. But this is nice.

A little bit of cool is good for the soul. Helps you get your mind together. Put things in perspective."

The three women stared at him without a response. He seemed to be speaking more to himself than to them. The silence was palpable. Tyrone cleared his throat.

"Any of you need anything?" he said, walking to the door.

"Not me," Misty said. "But don't eat. I'm going to be cooking lunch in a little bit."

"I'm okay, Daddy," said Reesy.

Tyrone felt as though his heart would burst. She didn't call him Daddy often. He could count on one hand the number of times he'd heard it come from her lips in her thirty-two years of existence. Even if she referred to Tyrene and him as Mom and Dad when she talked to her friends, she kept her formality in their presence. It was one of the last vestiges of her childhood rebelliousness.

"You going to smoke?" asked Tyrene. "Because this is the worst possible time for you to—"

He held up his big paw of a hand.

"Please, Tyrene. Not now, okay? Could you let me have just one second of peace?"

Reesy glanced at her father, then her mother. This exchange was something new. It had always been the two of them pitted against a common adversary. She'd never seen them be adversarial to each other.

Tyrone was out the door.

"When are you guys going back?" Reesy asked.

"I don't know," Tyrene said. "I figured we'd stay here with you a few days and make sure everything's okay. We can afford to leave the office for a while."

Reesy's legs were stretched out long on the sofa. She wore cozy one-piece pink fleece pajamas with feet. Dandre had bought them for her a couple of months back. They would have taken her clear through at least the fifth month of pregnancy. She was still attached to the damn things. They were the warmest, most comfortable pajamas she had.

"You don't have to stay," she said. "I'm really okay, right, Misty? Tell Tyrene that she and Tyrone can leave."

Misty was in the kitchen making a pot of chicken and dumplings. She was rolling out the dough on a floured sheet of wax paper. She looked up, right into Tyrene's face.

"You can leave," she said, making her first real eye contact with Reesy's mother since the pimp slap. "Rick and I will make sure she's taken care of."

Tyrene's lips quivered like she wanted to say something, but she knew it'd be best to tread light, given the circumstances.

"Fine," she said after a moment. "Since you want us out of here so bad, we'll leave first thing in the morning. The office is probably a madhouse without us anyway."

"So you never told me what was wrong with you," Reesy whispered.

Tyrene was in the second bedroom taking a prelunch nap. Tyrone hadn't returned yet. The words startled Misty. She dropped the spoon she'd been stirring with.

"Are you crazy?" she asked Reesy, who was standing close behind her. Misty picked up the spoon and walked over to the sink to rinse it off. "What are you doing up? You should be laying down. Get out of here."

"I'm tired of laying down. That's all I've done for the past twenty-some hours. Shit." Reesy sat on one of the stools by the counter. "So what was up with you yesterday at the hospital?"

"What?" Misty asked. "Other than the fact that my best friend's wedding was turned upside down and she had a miscarriage? You don't think that was enough to stress me the fuck out?"

"Relax, Miss Divine, relax. Yesterday was crazy. But I'm not talking about just that."

"Then what are you talking about?" Misty said, turning back to the stove.

"Your cheek was all flushed, like you'd been slapped."

Misty dropped the spoon again.

"Aaaah," Reesy said. "So you thought I didn't notice that print on your cheek. So what happened? I already know it came from Tyrene."

Misty's heart thumped. She didn't want to have to tell Reesy about what she'd seen. Her stomach hadn't been right since. It was gurgling and hissing even now.

"My mother's prone to slapping. Some people have an itchy trigger finger. Tyrene's got an itchy trigger wrist."

"Emotions were high yesterday," answered Misty, tossing the spoon in the sink. "I said something flip to her, she said something back to me. I was keyed up, she was keyed up. Everything's straight now."

Reesy swung her legs about, staring at the pink material enclosing her feet.

"Yeah. I could tell there was some kind of tension between y'all. Tyrone must have been in on it, because he seems like he's ticked at her too."

"I don't know anything about that." Misty adjusted the temperature of the oven. "Stop swinging your legs like that before you do yourself more harm."

"It was about Dandre, wasn't it?"

"Wasn't everything yesterday?" Misty lied, taking a stack of plates over to the dining room table. "Get out," she said when she returned. "Get back on that couch and rest yourself."

"I'm getting out," Reesy said with a laugh.

She trudged off into the living room and eased back onto the sofa. She listened to the sounds of Misty cooking. The house was filled with the warm, wonderful scent of comfort food. Light from the window hit the diamond on her left hand. It glimmered. Reesy lifted her feet up onto the cushions and lay her head down.

"He's the first person who ever made me believe in love," she said, gazing at the ring. "I felt like I could do anything with him next to me. I can't believe it all turned out to be a fucking fraud."

Misty stood motionless at the stove.

"This is my karma, isn't it?" said Reesy. "This is my punishment for doing what I did to hurt him. That whole thing with Helmut is going to haunt me forever."

Helmut Wagner was a German financier who had wanted to take the play she was starring in, *Black Barry's Pie*, from off-Broadway to the big time. He was also very attracted to Reesy. She didn't find anything about him attractive, but she had found his interest in her fascinating. She'd never been with a white man, and when she got drunk one night while out with him, the unexpected happened. It was just sex, she had reasoned, but then it happened again.

She was dating Dandre at the time, and he was very much in love. He'd given her a car, a key to his place, and the key to his heart. It was a first for him, but for her it was all about revenge—a way to pay him back for getting her fired from her corporate job. The plan was to get him to fall for her, then dump him without ceremony.

But Dandre causing her to lose her job had been an accident. So was the fact that she found herself falling for him. Once Dandre had discovered what was up between her and Helmut, it was too late. By then she'd realized just how much she cared for Dandre, but it had taken everything to get him to open up to her again.

"This isn't your karma," Misty said, coming into the living room and sitting beside her. "This is just life working itself out. You still love him. He loves you. None of that has changed."

"Everything's changed." Reesy was crying into the pillow. "How can I be with him now, after a fiasco like that? All those people looking at those pictures of him. That woman in black at the church. Who was she anyway?"

Misty rubbed her friend's back.

"Does it really matter?"

Reesy sniffled, her shoulders shaking.

"I lost our baby. He made a fool out of me."

"That man loves you."

"It's over," she said.

Reesy sobbed into the pillow, trying to smother the sound. Her motions were so intense, she seemed to be choking.

"Oh honey," said Misty. "It's not, it's not." She kept rubbing Reesy's back. "You two have weathered so much. This is just another obstacle. It ain't over till it's over."

Reesy looked up at her with a wet face, the sobs coming in a wave of hiccups.

"This isn't a song, Misty. This is real life. My life. He and I are finished. There's nothing left. Me having a miscarriage was just the universe's way of making sure we were totally disconnected."

"Don't say that, Reesy. Neither you nor I know what God and the universe have in store for us. Don't try to predict it on your own."

Reesy sat up. "I don't need to," she said. "What's done is done."

Misty wrapped her arms around her friend.

"Don't speak so soon," she said. "Hold off a few days. Just wait and see how you feel. Life is full of mystery. You don't know what kind of plan is unfolding for you."

"Could you cancel my appointments for tomorrow?" Hill said into his cell. "I'm extending my trip an extra day."

He had dropped Alyssa off and was heading home. She hadn't talked much on the return trip, which was a relief to him. He'd been too mired in thought to entertain any extraneous input.

Hill needed some time to regroup and consider all that had transpired that weekend. He figured he'd stay home and get his head and emotions straight.

He was worried about Dandre and his state of mind. His son had taken a blow, and Hill knew he needed to be there for Dandre to help him get through it. But he kept flashing back to thoughts of the things he and Tyrene had done. He couldn't turn his mind off. It was rampant with images of wanton lust and bad behavior, and for that he was feeling ashamed. Not remorseful, just embarrassed.

Hill had never been with a married woman before. He respected the sanctity of that institution and what his own marriage had meant to him. There'd always been such a bumper crop of available young women for him to pull from, so there'd never been any need for him to wade in marital waters. When Eileen was alive, the idea of her with another man was enough to make his knees buckle. Yet here he was, guilty of that very sacrilege himself.

The fact that she was his son's fiancée's mother made an already complicated situation seem even more absurd.

Tyrene, as it turned out, was a dynamo, with the stamina of a twenty-year-old. She had shifted his entire frame of reference. His feminine paradigm was forever changed.

Older women weren't sexy. They were problematic, dried-out sacs of skin that required constant support from the likes of K-Y and poor lighting. At least, that's what they were supposed to be.

Not Tyrene Snowden. Nothing about her was dried out, from her firm, supple, resilient flesh to what he'd found to be the most irresistible zone—her lush, shaven loins. He'd wanted to lose himself in her valley of darkness, and told her so again and again as he sank into it. He replaced his old name for her—bitch—with a new one that night: the Liquidator. Not only was she a gusher, but she had drained him dry.

After she'd left, he lay in bed thinking of her, touching himself. It'd burned him to know she was just a few floors above him, inaccessible, cozied up with her colossus of a husband. Hill didn't sleep that night. Before dawn had a chance to break, he had gone up, roused Alyssa from her postsexual stupor, and checked them out of the hotel.

He couldn't bear the thought of seeing Tyrene with Tyrone, so he'd abandoned ship as quick as he could. He was back in Washington before Tyrene was even awake.

As he drove to his house now, he pictured her straddling him with those agile yellow limbs.

"This is awful," he said. "It's driving me mad."

She hadn't given him much to go on. No words of encouragement, no hints at any real fracture in her current state of nuptial affairs. But what about her actions? he thought. They seemed to say everything. The way she was on him and over him and into him had to mean something. When she kissed him good-bye in the lobby, he hadn't considered it a permanent separation. There was something in the way her tongue met his that didn't speak of finality.

"Good grief," he lamented. "What am I going to do about this tricky situation?"

Four days later, Reesy felt an irresistible urge for some answers. She had tossed the whole night, tormented by a replay of the events at the church. The sound of envelopes ripping open raced in her head, as did the image of herself tumbling down the stairs at the front of the church.

She threw on some sweats and sneakers, snatched her parka from the hook by the door, stuffed herself into it, and made for her car.

Dandre was standing in the doorway of his brownstone. Despite the bitter winter wind, he was engaged in what looked like active conversation with an attractive woman standing on his front steps. She looked familiar. Her fleshy round ass was what gave her away.

Reesy sat in the car, staring at what was taking place. She

had come to talk to him, but now that was moot. She had her answer. He'd been playing her all along, just as she'd suspected.

She pulled out of the parking space she had maneuvered into a few doors down from Dandre's house.

"Fine," she said to herself, her eyes flushed and stinging with tears. "Fuck him. He can have that woman. He can have whoever he wants."

# Sicker Than Your Average

"What happened to your hair?"

It was six days later and Misty was standing at Reesy's front door.

"I cut it."

She let Misty in.

"I see that. That's what I'm talking about. You didn't say anything to me about this."

She watched Reesy walk ahead of her, examining the back of her new pixie cut. They both sat on the couch.

"So do you like it?"

Misty reached over and touched it.

"It's fabulous. It suits your face. So when did you do this?"

"Yesterday. I figured I needed a wholesale change."

"What do you mean by 'wholesale'?" She noticed that Reesy was still wearing her ring.

Reesy didn't answer. She glanced around the apartment. Misty's eyes followed hers.

Boxes were everywhere, secured with packing tape, labeled in black Magic Marker.

"Uh, what's going on here?" asked Misty with unmasked surprise. "Are we moving?" She wondered how she had missed all the boxes. Reesy's new haircut was a vortex that had sucked up all her attention.

"We are."

Reesy got up and went into the kitchen. She opened a cabinet, reached in, and grabbed a box of apple cider mix and two mugs.

"And just where are we moving to?" Misty asked.

Reesy turned on the faucet and filled the kettle. She put it on the stove and turned up the fire.

"Reesy."

"What's that?" she said, turning around.

"Where and when are you moving?"

"Oh."

She tore open the packets and poured them into the mugs.

Misty knew this drill. It was the old I'm-going-to-tell-you-on-my-own-terms game. No sweat, she thought. They'd been playing it for years.

The kettle whistled. Reesy filled the mugs and stirred the drinks, dropping cinnamon sticks into each. She carried them into the living room.

Misty was sitting back on the gold couch, flipping through the current issue of *Vibe*.

"Would you do Jay-Z?" she asked.

"I don't know. Maybe," Reesy said, sitting the mugs on coasters. "There's something kinda street cuddly about him."

"Street cuddly. That's a new one."

Reesy leaned back into the cushions.

"Yeah, you know. Like maybe he spoons you when you sleep and gives you back rubs and shit, but he can still lay a muthafucka out if he steps to you wrong."

"Right," Misty said, putting down the magazine. "Hey, didn't you say once that you were going to stop cursing?"

"I said a buncha things once." She sipped her hot cider.

Misty checked her out, waiting, watching the mist from the mug steam her face a little. She picked up her own mug of cider.

"That look really does suit you. You have such a pretty face."

Reesy smiled, still sipping.

Misty was playing the game well. The rules were, no pressure. The informing party would tell when she felt like it. Reesy appreciated the fact that Misty was such an intimate friend. Misty knew most of her moves without having to be checked.

"What'd you do with the braids?" Misty asked.

"I burned them."

"Damn."

Misty put down her cider and sauntered around the apartment. She ignored the boxes, which were underfoot at every turn. She walked over to the window.

"We had snow in Connecticut the other day. It was beautiful."

"Yeah. We had some too, but it didn't stick."

"Neither did ours."

She kept looking out the window at the people walking by on the street below. They were bundled in thick coats and scarves, leaning their knit-cap- and hat-clad heads forward to cut the wind. She watched a mother go by with her four little ones. They all held hands like one big daisy chain.

Her stomach made a gurgling noise. She walked back to the couch and sat down. She picked up the mug and took another sip of cider.

"I'm moving to California," Reesy said.

"Oh really?" Misty said in a calm voice, still going along with things.

"Yup. I'm leaving tomorrow on a cross-country drive."

"Tomorrow?" Misty shrieked. Game over. She felt like Reesy's behavior was absurd. "You can't leave town tomorrow."

Reesy's legs were tucked beneath her. Her favorite afghan was pulled over them.

"Why can't I? There's nothing here to stop me."

Reesy hadn't told her about the incident she'd witnessed at Dandre's house between him and the woman. That had been the deciding factor. Her dignity had taken enough blows. Too many for her to want to talk about it anymore.

She stared at Misty, waiting for her to give an adequate reason why she should stay.

Misty's chin dropped. She felt limp, helpless in the face of everything happening around her. She ran her hand across her face, absently tracing the beauty mark on her cheek. Her hair was pulled back into a ponytail, but it felt tight, like she needed to loosen the elastic that was holding it together.

Reesy could almost see the thoughts turning over in her friend's head. Misty glanced up. Her almond-shaped eyes were absent of their usual sparkle.

"So what about me?" she asked. "You can't just leave me here. We've never lived apart before."

"You were in Atlanta for a while before I moved there."

"But you did ultimately move there, and we talked on the phone every day."

Misty's stomach was doing the bump.

"You have a husband now," Reesy said. "You need to focus on him and your new life. And last time I knew, they had phones in California, so I don't see it being a problem for us to still talk."

Misty stood again and wandered around the room.

"This is so ridiculous, Reesy," she said. "You can't just keep running from things."

Reesy seemed relaxed as she fingered her hair. It was apparent that she was at peace with her decision.

"I'm not running from anything. It's called getting a fresh start. I've done my time in New York. Like Julian always used to say, gotta make moves."

This is too much for me, Misty thought. Reesy and her mother were making her life way too complicated.

"I've been talking to Rowena," Reesy said. "She's gonna introduce me to some casting people and maybe try to hook me up with her agent."

Rowena had been the lead in *Black Barry's Pie*. After a grueling audition for the part, Reesy had taken over the role of Mimosa Jones when Rowena moved to California after she'd booked a part in a Hughes brothers film.

It had been a big transition for Reesy, considering she'd started in the play as a background dancer. Even though Reesy had a master's degree, for most of her adult life she had chosen jobs that didn't challenge her so that Tyrone and Tyrene wouldn't have any expectations. The first few years after she graduated from college they gave her daily lectures on why she should attend law school. She was heir to the Snowden & Snowden legal empire, they reminded her. It was pointless, and in time, her parents saw the futility of their pressure. *Black Barry's Pie* had been the first job she'd ever had in the theater. After years of drifting from job to job and a fleeting fling with stripping, Reesy had found her fit.

"But L.A. isn't really known for having a great theater market," Misty said. "New York is the center of the universe when it comes to that."

"Dreams change. I'll network with people in the film industry. And maybe I can book some work on TV."

Misty's stomach was on fire. Gas was bubbling up and now hovered at the edge of her throat, threatening to erupt. She swallowed a gulp of air to press the gas down.

"Don't you have to be in the unions for that?" she said as she swallowed. "You can't just go there and jump into—"

Reesy laughed.

"Same ol' Misty, always of little faith. You said something to me along the same lines as that when I told you I was gonna try out for the theater. If I believed everything you said to me, I'd never leave my house."

Misty sat on the arm of the chair.

"That's a terrible thing to say. I've always been so supportive of you."

The gas was burning her palate. The bubbling in her stomach could be heard in the room.

"What's wrong with you?" asked Reesy.

"I don't want you to leave, yet you make it sound like I don't believe in you. I've always believed in you."

Her midsection roared. The gas liquefied and bubbled up, racing to the inner edges of her mouth.

"Fuck that," Reesy said. "I'm talking about all those squirting noises and shit that are coming out of you."

A final noxious bubble burst upward, forcing Misty to rush from the arm of the chair to the bathroom. She bent over the toilet, opened her mouth, and, as if on cue, the contents fell out, hitting the water with a splash. Reesy was at her heels, worried. She hadn't anticipated her leaving town to have such a dramatic effect.

"What's wrong with you?" she asked. "Is it the cider? Is it my going away?"

Misty was crying hysterical tears against the bowl. She sat on the floor, exhausted, sick, her head buried in the crook of her elbow.

"Misty? Misty?"

Reesy sat on the floor next to her. Misty kept crying.

"Girl, stop being so silly and tell me what's wrong. I know you love me and all and we've been partners forever, but I didn't expect you to throw a fit like this." She put her arm around her. "C'mon, tell me. Is it me leaving? What's the matter?"

Misty realized she didn't know how to explain. The burden— the stress—it was all too much for her, along with everything else. This was the last thing Reesy needed to hear on the eve of a life change. Misty had been debating the *how* and *when* of telling her, in addition to the *if*, but she wasn't sure if her friend had even dealt with what had happened with her and Dandre yet. Their relationship had unraveled and they'd lost a child. Reesy hadn't addressed the issue since her parents left. Misty knew it was still troubling her; it had to be. There's no way, she thought, that Reesy can handle this other thing. It was just as sensitive and explosive, in the wake of all that had happened.

Misty kept crying, her hysterical sobs alternating with fits of retching. Reesy grabbed her shoulders with both hands and made Misty face her.

"Stop it," she demanded. "Stop it right now. Tell me what's wrong with you. Does this have something to do with that situation at the hospital and why Tyrene slapped you? You were never really straight with me about that whole affair anyway."

Misty leaned over the toilet and vomited again.

"Nah, see. This is crazy. Something is definitely up." Reesy hovered over her. "Something else went down that I don't know about, didn't it? C'mon. Stop fucking around. Tell me what happened Misty, or I'm gonna pick up the phone and call Tyrene myself. She might have smacked the fear of something into you, but I'm not scared of her. I never have been and I never will be."

She lifted Misty's chin. Misty stared at the floor, which was littered with stray tears.

"Look at me and tell me the truth, or I'm calling Tyrene. I swear I will."

Misty's sobs subsided somewhat, but she still didn't open her mouth to speak.

"Fine," Reesy said, getting up. "I'm gonna settle this shit once and for all. I'm tired of people walking around me with secrets and having them blow up in my face later. This has got to stop."

She made a move for the door. Misty knew she couldn't let her call Tyrene.

"I'm pregnant."

Reesy stopped in the doorway. She was facing the living room.

"I'm sorry," she said. "I think I misheard you."

Misty sobs began anew.

"I'm pregnant," she screamed. "And I don't want to have this fucking baby. The last thing I need is a baby right now."

The two women were sitting on the couch.

Misty was wrapped in Reesy's afghan, drinking the reheated cider. Reesy stared at the hardwood floor.

"I don't understand how it is you're not happy about this," she said. "You have a man who loves you. Everybody can see that. This was all you've ever talked about for years—having a husband and a family. I don't get you, I swear. I don't get anybody anymore."

Misty sipped her cider. She didn't get herself either. She didn't get Tyrene, she didn't get Hill, she didn't get Dandre. She didn't get why Reesy had to pull up roots, although it made more sense than everything else that was happening.

What bothered her most was Rick. She hadn't told him about the baby yet because she knew that, once she did, it was going to be on. He would flip into Daddy mode with a superhuman quickness. This was a role he'd looked forward to for most of his adult life. It was something he talked about at least once a day, and always at night. Before sex, after sex, during sex.

"I can't wait to see you barefoot with my seed in your belly," he would say once he was inside her. "What would you do if I knocked you up right now?"

He would talk about it over breakfast.

"How do you feel?" he'd ask.

"Fine. Quit drilling me," she'd say.

"No queasiness, no morning sickness?"

"Rick, we used a rubber. I'm not ovulating. Stop wishing that upon me. Watching what Reesy's going through with her pregnancy is enough."

"Just think—if the two of you were pregnant at the same time—that would be sick, wouldn't it?" His grin would border on diabolical glee. "Really. That would be some cool-ass shit."

"Eat your bacon."

"Yeah," he'd say with a dreamy gaze. "That would be cooler than a muthafucka."

She imagined him around the house, prepping for the new arrival. Everything would change.

Rick wanted several kids, so this would be the first of a series he would expect her to pop in rapid succession. That's why she wanted to wait. She didn't mind having them, but she did mind when. Misty still had career goals she wanted to meet. Her boss, Rich Landey, had hinted at the possibility of another merger— this time with a company in the Netherlands—which would catapult her into international terrain and a six-figure salary with a compensation package and stock options that had the potential to move her into the seven-figure zone. She was excited by what that would mean for her and Rick and their future security. She was also pleased about the European travel and the prospect of her employee/husband being able to accompany her. It would be like honeymooning, compliments of Burch Financial, over and over again.

All she needed was two years of this, she figured, and then they could talk about making babies. Besides, she liked the tradition of the bride and groom having the first two years of marriage to themselves, free to be with each other without the demands and encumbrances of children. Once little ones arrived, they would never have this kind of time to themselves again. She wanted to cherish it, not give it away just months after they'd said their vows.

Although they hadn't made a formal edict about their family plan, Misty believed her husband understood her position. And although she wasn't taking birth control pills, they had been using condoms coupled with the rhythm method and it seemed to be working. At least she thought so. It wasn't until the scene at the hospital made her sick and the nauseating feeling just wouldn't go away that she began to worry. It got between her and her morning grits. It kept her from the dinner roast. Sometimes just the sight of food was enough to trigger an episode of dry heaves. She hadn't eaten a whole meal in days because everything she tried to consume defied the laws of gravity.

Perhaps it's stress, she thought, but when her period didn't show up, she knew Tyrene and Hill were not to blame.

"So when are you going to tell him?"

"I don't know," Misty said.

"You are going to tell him, though . . . right?" Reesy searched her friend's face for a sign of something. Misty was always so transparent. For once, Reesy had no clue what was going on in her head.

Misty pulled the afghan tighter around her.

"You're not thinking of doing something stupid."

It wasn't a question. It wasn't a statement. It was a judgment. If Misty was thinking it, she realized, she wouldn't dare share the thought.

"I won't let you do it," said Reesy. "I'll tell Rick first. I won't let you do this to your baby."

"I'm not thinking of doing anything," Misty said in anger, "and if I was, it's not your call to get in my business."

"It is my call. I just lost a baby I wanted. I'm not going to watch you throw one away."

Misty's eyes welled up.

"You know I don't believe in abortion," she said. "How dare you fucking lecture me?"

"Didn't you guys talk about this kind of stuff before you got married?" Reesy asked. "Didn't you come to some agreement about when you'd start a family? This is not the kind of secret you keep from your husband. What kind of foundation is that for you to build on?"

Misty stared at the wall.

"I've been working most of my life. It helps me define who I am. I thought I could be married, have a career, be a mother—all that shit—but on my terms. None of this was my call. Rick wants this baby, I don't. We were being careful. I just don't understand how this could happen."

"You better be careful what you say. Life has a funny way of hearing you."

"What do you mean by that?"

"I mean you keep talking about not wanting this baby. What if something happens all of a sudden that takes away your ability to have a baby at all? I'm sure that wouldn't be on your terms either. You talked to me the other day about counting my blessings and shit, but you're just another talking head as far as I'm concerned. You don't even take your own advice."

Misty flung the afghan off and got up from the couch. She grabbed her coat and purse from the arm of the chair.

"I'm outta here," she said, and marched to the door. "Be careful. Drive safe. Make sure your broom is tuned up before you take off." She refused to turn and look at her friend. "However the fuck you're going, I hope you get there in one solid piece."

"I'm driving," Reesy said, following her to the door.

"Well, drive safe. See ya."

Reesy rushed up behind her, grabbing her arm before she could leave.

"I didn't mean to upset you, Miss Divine. Really," she said. "I love you. You're the only sister I've got."

"I love you too." Misty stared out the open door, still not facing Reesy, the cold air embracing her skin.

"Turn around and give me a real hug. Like I said, life is funny. We don't want to say good-bye on these terms. I don't want to have any regrets when I get on the road tomorrow."

Misty turned around and, still avoiding Reesy's eyes, gave her a tight hug.

"Look at me."

Misty was crying. Reesy's eyes were wet too.

"Promise me you won't kill your baby."

Misty took a deep breath and walked out the door.

# PART 2

---

## *Pluct*

# Hit the Road, Black

Reesy left Harlem at dawn the next morning, her trip laid out compliments of Mapquest.com.

She was taking the northwestern route, I-95 to the Jersey Turnpike, across the Delaware Water Gap, through Pennsylvania, Ohio, and Indiana, past Chicago, then Iowa, Nebraska, Wyoming, Utah, and Nevada. She was giving herself four or five days to get to California, no rush.

This was to be a trip of leisure, with eight-hour stopovers each night so she'd be well rested the next day. It was the thick of winter, but nothing on The Weather Channel indicated that she'd hit horrible driving conditions anywhere. If she needed snow chains, she figured she could stop in some city along the way and get them. Other than that, everything seemed copacetic.

It was just going to be her and Black, her Porsche Boxster—a gift from Dandre the first night she played the lead in *Black Barry's Pie*. The car was ready for the long trip ahead. He had been given a full inspection at the dealership the day before. He'd had an oil change, all the fluids were fresh, there were new spark plugs, belts, wipers, and tires. Black had been cleaned and was smelling quite spiffy, like pineapples, compliments of one of those ubiquitous car fresheners sold at the counters of gas stations and convenience stores. She'd stuck the scented tin under the driver's seat. By the time she got to L.A., she knew she would be sick of pineapples and tired of sitting hostage in Black.

She had a grip of CDs packed, her favorite stuff: Biggie, 'Pac, the Beatles, everything by Stevie Wonder, some Fleetwood Mac, Steely Dan, Jay-Z, Nas, Lauryn Hill's *Miseducation* joint, some Erykah Badu. And Maxwell. He was her Moses, and it was his music she planned to have playing as he led her on her exodus from the wilderness of the city off to freedom in California, with miles of distance—2,814.32, to be exact—between her and Dandre.

She had fried up a mess of chicken the night before and had it packed in a Tupperware container, along with a loaf of white bread and slices of Sara Lee pound cake. She had a small cooler stuffed with plastic bottles of Pepsi and tiny bottles of Cocola. All these things were more tradition than actual want. Whenever Tyrone and Tyrene took her on road trips as a child, this was what they had packed. The three of them would eat the cold chicken folded up in the light bread, wash it down with small bottles of Coke, then snack on Sara Lee. It was like an oil change—necessary for any drive that exceeded four hours.

Mapquest said her trip was an estimated forty-five hours and thirty minutes. She planned to stop for fast food and a few sit-down meals along the way, but things wouldn't feel right without the smell of cold cluck in the car. She needed all the accoutrements to bless the trip.

She hadn't told Tyrone and Tyrene about her plans. She'd deal with them once she was settled in L.A. To prevent them from calling her apartment and finding the number disconnected, she told them she was going away to a resort in the Poconos for a couple of weeks. They bought it, insisting she needed the peace of mind so that she could regroup.

"I'll have my cell with me," she said, "but it'll be off most of the time. If there's an emergency, just leave me a message."

"That's okay, baby girl," said Tyrone. "You take your time, we won't call and bother you. Do you need anything? Are you doing okay?"

"I'm fine, Tyrone. Really. I'm looking forward to the mud baths and full-body massages."

Tyrene, listening on another extension, had a flash of herself laid out on the bed at the Parker Meridien getting a full-frontal treatment at the hands of Hill.

"Well, good for you," her mother said. "Has your father told you about his problem?"

"Tyrene," he interjected with a growl as subtle as a bear's.

"What, Tyrone, what?" she said. "Teresa, you know your father's smoking again, don't you? All that secondhand filth in the air around here. I swear, it's like he's a different man. He doesn't give a shit about me."

"What the hell are you talking about, woman?" he said, his mouth away from the phone. "Why are you discussing this in front of Teresa?" He coughed and cleared his throat. "I wish I was going to the Poconos with you, daughter," he said into the receiver. "Goodness knows I could use some R and R, some earplugs, some something. Sela."

"Then go, muthafucka," Tyrene said. "There's no one here forcing you to stay."

"What's wrong with y'all? I've never heard the two of you act like this."

"It's all that damn cigarette smoke. He's sucking it in and blowing it out, and watch . . . I'll be the one with black lung and emphysema."

"Those are two different things," said Tyrone.

"Well, it all spells death to me," she shrieked.

The three of them were silent, the echo of Tyrene's hysteria lingering in the air. Each one held a receiver and stared at nothing, longing to be somewhere else.

"I need Misty's phone number," Tyrene said.

"What for?" asked Reesy, wondering if her mother would admit to their tiff.

"She had some legal issues at work she wanted to ask me about," Tyrene lied.

"Then won't she call you?" interjected Tyrone.

Good one, Daddy, Reesy thought.

Tyrene searched for a comeback, but Reesy gave her the number before she could think of something that seemed more convincing.

"I gotta go," Reesy said after giving her Misty's info.

"You're not going away with that philandering bastard, are you?" her mother asked.

"Tyrene," said Tyrone.

"Bye, y'all, I love you."

"And stop saying 'y'all,'" Tyrene commanded. "It's improper English."

"Oh," said Reesy, "but 'muthafucka' and 'philandering bastard' are okay?"

Tyrene gasped. Reesy clicked off before there was any further response. The last thing she wanted was another diatribe from her mother. No matter what they discussed, it would somehow weave its way to Dandre, and Reesy was not ready for that. It had required a herculean effort to shut him out of her head. She knew she hadn't dealt with what had transpired between them and that it threatened to erupt if she didn't, but there was time for that. The words of her favorite heroine from literature and film—Scarlett O'Hara—still held true: tomorrow was indeed another day. There was plenty of time to look into the belly of that beast.

Tyrene's rants were persecuting, a torture Reesy wouldn't wish upon the most wretched of souls. She pitied her father, who seemed to be rearing up and taking umbrage—at long last—at the incessant hooting of his wife. Tyrone was opinionated and, at times, quick to interfere, but he was slow to anger.

When he did blow, it was big, volcanic, and swallowed up everything in the vicinity. Reesy hadn't seen him come undone in years, and that was only once, after a teacher who'd made the mistake of calling ten-year-old feisty Reesy a "bad little nigger." Her father had threatened to dismember the woman, two limbs at a time: "I'll pry her apart like the fucking Barbie whore she is!"

According to Tyrone, people like Reesy's teacher should be the first ones culled from society. To him, she had represented the oppressive establishment. Dismembering her would have been the clarion call of a real revolution.

Reesy couldn't imagine what it must be like for him with Tyrene right there in his ear. All day long at work. All night long beside him in bed. They'd seemed like such a perfect match, the kind of Frick and Frack relationship she sought with her own life partner, whoever he turned out to be. The hint at a possible chink in their collective armor was disturbing, a shifting of absolutes that would have repercussions too infinite for her to ponder. It made her remember that moment in the movie *The Color Purple*, and the line that always struck her the most: "Pa ain't Pa."

Reesy needed Tyrone and Tyrene to be made for each other. How else, she thought, could she hope for the same for herself? They'd been so simpatico, even down to their names. She defined herself by their uncanny symmetry. If their duality wasn't real, she wondered if her own personal truths would be next to fall away.

She realized that she wasn't leaving soon enough. She shook her head and fingered her hair. The glimmer of her ring caught her eye as it passed.

Two weeks would give her an adequate break. She knew the next time she heard her mother's voice she would be telling them she'd moved an entire coast away, and the ranting would begin anew.

The thought of them made her head hurt. She took some Aleve to intercept the pain before she started on her way.

She and Black had made it through Des Moines and were headed into Nebraska.

It was late, almost eleven, and she figured she'd stop for the night.

Day two, and everything was par for the course. Her unscheduled schedule was on schedule. Because she'd gotten such an early start, the first day had taken her clear through Ohio and Indiana to Chicago. She'd spent the night at the Omni Hotel downtown, allowing herself a luxurious bath and room service.

She'd thought of calling Grandma Tyler, but didn't tempt herself. Her grandmother would know she was in town. Her spidey senses would kick in and she'd probe Reesy about her whereabouts. Reesy'd never been good at lying to her granny.

She'd call her later, she decided, once she was farther down the road. She was sure that Tyrone and Tyrene had already told the old woman that she was in the Poconos. When Reesy called her, she'd make it seem like she'd taken a break from the resort and gone for a drive. That way, she thought, it wouldn't be a lie if Grandma Tyler asked her if she was in the car.

"That'll work," she'd said, settling in for a toasty sleep beneath the sumptuous covers.

She had checked out by noon the next day. She gassed up, filled the cooler with more ice and Cocolas, and aimed for Interstate 80 again.

South Florida, though beautiful and diverse, always seemed to Reesy like the lowest chamber of hell. It was an isolated gulag shut off from damn near everything except Cuba. Just getting out of her native state took five to seven hours, depending on one's destination, and whenever she and her parents had taken a road trip, it had almost always been out of state.

Because of those childhood trips, she'd mastered the art of the long-distance drive. She understood maps, highways, and interstates and knew how to pass the time with music and thought. She expected her mind to be flooded with thoughts of Dandre and the baby. Instead she was tormented with visions of Tyrone and Tyrene.

"Out, out, damned spots," she said to the air. "Before you fuck up my head any more than it is."

Stevie Wonder was singing about love being in need of love. She wasn't in the mood for that sappy shit. She hit "random" on the CD player and heard discs shifting in the magazine. A few seconds later, out came the husky sounds of Biggie having a rap-off with Lil' Kim.

Reesy pumped the speakers and sang aloud with the music.

*"What do you do when your man is untrue? Do you cut the sucka off and find someone new?"*

Made sense to her.

She spotted an exit ahead and a La Quinta Inn. She was still in Iowa, but figured it would be the perfect place to call it a night.

When Reesy set out the next morning, there were just a few miles of Iowa left to conquer. She was relieved when she saw the Nebraska state line ahead, beckoning her forward from the dull jaws of the Corn State. The miles were going by like nothing. She was already more than halfway across the country.

The second she entered Nebraska, it was as though someone had dropped her into the bowels of the world. It stank to high heaven. The entire state was one long stretch of roadkill.

She wasn't even a mile inside the state before she swerved to avoid her first . . . something. It was medium-sized with stiff hair. Too small to be a deer but bigger than a beaver.

"What the fu—?"

Black made a bloo-bloop sound as she ran over something

else, before she could finish freaking out about the first lump of squashed hairy meat.

"My car's too small for this," she said. "Black, we're gonna have to pay attention, or these things are gonna fuck you up."

She didn't drive a straight line for the next few hours. Black bobbed and weaved his way across the state, with Reesy navigating the roadkill like a complex game on a Sony PlayStation. Every time she avoided a carcass, she felt she'd advanced to another level.

"Fuck Tomb Raider," she said to Black. "I'm the Meat Faker."

It was bad, as though someone had loosed a safari upon the highway and the animals were playing a dangerous game of chicken. They were all losing. From what Reesy could see, it was Cars and Trucks: thousands, Animals: zip.

Even though the huddles of cows must have known they too were destined to go, they mooed with what appeared to be indifference as they watched the road. Theirs would be a more expedient exit than the dreaded death-by-dumb-dash-and-mash they witnessed every day.

There seemed to be more scattered meat than visible asphalt. Reesy pulled over twice to unload the contents of her offended stomach. The lurching began anew when she walked to her car and noticed crushed flesh embedded in Black's new treads.

The smell of pineapple inside the car was a distant memory. It couldn't compete with Nebraska's meals on wheels.

By the time she hit Wyoming, she still wasn't hungry.

The pristine, clean, and expansive vistas were a literal breath of fresh air after the land of the slaughtered.

She passed a rock fixture shaped like Lincoln.

"Wow, look at that," she said to the car.

She needed someone to talk to because Black, for certain, could not talk back. She was glad he couldn't. Odds were it would sound like Dandre's voice.

Her cell had been ringing nonstop since the day of the wedding with calls of supplication and apology from Dandre. She couldn't bring herself to respond to his messages.

In order to escape the sound, she had turned the phone to vibrate mode. The sensation was soothing against her leg, sometimes bringing her back to active thought.

She needed the company of someone human.

She figured now was a good time to give her granny a call.

"You in the car, Tweety?"

"Yup. I needed to clear my head."

It was the truth. After all the carnage she'd just seen on the road behind her, her head was due a good clearing or three.

"So is your getaway working? Are you feeling better? You know, things ain't always as bad as they seem."

"I don't want to talk about that right now," Reesy said. "I called to check on you, pretty lady. What you been up to? You been leaving all them old men in Chicago alone? They'll give you worms, you know."

Grandma Tyler's laugh was part cackle, part wheeze.

"You always been crazy, Tweety. That's one of the reasons I love you so."

"I love you too, Granny."

It was brick outside, but Reesy was warm inside the car. The sound of the old woman's voice made her heart light and easy. As conversation dwindled, Grandma Tyler hummed an indecipherable tune. If Reesy hadn't been driving, she would have closed her eyes and lost herself in the rhythm of the soothing melody.

"Speakin' of crazy," Grandma Tyler said abruptly, "your mama and your daddy are two of the biggest nuts I ever done met." The announcement put Reesy on edge.

"I know," she said. "I don't know what's wrong with them. I think what happened messed them up so much, they don't know what to do. They're used to yelling at me, but they can't really do that right now because they think I'm fragile."

"You? Fragile? Not hardly," the old woman said. "My Tweety's a tough bird. Ain't no foolishness gon' break you down. You made-a the good stuff."

Grandma Tyler made a smacking sound with her lips. Reesy knew what that meant. The woman was bracing herself to spit out a mouthful, and she was warming up her trap so she could do it.

"So what makes you say they're crazy?" Reesy asked after a moment. "Did Tyrene say something?"

"I say they crazy 'cause they are. I called over there to see if they had talked to you, and they bust out and hollered at each other through the line while I sat there in the middle like a squirrel at a tennis match."

Reesy laughed.

"A squirrel, Granny?"

"Hell yeah, a squirrel," she said. "You know he sits out there on the court, thinking that's a big ol' nut being batted around. He just waits and waits, watching the nut go back and forth, fig-uring if he wait long enough, the nut's gon' drop."

Reesy gripped the wheel and gazed at the road, trying to fol-low her grandmother's visual.

"But you see, in this case, the nut ain't gon' drop," Grandma Tyler said.

"Why is that?"

"Because it's two nuts—your mama and your daddy—and I'll be damned if I'm gon' sit there like a stupid squirrel while they bat some bullshit across my head."

"Shut up, old lady," Reesy said, "before you make me crash."

"Your daddy said *sela* so many times, I thought he was Lionel Richie. I told him he can take his *sela* and stick it up his ass."

Reesy laughed so hard, she mashed the gas pedal by acci-dent. Black sped forward and hit an ice slick in the road. The car threatened to spin. It frightened Reesy enough to make her pull over onto the shoulder.

"Shit," she said, her head resting on the wheel. "You're gonna get me killed, lady."

"What you do, almost hit somebody?"

"Just shut up talking. You ain't got no sense."

"Neither does your mama and your daddy," Grandma Tyler said.

An hour later, they were still on the phone. Reesy told her about her new haircut.

"Does Tyrene know you did it?" Grandma Tyler asked.

"Heck no. That'd just be something else for her to fuss about."

"One-a these days, you gon' learn from what I say. Don't let them two bully you. I done told you before, they ain't no saints. You a grown woman. It's time you know that. Stop measuring your life against what they might or might not say. They didn't let nobody do it to them, so don't you let nobody do it to you."

Reesy was back on the road, headed toward Utah. She saw the reason for the absence of roadkill in Wyoming. Fencing separated the fields from the interstate. Nebraska, at least the part she saw, had been wide open and unfenced.

"That explains everything," Reesy said.

"Right. They was some wild ones, those two," said Grandma Tyler.

"I'm sorry, Granny. I wasn't talking to you."

"Well, who was you talkin' to? Somebody in the car witcha? That's a mighty long drive you been on," she said. "We been on the phone for a long time. They ain't gon' shut it off, is they?"

"No," Reesy said with a laugh. "The phone's okay. And I wasn't talking to anybody. I was just looking at the road and talking to myself."

"Oh."

The old woman started humming again.

"So, Granny, how wild were Tyrone and Tyrene? And what do you consider wild, because my definition might be different than yours."

Reesy knew Grandma Tyler might consider exotic dancing outré. There was no way her parents had her beat. Maybe they cursed a little too much back in the day, and Tyrone was back on his cigarette habit again. So what, she thought. She bet that showing her naked ass to men for fun and money was the height of edgy behavior for anyone in the Snowden clan.

The old woman cleared her throat.

"They was wild, baby. Back when they was Panthers, they was into all kinds of stuff."

"Like . . ."

Reesy checked the road signs while she waited for her grand-mother to deliver the shocking goods.

"Like sharing partners."

"What do you mean, 'sharing partners'? Sharing them how?"

"I mean swappin' each other off for sex. Tyrone used to be a big cocky so-and-so, and them Panther men liked to rule they women. A few of 'em went through your mama, and your daddy let 'em have her. It was all 'for the cause.' Meanwhile he was rakin' his share of fat fannies 'cross the coals."

Reesy's eyes were fixed on the broken white line down the middle of the road. She couldn't imagine the things her granny was saying. Tyrone and Tyrene were much too prim and judg-mental to get down like that.

"Were they married then?" she asked, not sure she wanted to know the answer.

"Married?" Grandma Tyler said with a cackle and a rasp. "Them two?" Reesy couldn't tell if the old woman was laughing or coughing. "Them fools put the 'common' in *common-law*. It was your mama's big secret, that's why you ain't never seen a wedding picture round the house. I don't know why she kept it from you. They been together so long, what difference does it make that they ain't have no real ceremony?"

Reesy couldn't find the wind in her lungs to form words.

"Shit," Grandma Tyler said in a small voice. "I wasn't supposed to tell you that. I promised your mama I never would."

Reesy's ears were ringing.

"Well, you're grown now, Tweety, and you was bound to find out one day. Better to hear it from me." She cleared her throat. "That's why Tyrene was so upset that you had everybody in white at your wedding. It was her first real chance to see it done right. She wanted you to do what she didn't, but that's too much pressure to put on somebody."

Reesy was on the shoulder of the road now. Black was low on gas, but she didn't notice. The car idled while she leaned back against the headrest, her eyes closed.

"I'm not saying nothing your mama won't confirm. She knows she can't lie 'bout it, but ain't no way you'd know none of it if I didn't tell you. It makes me sick to seem them hold you to standards they wouldn't answer to themselves. It's time to put a stop to it. I'd spin in my grave knowing I left this world without you ever knowing the truth."

"Stop talking like that," Reesy said. Her eyes were still closed. She tried to picture Tyrone and Tyrene with people other than themselves. "I can't wrap my brain around this," she said with a whisper. "I feel like I'm in the Twilight Zone."

"I'm just sayin', don't let them make you question your life and your decisions," said Grandma Tyler. "They was rapscallions then, and they rapscallions now. They just rich ones, that's all. That's why I get so hot when they get on you 'bout stuff, all judgmental and intolerant. If I had a dollar for the times I smelt weed on your mama back in the day, or hell, a quarter for every time I heard them talkin' 'bout an orgy—"

"Grandma, stop."

"I'm sorry, Tweety," Grandma Tyler said. "I hope I'm not upsetting you. I'm just fierce when it comes to my tugar. I done watched them try to run roughshod over you for years and I can't take it no mo'. I done had my fill of this madness. My fill, I tell you."

"Right."

Reesy realized her theory about the ideal couple, well matched down to their near-identical names, was history. Gone in the twinkling of an old woman's attempt to protect her from harm.

Oh my God, she thought, my whole life is a fraud. She sat back up, leaning her head against the wheel.

Reesy imagined she could feel the universe shifting. Her molecular structure was being realigned into the creature she was supposed to be, something leagues away from the being she thought she was. It was like the girl in *Shrek:* princess by day, ogre by night.

She raised her head and stared at the highway.

All this time she had felt like a princess. Now she learned she'd been raised by two ogres. Which made her an ogre. Which, she figured, was pretty fucked up.

She stared at a FedEx truck that passed by. She focused on the back of the vehicle, her eyes fastening on the deepest color . . . purple.

She started to cry. It was bad enough to learn that Pa ain't Pa.

Who the fuck was Ma, was what she wanted to know.

Her hands were against the steering wheel. The ring twinkled through the kaleidoscope of her tears like a million stars in an open sky.

# I'll Take Manhattan
## . . . Beach

Although the rest of the drive was beautiful, it was unmemorable; a mere wrinkle in what Reesy considered a disastrous stretch of discoveries.

The Great Salt Lake went by unnoticed, and she rolled through the neon heart of Vegas without as much as a blink.

When the Los Angeles basin loomed ahead, Reesy was grateful to see the finish line, but blank about everything else. Grandma Tyler's confession had stunned her into a driving stupor. The old woman had thrown her a tennis ball–sized nut that would take her days to digest. The nut sat churning in her empty belly.

She had reached California with perfect timing. She needed to be far away from her farce of a former life. The damp streets of L.A. seemed as good a place as any for her to start over.

She exited the 405 at Rosecrans.

She took a right and hustled her way into the thick of traffic. She was just a couple of exits down from LAX. She knew that, wherever she settled, it had to be near the airport. Not so close that she was tortured by the perpetual sound of low-flying

97

planes, but not so far that the thought of leaving town or picking up a guest was out of the question. She didn't know where the hell Rosecrans was, but the signs around her indicated it ran through Hawthorne, Manhattan Beach, or El Segundo. She wasn't sure which.

She didn't know anything about Hawthorne or Manhattan Beach, and the two things she knew about El Segundo were unnerving. The first was that when she used to watch *Sanford and Son*, El Segundo and Julio were always the brunt of Fred Sanford's jokes. The other reference came from Q-Tip, along with his cohorts in the hip-hop group A Tribe Called Quest. Tip rapped about leaving his wallet in El Segundo. And he had to get it, had, had to get it. The mission to retrieve the wallet sounded like a dangerous thing. Just the thought of going back seemed to give them all pause.

Well, Reesy thought, if this was El Segundo, it didn't look like the hood. It was obvious Rosecrans was a main drag. She passed a sprawling parking lot for the Costco to end all Costcos, a big hub of concrete that looked like a place where smaller Costcos were hatched and disbursed. An army of cars circled and jock-eyed for position, duking it out for parking spaces and their God-given right to supersized savings. She drove on.

There was an Old Navy, a Barnes & Noble, a couple of gyms, a grocery store, a swell of fancy restaurants, more grocery stores, some eatery owned by Wolfgang Puck, a Bookstar, and a shitload of office buildings.

This was yuppieville. There were no mangy goats or Chicano babies with bare asses running around, as Fred Sanford would have her believe. What had all the fuss been about?

A huge movie theater complex loomed ahead to her right and a television complex beckoned on her immediate left. Manhattan Beach Studios. So she was in Manhattan Beach.

She was relieved to at least now have a point of reference.

*    *    *

She looked around as she drove down Sepulveda. A soft drizzle was falling that made the roads slick. Cars were moving with hesitant care, which gave her the chance to get a good look around. She was comfortable driving in the rain. The way she saw it, anyone from Florida worth her salt had long ago mastered the art of navigating tropical storms. This bit of dampness was child's play to her.

It was a typical beach city, much like the Fort Lauderdale of her youth. The difference was in the lay of the land. South Florida was a flat, sandy place, below sea level, she'd always heard. As a child, she feared it would sink and she'd be eye to eye with Flipper and his friends. California was different. She'd seen desert and snowcapped mountains during her drive, and now she was by the ocean. Every type of terrain seemed to be within reach. She noticed a big, solid rock of a mountain on the horizon ahead, surrounded by fog. It was beautiful and mysterious, like something out of an old Hitchcock film.

*Maybe I'll check around here*, she figured as she cruised past the sleepy little businesses and restaurants mingled with fancy car dealerships. She turned off Sepulveda onto Manhattan Beach Boulevard, stopping at the first apartment building with a "For Rent" sign.

"It's how much a month?"

Reesy wondered if she'd gone deaf.

"Eighteen-fifty," repeated Judy, the sophisticated young building manager, as she led Reesy around the tiny apartment. "Plus first, last, and security."

The place was pretty enough, with a fireplace, beige marble floors, and a vaulted ceiling, but the extra space that led up to the skylight wasn't livable. High ceilings meant nothing if all you had to work with below was under seven hundred square feet. And it was just a one-bedroom with a patio that wouldn't hold two people.

Eighteen-fifty, my ass, Reesy thought. Judy couldn't be serious. But she was. She said eighteen-fifty like she was saying two
dollars, with a smile. Like everybody had eighteen-fifty just lying
around.

"Manhattan Beach is, of course, one of the nicer areas in the
South Bay."

"What's the South Bay?" Reesy asked.

"Oh," Judy said with a pleasant smile. "You must be new to
L.A."

"Yes."

"Where are you from?" she asked, checking out the impres-
sive ring on Reesy's left hand.

"New York."

"New York is lovely," Judy said, leading Reesy out of the
apartment to the front of the building. "It's so fabulous there.
But, my goodness, it's expensive. Much more expensive than it is
to live here. Well, certain parts of L.A. are very expensive, of
course, but New York overall is so costly."

"Not in Harlem, it isn't," Reesy said. "You could rent a whole
floor for less than eighteen hundred bucks. Three bedrooms, a
kitchen, den, living room, a backyard. You get a lot of space for
your money."

"Yes, but who wants to live in Harlem these days?" Judy
asked. "Isn't it . . . ," her forehead crinkled as she chose her
words with care, " . . . rough there?"

"The white folks and the banks that are buying up everything
don't seem to think so," Reesy said, not choosing her words at
all. "In five years, Harlem's gonna be whiter than Utah. It's a
shame what's going on up there."

"Ohhkay." Judy looked down, unsure what to do with herself.
"Maybe you'd be more interested in Ladera or Inglewood?"

"Those must be black areas of town," Reesy said.

Judy's eyes widened and she coughed. Reesy spoke before she
could say anything to recover.

"I was born and raised in a beach town, Fort Lauderdale. It doesn't matter to me who lives around me, as long as they're decent and I feel safe. But I would like being near the beach and, if I had my druthers and it's going to cost me eighteen hundred dollars, I'd like a place with a yard. Maybe a rental house, you know?"

She smiled at Judy, who was still in a bit of an embarrassed stupor. Reesy watched Judy struggle to read her, as if she was unsure of what to say next. Reesy smiled again with reassurance and touched her on the arm.

"You know," Judy began, "I didn't mean anything . . ."

"It's okay," Reesy said. "You don't know me. For all you know, perhaps I would feel better in Linglewood."

"It's Inglewood."

"Well, there too," Reesy said with a laugh. Judy smiled. The two women walked to the front of the building and stood beneath the eaves, out of the rain. Reesy pulled her keys out of her purse and clicked the car alarm. Judy glanced in the direction of the responding chirps. She saw the black Porsche sitting by the curb.

"I think I might know of a place you'd like," she said. "It's more expensive, around twenty-one hundred, but it's a back house not far from the ocean. It's got three bedrooms, two baths, and a decent backyard. You want to see it? I know the owner pretty well. Things don't stay available around here for long."

"Thanks, Judy. Sure. I really appreciate your help."

The two women again smiled at each other.

"Um, Teresa," Judy said, "can I ask you a question?"

"Sure, but you have to promise to call me Reesy first."

"Okay . . . Reesy." Judy opened her mouth, then closed it, feeling a bit silly.

"Go on," Reesy said. "Ask me. We've obviously addressed the awkward stuff."

"Okay," Judy said. "I know this is going to sound crazy but, what are . . . druthers?"

Reesy smiled, realizing she'd just made her first L.A. friend.

* * *

The house was perfect, even though it cost a grip.

It was an older place, full of light, with lots of windows, hard-wood floors, spacious rooms, and cabinets everywhere. It was rich with character. There was a decent-sized front yard and a gate that led to a garden path and a secured backyard with ivy growing up the brick walls that enclosed it.

True to her word, Judy had called up her friend and he met Reesy at the property. He owned the house in front, which gave her an even greater sense of security.

Kent Sommers was a handsome thirty-something man with sun-drenched blond hair and a tan so golden, he made Reesy look pale. He was a family man who loved to surf, as evidenced by all the boards lining the side of his house. His wife, Barbara, was just as striking and golden, as were their two beautiful boys.

Reesy liked them at once, as they did her. They all sat together in the living room of their house, which was as open and airy as the one she hoped to rent. Reesy played with the children, five-year-old Colin and three-year-old Dean. Barbara made chai tea as they waited for Kent to do the requisite background checks.

Reesy hung out with them for three hours while he made calls to her prior landlords back in Harlem, Atlanta, and Fort Lauderdale. She and Barbara talked about Broadway, and life in New York versus life in Southern California. Barbara noticed the ring on Reesy's finger—and Reesy noticed her noticing—but neither woman spoke about it. They drank their tea as Reesy watched the boys playing with the family dog. Meg, a year-old Jack Russell, was a bright, wiry little thing that scampered about and did somersaults at will. Peals of laughter could be heard as the boys chased after her from room to room.

At least their family is real, she thought. Not like the counter-feit family she'd been brought up in.

Reesy wondered what her own marriage and family might

have been like, had the wedding commenced uninterrupted and the baby lived. No matter, she thought. It wasn't supposed to be.

When Kent returned smiling, she knew everything was a go. She was ready to move on with her life. There was no better time and no better place to start than right there.

She loved the rental house. It was far enough back so that she had privacy, and sound enough to buffer noise coming in and going out.

She liked it so much, she didn't even sweat what it was going to cost.

"Do you mind if I pay you several months in advance?" she asked Kent.

He and Barbara looked at each other.

"No," Barbara said. "That's not a problem at all."

Reesy had her cache of stipends, years' worth of checks for ten thousand dollars each that her parents had been sending every quarter since she'd turned eighteen. She had been investing that money for the past fifteen years, even though she had tapped into some of it in the last year to pay for rent and living expenses in Harlem. The stipends and dividends were now well into the low seven figures, a secret that Reesy kept well. Her ability to manage the funds and make smart decisions was a quiet source of pride. She had her parents' business acumen and a knack for numbers. Financial security was important to her, and while she wanted a partner to have her back on many levels and had looked forward to that with Dandre, it gave her a strong sense of satisfaction to know that she could always take care of herself.

So what if it was with her parents' money, she figured. As far as she was concerned, what they gave her was seed capital. It was her eagle eye that had turned it into greater profit.

She opened an account at a nearby Washington Mutual and transferred funds from her bank in New York. She returned later with a cashier's check for twenty-one thousand dollars. First, last, security, and seven months' rent. It sounded like an awful lot of money, enough to put down on her own piece of property, but she didn't know if she liked California that much just yet. She figured seven months would give her ample time to get settled and see if Manhattan Beach was where she wanted to be.

Reesy moved in that same day.

"The side door that leads to the back sticks a little," Kent said. "The wood swells. Winter's the rainy season and this is an older place. If it gets to be too much of a problem, let me know."

"Okay."

Reesy didn't expect it to be a problem. She didn't plan on spending that much time in the backyard anyway.

She called Misty the next morning to give her the address.

"Make sure you remember the half," she said. "It's six-oh-three and a half Bern Street."

"I got it," said Misty. "Are you sure you're okay out there? Do the people seem nice? I heard they're kind of superficial."

"I've been here one day. So far everything's fine."

"And your landlords' names are Ken and Barbie? That's crazy."

"It's Kent and Barbara," she said. "Look, I don't have time to talk now, but boy, do I have some heavy shit to tell you."

"About what, you and Dandre?"

"There is no me and Dandre, so I wish you wouldn't mention it again," Reesy said. "It's about T-n-T."

That was a nickname the two girlfriends had given Reesy's parents years before. Misty was silent on her end.

"Anyway," Reesy said, "I'm in the thick of traffic. I'll call you later. Just make sure my stuff goes out today, okay?"

"Okay."

"Hey."

"What?"

"You didn't do it, did you?"

Misty let out a heavy breath on the other end and, once again, there was silence.

"No, I didn't. I'm not going to."

"Thank God. You're doing the right thing."

"Look, Reesy—"

"No, you look. Whatever you do, don't ever tell Dandre my whereabouts. You got that?"

"Like I would tell him," Misty said.

"Just checkin'. Love, baby. I'll holla later."

Reesy went by a florist and ordered an enormous thank-you basket for Judy. She had one sent to Misty as well.

Then she went about the task of getting the basics from the Target on Sepulveda—pillows, a comforter, plastic cups and plates, snacks, and a little TV—enough to tide her over until her things arrived from New York.

Her stuff came five days later. By then her cable service had been set up, as well as her phone, power, gas, and the installation of appliances. Her first major L.A. lesson was that rentals didn't come with a thing. She had to buy a fridge, a stove, and a microwave.

The Sommerses' new vehicle—a shiny light blue SUV with a top rack packed with shiny new surfboards—arrived the same day as the freight truck with Reesy's belongings. She was beginning to realize one of the reasons why they loved her so. Her big fat check had given them a new car lease on life.

"Have you said anything to my daughter?"

Misty was at home in Greenwich, Connecticut, holding a pair of tongs, standing over a skillet full of hissing grease. Rick was stretched out on the couch, channel-surfing between news programs, waiting for her to serve up his favorite dish—fried chicken, homemade biscuits, fresh creamed corn, and cabbage with onions. The meal was heavy for the middle of the week, but he'd asked for it, and Misty wanted to please her man. She held the portable phone in the crook of her neck as she tried to keep from getting splattered.

"What do you want, Tyrene?"

"I want to know if you told Teresa what you saw."

She had Misty on speakerphone as she sat at the desk in her expansive office on the top floor of the Snowden Building in the heart of downtown Fort Lauderdale. Tyrone was in Miami Lakes briefing one of his clients, Trini Thompson, a popular, high-profile seasoned player for the Miami Dolphins.

Trini and his wife, Elise, were in the middle of a nasty divorce. After months of tailing her, to the detriment of his performance on the field, he'd caught her and her lover in flagrante delicto in a tiny motel in Islamorada. Tyrone had gone with him, afraid of what his close friend might do. His being there saved Trini's life, for had Trini been alone, he would have ended up in prison. He wanted to kill Elise and her lover, but Tyrone had stopped him. Now a tearful Elise was talking to every sports show, news channel, radio host, magazine, and newspaper that would listen. She was the remorseful wife, crying neglect because her husband was always on the road. Trini seemed like the villain. Tyrone was strategizing every way he could to turn the sentiment of the public and courts back to Trini's favor.

Tyrene knew it'd be hours before Tyrone returned. The two men would have dinner, drinks, and small talk before Tyrone broached the subject of business.

Misty maneuvered pieces of chicken out of the pan and onto paper towels. She lifted the lid on the corn and stirred. She couldn't believe this woman had the gumption to ring her up.

"I don't have anything to talk to you about," she said. "You should be getting your house in order, not questioning me."

Tyrene leaned forward, her palms on her desk.

"Now listen here, young lady," she said. "My daughter's had her share of trauma and crisis, what with that fool she almost married. The last thing she needs is a red herring thrown her way that has nothing to do with anything. It was an insignificant, unfortunate mistake, and none of us should ever be troubled with hearing about it again."

"Then why are you calling me?"

Tyrene slammed her right palm flat against the desk.

"Dammit, Armistice Fine, don't you get snippy with me."

Misty fumed at Tyrene's blatant refusal to acknowledge her married name.

"I'm calling you because I want an end to this. You've been like a daughter to me and I don't want any friction between us. If you love Teresa—if you love our family—then let this thing lie. We must promise to never speak of it again."

"Honey," Rick yelled from the other room, "is it almost soup yet?"

"Yeah, baby," she said. "Gimme a minute, I'm on the phone."

"Don't tell him you're on the phone with me," said Tyrene.

Misty set the tongs down and focused her attention on the conversation.

"So now you want to tell me what I can and can't say to my husband?"

"I'm telling you this is none of his business, and I hope to God you haven't said something to him already, because that would be very dangerous and foolish of you."

Misty laughed, her tone bitter.

"No disrespect, Mrs. Snowden, but you've got problems."

"Who do you think—"

"No, who do you think you are, calling me up and telling me what I'm allowed to say and who I'm allowed to say it to? I'm not a child and I'm not your child, so I suggest you take this bullying attitude of yours somewhere else."

Rick was standing in the kitchen doorway, watching his wife.

"Who dat, baby, Reesy?"

Misty shook her head and waved him away. He came over to her instead, stood behind her, and wrapped his arms around her waist. He palmed both breasts, then slid his hands down to her belly and rubbed it. She pried herself free from him and turned back to the stove.

The sound of Tyrene's ranting voice could be heard through the phone.

"What's up?" Rick asked. "Sounds like somebody's going off."

"Baby, give me a minute," she said. "The food'll be on the table in two shakes."

"Of that ass?" he asked.

"Yeah," she said, annoyed at his indifference to what she was experiencing on the phone.

Rick reached around her, his movements too quick for Misty to notice. The purloined wing burned his clenched palm as he rushed away.

"Oooch, oooch," he cried, tossing the blistering chicken from hand to hand.

Misty waited until he was out of the kitchen before she responded to Tyrene again.

"I'm hanging up now," she said into the phone, "and I suggest you not call here and threaten me again."

"It's not a threat."

"I don't care what it is, but if you call back with this nonsense, I will tell Reesy. And Tyrone. And Rick and Dandre. I'll round up everybody for one big conference call and get this . . . *situation* . . . out in the open for once and for all."


"What was that all about?" Rick asked, his cheeks full of bird. He shoveled more food into his mouth before he swallowed what was already in it.

"The Larchmont account," she said, staring into her plate. She didn't want lying to come as easy as it had of late in her marriage. It wasn't a smart foundation to build upon, she knew. But this was a small lie, she thought, so there was no harm that could come of it. Besides, she didn't have the energy to deal with what it would mean to disclose the truth about Tyrene's call.

"I heard you mention something about somebody having a bullying attitude," Rick said.

"It was nothing, baby." She picked at her biscuit. The sight of the food was making her sick. "Just one of the tenants. I told the on-site people to handle this. It should have never made its way up to me."

"But Larchmont's in my portfolio," Rick said. "Why didn't I get the call?"

"Who knows? Fuck it. It's no big deal."

Rick glanced up from his plate into his wife's face. Her eyes were troubled and she seemed tired. Her language was even a little harsher than usual. I'll give her some extra loving tonight, he decided. That might put some life back into her. He figured he'd start with running her a hot bath, then he'd give her a nice long massage. And then it'd be on.

Yeah, he thought. A long night of loving was just what Misty Hodges needed.

Tyrene was still at her desk two hours later, the lights of the city behind her the sole source of illumination in the room. She tapped her fingers with their excellent manicure against the desk. She was vexed, at a crossroads with herself. Why am I doing this? she thought.

"I don't like him," she said aloud. "But I don't know how to leave him alone."

She was still upset at Tyrone for what had happened between them in New York. She was accustomed to the two of them handling situations in tandem. That was their rhythm, bad cop–bad cop. Tyrone would rumble the trunk of the tree and she would make sure the branches fell. She didn't like weakness in men.

She couldn't afford it. Deep inside herself, Tyrene believed she was too weak to face the world without the support of someone strong. That was what had attracted her to Tyrone in the first place.

Even in the earlier days of their relationship when there had been so much free sex, it was an environment thick with machismo. Together they'd planned to be instrumental in the revolution, but their leaders would be chest-beaters, men who weren't afraid to step up to the challenge of building a new world order.

Tyrene felt Tyrone had carried those very principles into their practice. With her by his side, the two of them had created a revolution of their own.

But in a moment of unexpected weakness, he had abandoned her and their established rhythm. He'd left her out there, giving her the appearance of a shrieking loon. Tyrene had always been able to count on his booming voice to cover her own. Instead, everyone at the hospital had treated her like she was some type of hysterical shrew, and Tyrone's standoffish behavior and resonating "fuck you" had made it seem as if he concurred.

She wondered what would happen if Misty chose to say something to her daughter. She couldn't imagine what Tyrone would do.

Tyrene wanted to believe that Misty wouldn't say anything about what she'd witnessed. She was a nice, meek girl who didn't like drama and was quick to back down whenever Tyrene stepped to her about something she deemed inappropriate. This thing with Hill wasn't serious, she knew. It was a heady moment in her life that was compensating for several things, one of which included resenting Tyrone for smoking again. Her fascination with Hill would pass soon. She couldn't let it escalate to something unmanageable. Tyrene vowed to herself that she would let go before it threatened to jeopardize her relationship with Tyrone.

The first line of her phone rang. She picked it up at once.

"Tyrene," she said.

"What are you wearing?" asked the voice on the other end.

She leaned back, a twisted smile on her face, relaxing her legs into an open position.

"I wondered what was taking you so long."

"You miss me?"

She gave a cavalier laugh.

"Yeah," Hill said. "You miss me, old bird."

"Don't get cocky," replied Tyrene. "All I miss is your raggedy dick."

# I'm Going Going
## Back Back 2 Cali Cali

"Are you sure that's the address and phone number?"

"Yeah, man," Rick said. "Misty had it written on a notepad by the phone. She had to call the freight company so they'd know where to send Reesy's stuff."

The two friends sat across from each other in Swank's, one of their favorite uptown haunts. It was a dark place with dim lighting, a bar and grill designed for secrecy and conspiring. Swank's was where they used to meet to plan dirt, back in the days when they were apt to get dirty. It was a spot where they had taken chicks they didn't want to be seen with in the light of day. It was a place where they were assured discretion. Those days were long past.

This meeting wasn't about conspiracy. Dandre just wanted to get his woman back.

His face was weary and his eyes had been bloodshot every day since the-wedding-that-wasn't. He'd grown a beard. It would have suited him, Rick thought, if it weren't so unkempt and he didn't look so distraught.

"Shave that shit off before you head out to see her," Rick said. "You look like a two-dollar Danny Glover."

113

"Fuck Danny Glover," Dandre mumbled, downing his fifth warm scotch in less than twenty minutes. He signaled to the waiter.

"Hey man," Rick said, "Danny Glover's cool people. Because of him, you stand a better chance of getting a cab in this town."

"Then fuck you."

"Right," Rick said, leaning back against the cushion of the booth. "Fuck me. After I just gave you her address. As if enough people haven't been fucked already."

The waiter approached.

"Another scotch, no chaser," Dandre mumbled.

"Bring us some bottled water," Rick said. "No more drinks for this guy. And maybe some chicken wings and a basket of fries."

The waiter nodded and left.

"I don't want any fucking fries."

"You need to eat. When was the last time you had a decent meal?"

"Scotch is food."

The waiter returned with two glasses and a bottle of Pellegrino.

"I hate that shit with the bubbles," Dandre said to Rick. "You know that."

"I'm sorry, sir," Rick told the waiter, "could you bring us something noncarbonated?" The waiter reached for the Pellegrino. Rick slipped him a five-spot in advance of the tip that would be forthcoming. The guy had been putting up with a lot from Dandre. "We appreciate it, man."

"No problem," the waiter said.

Dandre smirked. "No problem. Right. His whole life wasn't just turned on its ear. What the fuck does he know about problems? I wish I had no fucking problems."

Dandre's shoulders slumped and his eyes grew teary, something that had been foreign to him before he got involved with Reesy. Now it seemed to happen all the time.

The first time he'd cried was when he'd learned she was playing him as payback for costing her a job. She had blamed him for her getting fired from her job as an administrative assistant when he complimented her on being such a talented stripper. His words weren't intended to be malicious. When she used to dance at the Magic City in Atlanta, she'd been one of the best he'd ever seen. But he'd acknowledged that fact in a roomful of people at Burch Financial, where she worked.

That's when she had laid out her plan for revenge against him. She wanted him to fall for her, and fall he did.

When he'd come upon Reesy and Helmut naked at her place in Harlem, he thought he'd never get over it. Instead, after days of being separated from her, his heart had opened even wider. That's what made him go to her in the middle of the night and propose. He'd gotten her pregnant that same night; he was sure of it.

All of it was still fresh in his mind because everything had happened just three and a half months ago. Reesy and Helmut. The pain in his heart. It took the devastation of that moment for him to realize that he didn't want a life without her in it. Now that was just what he was facing . . . again.

His shoulders shook and tears spilled onto the table. He didn't bother to wipe them. He just let them splash and fall into his empty glass.

The waiter returned with a bottle of Evian. Rick opened it, poured some into a glass, and pushed it in front of Dandre. The glass sat there, untouched, as Dandre's tears ran down his face, snagged by the tangle of his ragged beard.

"Rejeana came by," Dandre mumbled.

"What? Are you kidding me?"

Dandre nodded.

"So that was her at the wedding," Rick said.

"Yep."

"Shit."

Rejeana had been one of Dandre's old steadies. Not a real girlfriend, he'd never had one of those before Reesy. But she was someone he'd kept on rotation. She'd been on rotation for years.

Two years back, she'd gotten it into her head that she and Dandre were going to the next level. Rejeana had begun demanding more time and access. She'd started showing up places when he was out with other women, always confronting the women, never Dandre.

For a while it had amused him, until the night she showed up at One Fish, Two Fish, whipped out a knife amid a roomful of people just trying to enjoy their dinner, and threatened to cut Dandre's date. He hadn't dealt with her since and Rejeana, he believed, had just gone the way of dropped broads and the dinosaur.

"Why'd she do it, man? Were you seeing her again?"

Dandre glared at Rick. Rick shrugged.

"I'm just asking. You were about to get married. Sometimes the thought of that makes a brother revert."

At the words "about to get married," Dandre's eyes began to tear again.

"I wasn't fucking around on Reesy. Especially not with Rejeana. She just wanted the last word." He reached for the glass of water. "The bitch just had to have the last fucking word."

"What'd she want?" Rick asked. "Did you wring her fucking neck for what she did?"

Dandre knew Rick was being dramatic. That kind of thing wasn't a consideration for either of them. But his palms had been itchy when he saw Rejeana standing on his doorstep. If she'd been a man, he would have folded her whole body up into that big bubble ass.

"She wanted to say she was sorry," he said. "That she was still in love with me and was jealous because of how I dumped her and was marrying somebody else."

"But you dropped her ass two years ago."

"The bitch is crazy. That's why I stopped messing with her to begin with."

Rick stared at the table.

"Tell me something," he said. "If she was so damn jealous, how'd you get her to do that whole threesome scene?"

Dandre shook his head, flinching at the memory.

"She did it for me. She was down for anything she thought would make her top dog."

"Damn."

Dandre drained the glass of water and reached for the bottle of Evian.

"I told her Reesy had a miscarriage. You know what she said?"

"What?"

"'Good.' That lunatic looked me right in my eye and said, 'Good.' I wanted to strangle her, Rick." He clenched his fists in front of him as if he had the real Rejeana in his bare hands. "I wish I could have just squished the living fuck out of her. At least I'd feel halfway better."

Rick watched his friend across the table, remembering a time in his life when he'd gone through something just as traumatic. It was long before Misty, and was an epic loss that had upended everything in his world. Back then he couldn't imagine things ever getting better. But they had, and he wanted his friend to realize that the situation he was in would also pass.

Dandre had been with him through those terrible moments. He was the one who rescued Rick from a year-long abyss of self-pity, isolation, and borderline alcoholism.

As far as Rick was concerned, Dandre had saved his life back then, and now he was going to do everything in his power to return the favor. Even if it meant incurring the wrath of Misty, to whom he'd sworn not to tell of Reesy's whereabouts.

"We shouldn't get involved," she'd said.

"But, baby, he loves her."

"Then let's let them try to work that out. They've got enough complications already without us getting in the middle."

There'd been a resentful, almost angry undertone in his wife's voice when she said those words, which surprised him, because he assumed she was sympathetic to Reesy and Dandre's plight. Rick didn't take the conversation any further.

He knew how Dandre felt about Reesy. He'd known Dandre forever, it seemed, and no woman had ever affected him the way this one had. Rick was going to help, if he could, starting with giving him Reesy's address. He didn't break his promise to Misty. He didn't tell Dandre. He wrote the address down and handed it to him.

After that, it was on Dandre.

Rick just hoped he could get it together enough to make the right moves.

"So what are you gonna do when you get there?" Rick asked as he pulled into JFK, headed for the American Airlines terminal. "You can't just pounce on her, you know. That'll make things even worse."

"I know," said a clean-shaven Dandre. His eyes weren't as red, compliments of Visine. The weeping wasn't over, he'd just gotten better at hiding it. "My dad has a place on Hermosa Beach, which is right next to Manhattan Beach. My cousins have been staying there."

"The twins?" Rick asked, looking over at him.

"Yeah. Zoe and Chloe have been in the house since they first moved to Cali."

Zoe and Chloe Renfro were video hoes; starlets on the make, twin visions of walking, talking sexuality. The girls had been featured in a host of rap videos, from Snoop Dogg's to Master P's. Their specialty was straddling the hoods of expensive cars and flashing their breasts.

They were statuesque, free-spirited girls with honey-brown

complexions and corkscrew curls of auburn hair tumbling every which way. Their doe-eyed expressions belied their zest for freakiness. The tattoo on the left cheek of each girl's ass—a pair of red lips with a big, bright outstretched tongue—hinted at their true, wanton nature.

During Rick's period of depression, Dandre summoned Zoe and Chloe to help rescue him. Dandre drove Rick to his place on Martha's Vineyard, had Zoe and Chloe flown in, and—within the course of one bizarre hedonistic afternoon—Rick had experienced a mental and physical rebound. Dandre had admitted to partaking of the two women himself in past crazed encounters. He did it again that day at the Vineyard. He claimed they were distant cousins, so distant, he never even bothered to mention them to Reesy. Rick always suspected distant just meant they lived three thousand miles away.

"So you're sure that's gonna be cool?" he asked. "Those girls are probably into some pretty wild shit. Who knows what goes on up in that house? The last thing you need is for Reesy to get wind of it. That's why this whole situation went down to begin with."

"I'm not trying to be up in any mess," said Dandre. "It's a big, two-story house on the Strand, facing the water. I'll crash there for a while in one of the rooms upstairs. I figure I'll stay as long as it takes."

He had one carry-on bag with him.

"By the looks of things, you don't expect it to take very long," Rick said.

"I can buy whatever else I need when I get there. I wanna travel light." Dandre glanced over at this friend. "I just want her back, man. Do you think there's any chance I can ever get her back?"

Rick put his hand on Dandre's shoulder.

"Of course there is. As long as you have faith and your heart's in the right place, you can do anything, and that includes getting your woman back."

"Right."

"One more thing," Rick said.

"What's that?"

"Whatever you do, don't cry too much. Reesy's tough. You know that. She's already seen you cry and she left anyway. Restrategize. Don't be too hard, but don't punk out either."

"I'm not a punk," he said, his eyes growing red again. "You've known me all my life and never saw me go out like that. How can you call me a punk?"

"I never said you were. I'm just saying . . ." He watched Dandre pull the Visine from his pocket and squirt it in his eyes.

"You cried every day for a year after what happened with Keisha," Dandre said.

Rick grew quiet. That had been a very hard time for him. The pain he felt back then was real, and nothing about it had to do with being weak. He lost Keisha right when he realized how important she was to him. He never wanted to make that mistake again. He thought about the desperate measures he was taking now to make sure that would never happen with Misty.

"You're right, man," he said. "I'm sorry."

"Reesy's the one. I can't lose her." Dandre cleared his throat, choking back his emotion. "This shit is tearing me up."

"I know," said Rick. "Just think about how you're gonna step to her. This might be your last shot. Don't blow it again."


"Puppies," he said.

"What's that?" asked the flight attendant passing his row in first class.

"Huh? Oh. Nothing," Dandre answered, shocked to discover he was thinking aloud. He was three hours into the more than five hour trip, and he'd been searching for some kind of icebreaker that would allow him to contact Reesy again.

The woman gave him a questioning look, then went on.

Puppies, he mused. Yeah. That's how he would make his way

120

in. As hard as she tried to act like she wasn't, he'd discovered that Reesy was a real softie. Once they'd become open about their love for each other, she was affectionate and nurturing, a real homebody with a domestic streak. She had babied him and had been planning to baby the baby even more. They had talked about having the whole shebang, the two-point-five kids, the white picket fence, and even a dog. He was looking forward to all of it. He'd never had a pet as a child, but always loved animals. Reesy seemed to love them too.

I'll get her a puppy, he thought. That would give her something to pour her love into, and open the door for them to have dialogue again. He settled back in his seat, proud of himself.

Puppies were the answer to everything, he realized. There wasn't a person alive who didn't like them. He'd even read somewhere once that a post office brought them in for stressed-out employees during peak times like tax season and busy holidays. The puppies kept them from going postal. No matter how upset an employee became when overwhelmed with work, something about a bouncy bundle of fur just made it all seem better.

Dandre smiled as he reached in his pocket for the bottle of Visine.

It was after 8 P.M. when his flight landed. He rented an Explorer and drove straight to Manhattan Beach. He'd done Mapquest before he left New York, so he already knew general directions to where she lived.

He was careful not to appear conspicuous, lest she be outside or someplace where she would notice him. He wanted his first contact to be well planned.

His pace was slow as he drove past the address. The roads were slick and a slight drizzle was falling. The lights were on in the house in front. There was a side path that led to the back house, which he assumed was where she lived.

He pulled over to the side of the street, hit the lights on the truck, got out, and approached. The sound of barking could be heard from the front house. Dandre ducked behind a nearby tree. It was chilly and drizzling, and he was getting wet. He peered around the tree, toward the back of the house.

There was Black, parked deep inside the driveway, his New York plates in plain view.

"Perfect," he said.

He rushed back over to his rental, turned on the lights, and pulled off. He'd make his move tomorrow, he decided. First, he needed a long night of rest and a chance to reacclimate himself to the world of Cali. It had been a while since he'd been on the left coast.

He could hear the dull thump of music as he walked up to the house. The silhouettes of swaying bodies were visible through the windows. He put his key in the lock, but it was already open.

It was cold outside, but it was warm inside the house, and the air was thick with the stench of primo chronic. People were everywhere, walking, talking, dancing, and lying about as if they were at home. Containers of half-eaten pizzas and buckets of wings were on the coffee table, along with empty bottles of beer and liquor.

A stunning assortment of bikini-clad and topless women made out with various men and each other to the sounds of Snoop pumping through the stereo system. Zoe and Chloe— both topless—were dancing in the middle of the room. Sandwiched between them was a Suge Knight lookalike, a bald and bearded guy chomping on an unlit stogie.

"Go Sleazy, go Sleazy," they chanted.

Dandre stood in the doorway watching them.

"C'mon in, man," someone yelled. "Shut the door, it's cold."

Zoe and Chloe looked in his direction.

"Dandre," they yelled, running over to him, abandoning Sleazy to grind alone with his cigar.

"Who's that cat?" asked a guy on the couch. He was rolling a blunt the size of a hot dog.

"I own this place," Dandre said. "Who the hell are you, and why the fuck do you have all that weed in here?"

The guy raised up off the couch, ready for beef. Dandre dropped his bag at his side, sizing him up.

"Stop it, Ebay," Zoe said to the man, her bare breasts heaving. "This is our cousin Dandre Hilliard from New York."

"Cousin?" asked Sleazy, cocking his head at the girls as they stood beside Dandre. "Now this is kinda freaky. He don't seem too shocked to see your titties hanging out like that."

"We're distant cousins," said the twins and Dandre.

"Oh," Sleazy said. "Well, whatup then."

Random people in the room gave a nod and said what's up. The rest continued with whatever they were doing. Ebay sat back down, licked the blunt to seal it, and lit up. Sleazy went back to dancing, his eyes closed as he waved his cigar in the air.

"How come you didn't tell us you were coming out?" asked Chloe.

"Perhaps I should have," Dandre said. "Now clear this place and go put some clothes on."

Both women groaned and began to complain in unison.

"What? Why you trippin'? It's not like you haven't been in this kind of scene before. This used to be how you liked to get down."

"Not anymore," he said. "Get 'em out."

Dandre turned the dimmer switch in the living room to high. People began to cower and cover their eyes.

"What's going on?"

"Shut that light off."

"Whodafuck?"

"Yo, who got my weed?"

"Y'all, the party's over," Chloe said.

"Yeah," said Zoe, "y'all gotta get out."

The guests moaned and griped as they snatched up their

123

clothes, half-full liquor bottles, and unclaimed blunts on the coffee table.

Dandre walked past a couple going at it on the staircase.

"Time to break out," he said, tapping the man on the shoulder as he passed.

He walked up to the landing, then down the hall to the master bedroom. The door was open and the scent of marijuana was thick. From the way the bedsprings sang, he knew he didn't need to proceed any farther. He went back down the stairs. Zoe and Chloe had rustled most of the people out, barring a straggler or two.

"Handle that situation upstairs," he said.

Zoe and Chloe looked at each other.

"The Tonies," they said, and bounded up the staircase.

Dandre didn't want to know who or what the Tonies were. All he knew was that it was going to take a concentrated cleanup effort and some strong fumigation to get the place back to a decent, livable state.

The twins had turned the expensive beach house into a hoe haven and roughneck central. Dandre couldn't imagine why the neighbors didn't complain. Perhaps they had and the girls kept it to themselves. Perhaps Hill knew and had bumped heads with them before.

The Strand was a renowned section of the beach, checkered with older homes, fabulous new ones, and some even more magnificent that were under construction. Hill had built this house five years earlier, after tearing down the original property. Zoe and Chloe, both twenty-three, had been living there rent-free and unchecked. All they paid were utilities. They had moved out West at the age of eighteen, determined to sparkle in Hollywood like the twin orbs of light they deemed themselves to be. So far their twinkle had been dim, but they were an obvious hit with the do-me crowd.

\* \* \*

"Can I go to bed now?" Chloe yelled. "I've got an audition in the morning at eight. My nails are gonna be jacked up from this."

She was wearing a sweatshirt without a bra and a pair of shorts, and was on her knees scrubbing the floor. Zoe was in the kitchen with a mop. Dandre was upstairs changing the sheets and covers.

"No," he replied. "Not until this house is clean. This is ridiculous."

"No, you're ridiculous," Zoe mumbled from the kitchen. She walked out into the living room and over to her sister. "He's trippin'. What do you think is up with him?"

"I don't know, girl," Chloe said. "I thought he was getting married. I don't know what he's doing out here. Maybe he wants to use it for the honeymoon."

She threw the scrub brush into the bucket of soapy water sitting beside her.

"Then where are we supposed to go?" Zoe asked. "He can't just come kick us out like this with no advance warning. We should call Uncle Hill."

"Call him all you want," Dandre said, coming down the stairs with an armload of dirty sheets and blankets. "This place is mine too." He dropped the linens on the floor in a heap. "And I'm not kicking you out. I just need a spot for a few days, until I straighten some things out."

"Just a few days?" they asked.

"Yeah, but those parties are history. There'll be none of that action going on up in here again."

"But, Dandre," Chloe whined. "Everybody considers this the spot."

"Well, everybody's gonna have to go somewhere else. I need this place to be peaceful. I've got some important work to do while I'm here, and the last thing I need is that kind of chaos to fuck it up. You understand?"

They stood before him nodding their heads.

"Then say you understand."

"We understand," the twins chimed.

"Tomorrow we're draining that hot tub," he said.

Dandre went back up to finish the room.

"Yeah, right," Zoe said. "He done went mad if he thinks this is the last time there's gonna be a party up in here."

"You know?" replied Chloe.

Dandre stood in front of the house. It was still cold and rainy and the twins had long gone to bed. A beanie was pulled tight over his head, and his hands were stuffed into the pockets of his sweatsuit. He was getting soaked, but he didn't care.

He contemplated the roar of the ocean before him. Even though it was dark, he could still make out the foam crests of the waves as the choppy waters crashed against the shore. The salty scent of the sea was comforting.

"I'm getting her back," he said. "Watch."

It was a statement to the heavens. Dandre wanted the universe to know that no distance and no thing could stand between him and his woman.

"It's time to put away childish things and step up . . . be a man."

The crashing sound of the waves was the sole reply.

# Three Dog Night

At noon the next day, Dandre was at a place called the Pet Sanctuary. The dogs were gathered together by breed in little playpens; so were some of the kittens. The place was filled with the happy sounds of yipping and screeching, barks and meows.

"How are these?" he asked the saleswoman, pointing at a batch of small, barking dogs.

"Miniature schnauzers are great," she said. "They're very friendly and alert, but they do tend to be a little noisy. Do you mind a barker?"

One of the schnauzers had the lungs of Pavarotti.

"What's that?" he said, pointing at the face.

"The bushy eyebrows and muttonchops are very typical of the breed."

"Oh. So it would look funny if I shaved it off?"

The woman glanced at him with surprise.

"I don't think you want a schnauzer, sir."

They walked farther down to a pen of beautiful little white dogs.

"What are those?"

"Some are bichon frises," she said, "and some are Maltese."

The dogs all looked the same to him.

"How can you tell them apart?" he asked.

"Bichons have curly hair. The Maltese, as it gets older, has straight hair. They're related breeds and both have excellent temperaments. They're also ideal because they're hypoallergenic."

"How's that?"

She reached into the pen and handed him one of the dogs. It was a bundle of little curls with big black bright eyes.

"This one's a bichon. They have silky hair, just like the Maltese, so they don't shed. They do require their fair share of grooming, though." She took the squirming dog from him. "They've got a top coat and an undercoat, and if it's not cared for properly, matting can be a real problem."

Dandre imagined Reesy cursing him out for giving her a pet that needed its hair done more than she did her own. He wandered over to what looked like a pen of little foxes. There were only three of them—two that were a beautiful red sesame color and one that was black and tan. They flashed what appeared to be wide-mouthed grins when he approached.

"Now these are cute," he said. "What are they? I've never seen them before."

The woman put the bichon away and came over to him.

"Aah . . ." she said. "These are my babies. They're very, very hard to get. I couldn't believe these three even came through. They've only been here for a few days, but they're inseparable."

Of course they are, he thought, they're together in a pen.

She knelt down, playing kissy-face with the puppies. "Aren't you inseparable, my cute little munchkins?"

The foxettes leapt and grinned at her. They didn't bark like the schnauzer and, without all that silky hair, they didn't seem as high-maintenance as the bichons and Maltese.

"What are they called?" he asked. "Do they get very big?"

Reesy wouldn't want a big dog. He was sure of that.

The woman picked up the black and tan one. It pinned its ears back and tried to lap her face. She handed the dog to Dandre.

"These are shiba inus," she said.

"Shiba what?"

"Inus. They're related to the Akita, although much smaller and with much better temperaments. They are a very happy, friendly breed by nature. They're indigenous to Japan—the most common breed there—more than a million, I think."

"Wow."

Dandre petted the puppy's head. It looked him in the eyes and grinned.

"Awww," he said. "It's smiling at me."

"She likes you," the woman decided, taking the dog.

She handed him the other two. Both puppies lapped his face and grinned, their ears also pinned.

"Oh, this is awful. Why'd you hand me these two? They look so cute when they lay their ears back like that. There's no way I can decide on one."

At that comment, the smaller red sesame puppy let out a yip.

"It's okay, baby," the woman said, rubbing the dog's head. "He might not split you up. He's still looking. It's okay."

"What do you mean, 'he might not split you up'?"

"Well," she said, "they're so close. The two little ones are lit-termates—you know, siblings. The bigger one is from another litter, but these two took right to him like family. I've never seen three dogs so attached to each other."

Dandre stared at her. The two red sesames licked his cheeks. She held the black and tan dog in her arms. It flashed him a white-toothed grin.

"They're gorgeous, aren't they?" she said. "They don't bark at all, unless it's to alert you to something. Every now and then you find one that has a curious bark, but that's rare."

"A curious bark?" he asked. "What do you mean by curious? Like this yipping? Because that's not a problem. It's kind of cute."

"Oh, don't worry about that other thing," she said with a wave of her hand. "It's nothing. These dogs are a joy. Very feline. They even clean themselves like cats, so bathing won't be a big problem at all. They almost kind of look like cats, don't you think?"

She played with the black and tan one's curled, bushy tail.

"They're not high-maintenance. And as long as a shiba has room to play, he's happy. Well . . ." She looked at the puppies. " . . . as long as they're together," she said in an exaggerated baby voice.

Dandre thought of Reesy and how she might react to such a thing.

"How old are they?" he asked.

"The girls are two months and the boy is four months."

Dandre coddled the dogs. They were reeling him in. The woman said nothing to him for a while as she watched him playing with the happy puppies.

"So how much do they cost?" he said at last.

"Six hundred."

"Together?" he said with shock. "Man, they're expensive. That's two hundred a dog."

"Oh my goodness, no," she replied with a laugh. "They're six hundred apiece."

Eighteen hundred–plus dollars, twenty minutes, ten pounds of puppy chow, six chew toys, three collars, three name tags, three puppies, and one baby pen later, Dandre emerged from the pet store. The woman stood in the doorway waving good-bye.

"She's gonna kill me," he said to the dogs. "I came for one of you. How in the world did I end up with three?"

The smaller red sesame shiba yipped. She sported a collar and tag with her new moniker—Harlem—named for her soon-to-be owner's former place of residence. The black and tan one was dubbed Peanut, in honor of Reesy's stage name as an exotic dancer, Peanut Butter. The larger red sesame shiba—the lone boy—was called Dante, a blend of Dandre's name and Reesy's real name, Teresa.

"Yeah," he said to the puppies. "I got played, right? That's what you're trying to say."

The three dogs yipped and wagged their curly tails.

He loaded them into the rented Explorer.

The woman watched him for a moment, smiled, then walked back inside the store.

"I can't believe he took all three," she said to her assistant. "That don't-split-'em-up bit hasn't worked in years."

The puppies were running around the beach house, pissing and shitting on everything that didn't move.

"You just had us up all night cleaning this place," Zoe said. "How you gonna bring these rats up in here and let them loose on everything?"

"For real," Chloe said. "I'm not getting on my knees again and scrubbing these floors, that's for damn sure."

Harlem ran toward her and leapt in her arms with surprising agility. She lapped Chloe's face and tugged at her curls. Chloe laughed.

"Get off me, you little house of shit. That's not gonna win me over."

Harlem kept licking. Chloe cradled the dog like a baby and walked upstairs.

Dandre watched her as he sat on the couch writing out a Mahogany Hallmark card to Reesy. The twins were not animal people at all. If the dogs could win them over, he knew they'd be his way back into Reesy's heart.

He waited until nightfall and the dogs were tired. They slept in fits, he discovered, like human babies. They would play very hard for a solid thirty minutes, then sleep for two hours. After their last burst of energy—around ten-thirty—he put the dozing bundles of hair into a box with holes cut in it and a big red bow tied on top. He loaded up the baby pen, chew toys, and dog chow.

He drove with caution down Sepulveda, not wanting to wake the dogs. The wipers were on "slow intermittent" to minimize the noise. The rain wasn't heavy enough to warrant the wipers to begin with.

He pulled past the house, looking for a sign of the car. He got out and ran over to the tree he had hidden behind the night before.

Black was deep in the driveway. He could see one light in the main house, but no lights seemed to be on in the back house. He imagined she was in bed asleep, still adjusting to the time change. At least, he hoped that's what she was doing.

He opened the back door of the truck and lifted out the box. He tiptoed across the street, past the front house, down the side driveway. The puppies didn't stir. He sat the box on Reesy's front step. A part of the roof jutted out over the box, protecting the dogs from the rain.

He rushed back to the truck and grabbed the other items. He deposited them beside the box and dashed away. He had almost made it when he heard the sound of barking. It wasn't coming from the puppies. It came from the main house.

"Shit," he said, bolting for the Explorer. "That's gonna wake the dogs up for sure."

He already expected them to be up soon. That was a part of the plan. They would whine, yip, and scratch at the box, and Reesy would hear it and come to the door. The barking dog altered his plan somewhat. He figured it best to get out of there before Reesy saw him and nothing ended up going as it should.

Reesy had the covers pulled over her head when her phone rang. It rang three times before it registered. She reached her arm from beneath the covers and picked it up before it could roll over to voice mail.

"Hello?"

"Hi . . . Reesy? It's Kent."

"Kent who?" she asked, her voice muffled by the comforter over her head. She was borderline delirious. She had joined a nearby gym and was exhausted from the workout. She did two classes, one at the insistence of a black girl named Rhiannon that Rowena introduced her to.

Rhiannon lived in Lawndale and went to the same gym. She insisted Reesy try the kickboxing class. She did and loved it. Rhiannon helped her get through some of the moves and keep up with the teacher.

When Reesy got home, she hit the bed within minutes of showering and was asleep by nine o'clock. It seemed like midnight to her. She was still operating on New York time.

"It's your landlord, Reesy."

"Oh. Shit. My bad." She sat up in the bed, rubbing her eyes. "What's up, Kent? Is everything okay?"

"Uh . . . well . . ."

Reesy could hear yipping.

"What's that noise?"

"Could you come to your front door?"

"Sure," she said. She hung up the phone.

Reesy was in her pink fleece pajamas. The ones with the feet enclosed. Kent would get a kick out of that, she figured.

"So what?" she said, scratching her fleecy ass as she made her way to the living room. She flipped on a light and went to the front door.

She opened it and a cold burst of wet air rushed in. Kent was standing on the front step in a raincoat, holding a box wrapped in a big bow with something scratching inside.

"Meg wouldn't stop barking, and then they started in. I'm surprised all the noise didn't bother you."

"Who is 'they'?"

"This box, and all this other stuff," he pointed at the dog chow, baby pen, etcetera, "was sitting at your door."

Reesy stuck her head out and looked. There was a big bag of

something and a folded object, but it was too dark and rainy for her to make them out.

Perhaps, she thought, this was a gift from Judy, the woman who had referred her to the Sommers. Or maybe from Misty. She had sent both of them gift baskets. But what was it, she wondered, a boxful of hamsters?

"I'm assuming you weren't expecting this," Kent said.

"Not at all. I'm sorry for the disturbance."

He handed her the box.

"No problem," he said.

He brought the things from the porch inside while she took the box over to the couch. She set it on the floor beside her. The yipping wasn't as bad but the scratching was frantic.

She noticed the card attached with her name, now smeared from the rain.

She tore the envelope open.

Kent was standing in the doorway.

"Sounds like whatever's in that box is itching to get out."

"I'm sorry about this disturbing you."

"It's okay," he said. "I'm just a little concerned. Were you planning on having pets?"

"I hadn't thought about it."

Kent gave a pensive nod.

"Am I allowed to have one?"

"Yeah . . . well . . . it's okay if it's small. I just don't want anything that's going to destroy the house or the yard."

"I promise I won't let that happen," she said, hoping she was telling the truth.

Kent nodded.

"Alright," he said. "It's late. Why don't we just take it as it goes."

"Thanks, Kent. I appreciate it."

The critters kept yipping and scratching.

"Think you can take it from here?" he said.

"Yeah, I got it. Thanks for coming over and, again, I'm really sorry about the noise."

"No problem," he said. "I'm up front if you need me." He was almost out the door. "By the way, that outfit is cute. It looks pretty warm. I'd like to get one for Barbara."

"It was a gift," she said.

"Seems that people like giving you things," said Kent.

Whatever was in the box was threatening to claw its way out.

"Looks that way, doesn't it?" Reesy replied.

The card was from Dandre. She hadn't paid attention to the other stuff Kent had brought inside, but the frenzied scratching was enough to make her believe what was in the box was a manic kitten, or a cat.

*I hope you love them an eighth as much as I love you, which is too infinite to measure,* the card said.

"Oh brother," said Reesy. She finished reading it.

*Please, please forgive me. Your lover for life, Dandre.*

She flung the card to the floor.

"I can't believe Misty gave him my address. I'll deal with her in the morning."

She undid the bow and pried open the top. The three things looked up at her, leaping and yipping in unison.

Cats. He had given her cats.

Great, she thought, as if the foiled wedding and miscarriage weren't enough to cement her fate of being alone forever. Now she'd have a houseful of cats to seal the deal.

The black and tan one reached its paws out for her. It was too irresistible for her not to pick the thing up. She looked at the tag on its collar.

"Peanut," she said. "Okay, that's cute."

She put Peanut in her lap and reached for another. She studied its tag.

"Dante. Ohhhhhkay."

It didn't take much for her to figure out the origin of that.

She put Dante on the floor. He rubbed against her leg and lay down, resting his head on her foot.

"Oh, how sweet," she said. "What a sweet, sweet boy kitty."

The last one jumped out of the box before she could pull it out. It made a mad dash around the room, then raced over to Dante and pushed him off her foot.

"Goodness," she said. "And who the hell are you?"

She grabbed it and brought it close to her face.

"Harlem. I guess you're a girl." She shook her head. "This is ridiculous."

Harlem stuck her tongue out, trying to lick Reesy's face. Reesy put her back down on the floor and Harlem took off. She stopped by the dining table and let go a puddle.

"Oh my gosh. Now I gotta deal with this."

She picked up Dante and Peanut, then stood and went over to Harlem. She scooped her up and led them over to the side door that led from the kitchen to the garden path and backyard. She positioned all three critters so that they were under one arm, unlocked the door, and pulled. She pulled again. The door was swollen from the rain. Dante, Peanut, and Harlem squirmed under her arm.

She set the animals on the floor, grabbed the knob with both hands, kicked it, and pulled. It popped open, a thin mist of rain coming in with it. She turned around for the trio, but they'd all scattered. The kitchen was empty except for her.

She pushed the door so that just a crack was open and ran into the living room. Dante was on the floor rolling on his back and Harlem was doing her best to rip a hole in a pillow. Peanut sat on the couch with her paw on the television remote.

Reesy rounded them up and went back to the kitchen. She shoved them all out.

"Go take care of your business," she said. "And hurry up . . . it's cold and it's wet."

Dante, Harlem, and Peanut sat on the back doorstep, staring at her.

"Go," she said. "Git. Go pee."

They sat there, getting soaked by the rain.

"Oh brother," she said, scooping them up. She kicked the back door closed and gave it an extra shove with her foot. She fastened the lock.

"If you guys mess up this house, it's on."

Dante and Harlem licked her arms. Peanut cocked her head.

She walked into the living room, over to the things Kent had brought inside. She saw the baby pen.

"Aha. Here's your bed."

She wanted to sit them down, but was afraid they'd all disperse again. Reesy thought for a moment, then walked back into the kitchen. She sat them on the floor.

"Wait in here," she said. They charged at her, but she closed the kitchen door before they could get through.

"Damn."

She went over to the baby pen and grabbed it. She carried it into her bedroom and unfolded it, snapping the hinges into place. She put it near her bed so that she could look down into it.

"I can't believe him. Giving me a damn herd of cats."

Reesy wondered how he'd got them there. For the first time, the thought entered her mind that Dandre might be somewhere near.

"Tomorrow," she said. "I'll think about that tomorrow."


Dandre wondered how Reesy was reacting to the dogs. He lay in bed smiling at the thought of her discovering them. He realized that he'd forgotten to give her the folder with all their paperwork—their descriptions, ages, dates of birth, parentage, and medical information. All the puppies had been given their primary shots, but they'd be due for new ones in a few months.

They'd be back together by then, he thought. He'd handle all that. She'd still need the paperwork.

He figured he'd get up very early and leave it at her front door. It was too risky to go back now. Reesy might still be up, getting acquainted with her new little brood.

The cats were barking.

Reesy threw the covers back and flipped on the light. She was beat. She hadn't had more than two consecutive hours of sleep since she'd come home from the gym.

She looked down into the pen. Harlem and Dante were looking up at her, making barking sounds.

"Ssssh," she said. "Stop it. Cats don't bark."

The black one was ghost. Reesy hung over the edge of the bed and looked beneath it. The varmint was sleeping on the floor.

Let her stay there, she thought, I'll get her in the morning.

She turned off the light, pulled the covers over her head, and went back to sleep.

When she awoke the next morning, Peanut was curled on top of her stomach. Dante and Harlem were in the pen, looking up at her with white-toothed grins. They stretched and made yawning sounds as they watched her get up. Peanut sat on the bed gazing down at the other two as though she weren't one of them.

"I know you guys need to go to the bathroom by now," Reesy said.

She grabbed Peanut under her arm and walked into the living room. She went to the window.

"It's still raining. Sheesh. This is like being in Florida."

The critter cocked its head at her.

Reesy opened the front door and stood on the step. The air was chill and everything in the outside world was soaked.

She was about to go back inside when she noticed a big white envelope by the side of the door. She reached down and picked it up. The words DOG PAPERS were written on the outside. She looked at Peanut.

"Y'all are dogs?"

Peanut yipped.

Reesy went inside and shut the door. She sat the puppy on the floor. Peanut scampered off to the bedroom to join the other two.

"That muthafucka gave me three dogs," Reesy said, still standing in the living room. "I can't believe that muthafucka gave me three dogs."

# PART 3

*Fuct*

# Sex and the Titty

"I swear I didn't give him your information," Misty said. "I had it written on a notepad. Rick must have gotten it, although I thought we agreed we'd both stay out of it."

"Is he in California?"

"I don't know. I didn't even know he had your address until five minutes ago when you told me about the dogs."

Reesy ran her hand across her cropped hair.

"You need to check your husband," she said. "You guys don't seem to understand each other when it comes to making agreements. Give him something else to stick his nose into besides my business. You tell him you're pregnant yet?"

"No."

"Any idea when you plan on doing that?"

"No."

"Umph," said Reesy. She heard a rough chewing sound. She turned around. Harlem was eating a hole into the hardwood floor. "What the fuck kinds of devil dogs are these?" she screamed. "What was he thinking, giving me a pack of wild animals? I was lucky I talked my landlord into letting me keep all three. He's gonna kill me when he sees the floor."

She ran over to the dog and put her in the baby pen, which

she had moved into the living room since it was no longer night. Peanut was sitting on the sofa watching *The Young and The Restless*. Dante was by Reesy's feet.

"This is ridiculous," she said, sitting down on the couch. "They're not housebroken, they're eating up the fucking wood. He just dropped the damn things off and left me with something that I really don't need."

"So call him and tell him to take them back."

Reesy rubbed Dante's back with her big toe. He leaned his head against her leg.

"Well . . . they're kinda cute."

"Then call him and thank him," said Misty.

"How about I not call him at all?"

"Reesy, those pictures were old. He told me that and so did Rick."

"And, of course, men don't lie or protect each other."

"You know he wasn't lying," Misty said. "He was with you every night. If you're scared, just say you're scared. We both know that's why you're running. But don't put something on Dandre that you know isn't true. Don't pretend he's still a player. You know he loves you."

"I didn't call you for a lecture."

Her phone beeped.

"That's probably Rhiannon," Reesy said.

"Rhiannon? Like the song?"

"Yeah," Reesy said with a laugh. "Like the song."

"Who is she?"

"A girl I met at the gym. We're supposed to hang out today."

"Is she black?"

"Yeah."

"She is?" Misty asked with disbelief.

"Hold on."

Reesy clicked over.

"Hello?"

"Hi."

Both ends of the line were silent.

"So do you like them?" Dandre asked after the moment of surprise had passed.

Reesy let out a deep breath.

"Why can't you just let me be?"

"Because I love you. I'm sorry about everything that happened. I don't want to lose you. I'm not going to lose you."

"Dandre, I'm not ready to talk to you just now."

"So when will you be ready?"

"I don't know. Maybe never."

"Reesy, I'm in Califor—"

"I've got Misty on the other line. I gotta go."

She clicked over.

"So was that your girl?"

"Shit."

"What's wrong?" asked Misty.

"The muthafucka's here."

Reesy put the puppies in the baby pen and laid two folding chairs across the top. She figured that would keep Peanut from getting out.

She went by Rhiannon's apartment in Lawndale. It was a roomy two-bedroom job with underground parking. Rhiannon's walls were covered with various head shots of herself, blown up and framed. The place looked like a gallery. Rhiannon was a beautiful girl who was quite photogenic.

"So have you booked much work?" Reesy asked as she walked around Rhiannon's place.

"Yep, I have. My agent's pretty good. I was an extra on *The Jamie Foxx Show*, and I had a speaking part on an episode of *Seinfeld* one time."

"Really?" Reesy said, turning to look at her. "What'd you say?"

Rhiannon put on her game face as if she were on the *Seinfeld* set. She positioned her shoulders and flashed her pearly whites.

"Coffee?"

Reesy waited, but there was nothing more.

The girl broke character and grinned. "That was good, huh?"

"Superb," Reesy said.

"Yep. I thought so too. I've got a callback tomorrow for this movie I auditioned for. I hope I get it. It's got Taye Diggs and Richard T. Jones in it. Don't you think he's cute? I think he's really fuckable."

"Who?"

"Richard T. Jones."

Reesy shrugged.

"To tell you the truth, darling, I can't answer that question, because I don't know who the hell that is."

They went to the Third Street Promenade in Santa Monica. The sun was out a little. They walked among the various shops, drifting in and out of stores. Reesy and Rhiannon both bought a few things.

"This place is nice," Reesy said.

"Yeah, it's a pretty cool spot. Everybody comes here."

They passed by a Borders bookstore.

"Hey," Rhiannon said. "Let's go in here."

Reesy lingered at the front of the store, checking out the new releases.

"I'll be over in the African-American section," Rhiannon said and walked off.

Reesy flipped through a book called *Cooking Italy*. She had just bought the book, two weeks before the wedding. Dandre loved Italian food and she had intended to master some of his favorite dishes.

"Whatever," she mumbled.

She wandered over to the African-American fiction section. An ocean of books stared out at her. Reesy took a step back, overwhelmed.

"Jeez, when did this happen?"

Rhiannon came up behind her.

"What are you talking about?"

"All these freaking books."

"These?" Rhiannon reached out and took one from the shelf, something written by one of those three-name authors that were all the rage. "These books have been here. How can you act like you don't know about black books? You seem so smart."

"I do know about black books. I just didn't know it had come to this."

Rhiannon held up the back cover of the one in her hand. Eric something-something. Reesy thought she saw the word *dick* in there somewhere. She was an expert at spotting dicks.

"I love him," Rhiannon murmured, stroking the man's face. "And he's really fuckable, don't you think?"

Reesy made a mental note to add the Dick writer to Rhiannon's ever-growing list of fuckable men.

"If it wasn't for these books, I wouldn't be able to sit through getting my tracks put in."

"You have tracks?" Reesy asked, startled out of her book daze. She studied Rhiannon's head for the telltale humps.

"Yeah." Rhiannon shook her lustrous mane of loaner hair. "You didn't even know, did you?"

Reesy looked closer, shaking her head. It was fabulous work. Imperceptible to the naked eye.

"Can I touch it?" Reesy's hand was already on Rhiannon's crown. She palmed the top, then felt along the back. Everything was smooth, barring the random surface variations that only a good palming would detect, and even then, those variations could pass as dips in the topography of Rhiannon's natural dome. The texture and color were seamless.

"It's good, ain't it?" the girl gloated. "I go to this chick on Sunset. She does all the stars. You wouldn't believe some of the people in this town who got weaves."

"What else on you is fake?" Reesy asked.

Rhiannon was stunned by the abruptness of the question. She'd never been asked in such a bald-faced manner.

"Well," she stammered, "it's not like I've had a buncha stuff done."

"What qualifies as 'not a buncha stuff' to you?"

Rhiannon's eyes went up a little to the left as she did a mental checklist. Her lips moved but no words came out as she began to count on her fingers the litany of physical tweakings she'd had. She double-counted and threw herself off. She shook her head and her hands and began her tally again, this time aloud.

"Let's see . . . there's my hair . . . my nails," she held out her fiery-red talons, " . . . and my titties are new." She cupped them as she said this. "Girl, this doctor's good too. He went in from the side, so I don't have that ugly nipple with the cut-around marks like Freddy Krueger's been at 'em or something."

Reesy checked out Rhiannon's showroom 36C's. They were nice, as tits went, but now that she was aware of their pertness, she was aware of their pertness.

Rhiannon paused, thinking again.

"I had my thighs sucked a little and my stomach sucked a lot . . . my upper back . . ." Again, the eyes rolling up to the left as she touched each part of her body she referenced. " . . . Oh, my bad, I almost forgot about this . . . I had my gums shortened and my teeth shaved down."

Rhiannon bared her teeth like a blue-ribbon mule.

"Damn," Reesy muttered, rubbing her chin. "A regular bitch like me just doesn't stand a chance."

"What do you mean, regular?" Rhiannon said. "You're not regular. You're gorgeous. Everybody's been checking you out everywhere we go today. Your guy in New York must be really good."

Reesy frowned. "What guy in New York?"

"You know, your plastic surgeon."

Reesy laughed, loud. Her voice was cacophonous and startling, even amid the choppy sounds of the Dave Matthews Band being piped everywhere, the clinking of espresso cups on tables, the foaming froth of the cappuccino machine, cash registers ringing, and the general din of scattered conversations. Reesy's laugh was rich and full of gravel, kind of guttural, almost angry—a wretched sound.

"Why are you laughing?" Rhiannon asked. "What, you think I might try to go to your doctor and get him to do me up like you? That's some *Single White Female* stalker shit. I don't get down like that. I was just giving you a compliment."

"Well, keep your compliment. I don't have a plastic surgeon, and I don't want one."

The left corner of Rhiannon's lip curled a little. She tilted her head and let out a soft breath.

"Okay. Whatever."

"Whatever, nothing. I haven't had any work done."

"Fine," Rhiannon said and walked off. She continued to mumble to no one in general or particular as she rifled through the shelves of books again.

"I can't stand people who wanna know all your business but they keep their shit to themselves like they're special or something. Like I'll tell her business. How stupid is that? Everybody's had some work done. What she wanna front for?"

Rhiannon stood among the books, giving no one a piece of her mind.

"This is unreal," Reesy said, laughing again. "Who the hell is she talking to?" She looked around. "Who the hell am I talking to?"

She went up to Rhiannon and put her arm around her.

"Sorry. I didn't mean to cut you like that. On the real, I haven't had anything done to me. That's the truth, I'm not trying to be tight about my business."

"Well, you must work out a lot."

"I've been taking dance lessons since I was two. I did it all through college. I did theater. I'm trying to do the movie and TV thing now, so I'm careful about eating right and staying in shape. That's all it is. I guess my body's just trained."

Rhiannon's expression indicated she still found Reesy suspect.

"Take my word for it. I don't have any reason to lie."

Reesy walked away to another section. She could feel Rhiannon watching her au naturel body in continued disbelief.

They were meeting a friend of Rhiannon's for lunch at PF Chang's.

"I think you'll like him," the girl said. "You're not looking for anyone to date. He's protective and he knows everybody. When you need a guy to hang out with without worrying about if he's gonna try to fuck you, Sleazy's your guy."

"Sleazy?" Reesy asked. "He doesn't exactly sound safe."

"Oh, he is. I mean, he'll come on to you at first, but that's just instinct. Once you check him, he'll be cool. Sleazy's got his share of women, so he'll probably appreciate having a girl as just a friend. I've known him for a few years and he's always had my back."

"Are you one of his women?"

Rhiannon smiled.

"We kick it every now and then. He's fun. But he's not the marrying type. Not right now. But then again, neither am I."

She flipped her mane.

Reesy thought about Dandre as she listened to Rhiannon. Perhaps that's how the woman from the photo thought of him. As somebody to kick it with. Fun. Not the marrying type.

"Sleazy's a comedian," Rhiannon said, "so that'll be a fun scene for you to check out. If you guys click, he'll probably take you around to some of the spots. You can meet the regulars on the Hollywood night scene."

\*     \*     \*

Rhiannon was right. Reesy and Sleazy clicked at once.

He had an easy personality, a blend of something both East Coast and West Coast, although he reminded her at every turn that he was from the great and wonderful land of Cleveland. Their conversation was seamless as they nibbled on seared-tuna-and-lettuce wraps. Rhiannon faded into the background, a bit annoyed that Sleazy was discussing things that he'd never broached with her before. She excused herself to the bathroom.

"Let me go check on her," Reesy said. "I think she's got a bit of a 'tude."

Reesy followed her.

"I'm not into him, Rhiannon," she said. "You said I'd probably like him. Well, I do. He seems like a fun person to hang out with."

"I'm not mad at you. It's just that he's talking to you about computers and movies and music and stuff, and you haven't even known him an hour. I've known him five years and he's never talked to me about any of that."

"Have you ever expressed interest in it?"

"No," Rhiannon said with a smile.

"Well then."

Both women laughed.

"Let's go," Rhiannon said. "He's probably hitting on the waitresses. Not that I care, but we need to save him."

"From what?" asked Reesy.

"Himself."

Rhiannon took off, leaving Reesy and Sleazy at the restaurant to continue their conversation.

"So how you adjusting, mami?" he said, chewing on an unlit cigar.

"I like it. I don't know about the rain so much. It reminds me of Florida. I thought it didn't rain in Southern California."

Sleazy's two-way pager beeped. It was sitting on the table between them. He checked it.

"It doesn't rain much here," he said, typing in a response on the tiny gadget. "Just in the winter. If we're lucky."

They ordered another round of drinks, and Reesy found herself talking to Sleazy as though she had known him for years. He told her how he used to hustle. She told him, without mentioning Dandre's name, that she had moved to L.A. to get away from someone who had broken her heart. She talked about her drive cross-country. She told him about the dogs.

"My ex followed me here," she said.

"Oh damn. Well, if you need some protection, just holla. I'm a big muthafucka. Folks tend to back off when they see my ass roll up."

"Thanks, Sleazy. I appreciate it." She took a sip of her drink. "Let me ask you a question."

"Alright." His two-way beeped again. "Hang on," he said. He read it, then typed something back in response. "Okay, mami. Shoot."

"Rhiannon said you'd probably hit on me. Why didn't you?"

He laughed, his big bald head tilting back like a heavy ball that might not rebound. His beard was salt-and-pepper. She didn't know how old he was. He could be thirty-three or forty-three.

"I love Rhi to death but she runs her mouth too much. She makes it sound like I holla at everything with a gap in its legs."

"She likes you. And from what I can see, you do holla at everything."

"Well . . . yeah. Just as long as it ain't got a dick."

"So?"

"So what, mami? You had me in the friend zone when I first sat down. I'm not stupid. I know a love-struck bitch when I see one. No offense. Plus this is a bit of a giveaway."

He tapped her left hand.

"That's a pretty big rock," he said.

"Yeah? And?"

"And, so, why do you still wear it if he broke your heart?"

"I don't know," she said. "Habit, I guess."

"Habit, hell. You're still hanging on."

Reesy stared at him. Sleazy stared back, his expression daring her to refute his words.

"You're hilarious," she said.

"I'm trying," replied Sleazy. "It's how I get paid. So look, mami, we gotta get you out. Get you into the L.A. groove. This is a filthy, rotten city, so brace yourself. But it's fabulous. The filthy and the rotten never looked so good."

"Bring it on," said Reesy. "I'm ready."

He glanced at the ring.

"You sure?"

In a grand gesture, she pulled at the thing. It didn't budge.

"My finger must be swollen."

"Yeah, right. Of course."

His two-way went off again. Sleazy checked it again. Reesy played with her finger.

It was somewhat pudgy. Not much, but enough to make the ring tight. Sleazy didn't know about her former pregnancy. Reesy tugged at the ring again, but it wouldn't come off.

"Forget the ring," he said. "That nigga's got you branded. Tell people you wear it to ward muthafuckas off."

"That's a thought."

"In the meantime," he said, "let's go out tonight. I'm thinkin' 'bout doing my thing onstage. You down?"

"Alright." She reached in her purse for money for the check.

"I got this," he said. "Sort of a welcome-to-L.A. treat, on me."

"Thank you, Sleazy."

"Right," he said. "Don't get too comfortable with it, though. I'm still on the incline. You're gonna have to get a rich dude if you're looking to get laced on the reg."

\*   \*   \*

When Reesy opened the door, one of the folding chairs was on the floor and all three dogs were out of the baby pen, nowhere in sight. Newspaper was shredded throughout the living room. There wasn't a square inch of floor space that didn't have a piece of the *L.A. Times.*

The smell of piss and feces dominated the air.

Reesy slammed the door. The three dogs emerged from places unknown and charged her like a pack of rats.

Dante let loose with an anguished sound, as if someone were stabbing him. Reesy jumped back in horror. Harlem and Peanut continued to yip, but Dante warbled and croaked as though he were on the brink of death.

She picked him up in her arms.

"Oh my goodness, what's wrong?"

He let out a wail that made her run to the phone and dial 911.

"I think I have a dying dog."

Reesy sat in the veterinarian's office. Barbara had given her the name and address of Meg's doctor.

Dante was sleeping in her lap. The moans had ceased once they got into the car. Dante had stood on his hind legs, staring out the window during the frantic drive over. He'd panted, looking back over his shoulder at Reesy. She'd kept expecting him to drop dead at any moment, victim to some mysterious newsprint overdose.

"I'm Dr. Cho," the Asian woman said to Reesy. She looked at Dante. "Oh, what a cute little shiba."

Dante wagged his tail as the vet lifted him from Reesy's arms.

"Come on back," Dr. Cho said. "Let's go in the examination room."

"So what's the problem?" the doctor asked, looking into the dog's mouth, then feeling his underside. She checked inside his ears and put a stethoscope against his fur.

"Well, he was screaming. It was a hideous sound. I thought he was dying. I don't know what's wrong with him."

Dr. Cho chuckled. She rubbed Dante's chin. He appeared quite happy. She scratched Dante behind the ears.

"There's nothing wrong with your dog," she said.

"Then why was he wailing like that? I've never heard an animal make such a god-awful noise."

"It's just something that shibas do," Dr. Cho replied. "Get used to it. He was probably happy to see you. Had you been away for a while?"

"Just a few hours."

"Then he was just glad that you were back home."

Reesy put her head in her hands.

"You mean to tell me this dog is going to do that every time I come home?"

"Probably, especially as he grows more attached to you. More than likely he'll do it every time he's excited about anything."

"Oh my goodness. I have two other shibas. Will they do it too?"

"Maybe, maybe not."

Dr. Cho handed Dante to her.

"There is one other thing about shibas that you also might not know."

"What's that?" Reesy asked, bracing herself.

"They can never be walked off the leash. Ever. No matter how well trained they are, there's always the chance that they'll dash off or run into the street. They have a very strong hunting instinct, so it's their nature to race off. You have to be careful with them."

"Great," said Reesy.

Dr. Cho smiled and put her hand on Reesy's shoulder.

"It's not a big problem. Just don't be casual about leaving doors open so they can get out."

Dante licked Reesy's face.

"This visit's on the house," the doctor said.

"I appreciate it." Reesy stood. "I'm sure you'll see me again."

She dialed Dandre's cell phone on the drive back home.

"These dogs you bought me are screaming lunatics."

"Whaddya mean?" he asked, surprised by her call. "The woman at the pet store told me they were low-maintenance. They hardly bark or anything."

"No, that's true. And except for the occasional hysterical wail from hell, they're perfectly fine."

"I don't understand what you . . ."

He flashed back to the woman's comment at the pet store. She'd said something about a curious bark, but insisted it was rare.

"I'm sorry, Reesy."

"Well, I just made an idiot out of myself at the vet," she said. "Thanks for making me look dumb once again."

"I didn't mean—"

"I saw you with that woman. I can't believe that after what happened at the church and me losing our child, you were still seeing her. What did you think I was, a fucking fool?"

"What woman? I don't understand what you're talking—"

"Fuck you, Dandre. What were you thinking? Huh? You think you can just come back into my life like nothing ever happened?"

"No, Reesy. That's not what I—"

"Were these three dogs supposed to take the place of our baby? Because if that's what you thought—"

She flipped the phone closed, her emotions snagging on the edge of her words, and flung it onto the passenger seat. Dante was standing at the window. He glanced back at her with a wide-toothed grin.

\* \* \*

Reesy was ready for a night out. After cleaning up behind the dogs and putting them and the baby pen in the kitchen, she had taken a long, relaxing shower. She pulled at the ring once more, but it would not be moved. She rubbed butter around her finger and still nothing.

"This is stupid," she said.

She got dressed and headed out to meet Sleazy.

He was standing in front of the club when she and Black pulled up. She parked the car and came over to him.

"You clean up nice, mami," he said, giving her a hug.

"So do you."

Sleazy was in a well-tailored suit and sporting a pair of gators. It made him appear even more imposing. The unlit cigar was in its usual place.

"You sure you're not cold?" he asked.

"I'm fine. Let's go."

He guided her toward the entrance.

"She's with me," Sleazy said to Derrick, the tall, fresh-faced, could-be-Latin-could-be-black ethnic crapshoot of a cutie collecting money from behind the Plexiglas.

"Yeah, I'm with the moulie," she said.

Derrick flashed an instant grin that lit up his questionable-heritage face.

"She got jokes."

"Yeah, man . . . she got mad jokes."

"Yum," Reesy mumbled, staring into Derrick's face.

"Stop it," Sleazy said through closed lips. "No fucking my friends."

"I don't know you well enough to know who's your friend."

"Then no fucking the help."

"So why am I here? And why is your mouth closed? What you are now, a ventriloquist? Are you about to ram your hand up my ass?"

Sleazy laughed as he pressed his palm into the small of Reesy's back, guiding her into the club.

"You're way too rowdy to be a girl, you know. And that pretty face is a straight-up lie. You're the devil, and I'm gonna find those sixes. I know they're on you somewhere. They're probably tattooed inside your—"

"Whatup, nukka," came a shout from the sidewalk. The two of them turned in the voice's direction.

Sleazy's buddies—an assortment of popular, unpopular, and waiting-to-become-one-or-the-other comedians—stood outside the club, checking out the newest sexy broad he was sporting at the spot.

L.A. weather was flaky as hell. Even though it was chilly, it was warmer that night than it had been during the day. Reesy had a wrap draped over a backless halter top—a series of strings fashioned after a cat's-in-the-cradle. She wore a pair of low-rider jeans that looked like she was poured into them. They show-cased the beginnings of the dimples on her high yellow bubble. Her feet were nestled in a pair of Manolos pointy enough to caulk a tub. It was later than they had agreed to meet, ten-thirty, the witching hour for the acts on stage. The nips of Reesy's tits were bullets, colder than Hecate's. A few gasps escaped as she weaved her way inside. None of the men even noticed her face.

"That nukka gets more pussy than the Crenshaw Clinic," one of the wannabes mumbled in awe.

"That's Sleaze for ya," came the drone of one of the famous. "I don't know why he still even bothers with comedy. He needs to just go get him one of them regulation caddies, set these hoes out, and go ahead get his paper on the level."

Still within earshot, Sleazy shot them a glance and flashed a quick wink, all over Reesy's shoulder.

"I hope they don't think we're kicking it," she said, breaking his rhythm.

He laughed. "I hope that big-ass rock doesn't make them think we're engaged."

"Please. You wish."

"These fools know better. Me and marriage? That's like pigs eating pork rinds. Ain't hapn'n. Just let a player roll. This is a win-win thang. Niggas see you with me and that raises your stock."

"My stock is doing just fine, thank you. I just hiked your portfolio, if you wanna be real."

"My nukka."

"Shaddup."

They disappeared inside the club.

Sleazy was funny. Reesy sat in the audience and watched him onstage. He was wry, deadpan, brooding, and dark. The women seemed to love it and the men found it cool. Much of his act centered on subduing women for sex and complaints against babies' mamas.

A lot of the other comics discussed the same thing. Reesy didn't realize there were so many hilarious variations on the same commonplace theme.

A man sitting alone at a table across the room caught her attention during Sleazy's act. She could tell he was tall, although he was sitting. He was bald and fair-skinned, with penetrating black eyes that twinkled, even though his expression was firm. His mustache and beard were trimmed low and neat. He was a stunner, so handsome she tried to downplay it, as though he were the most nondescript presence in the room.

She could see him watching her. It gave her a warm sensation, as if the hairs on her skin were being singed.

Sleazy came over and sat next to her after finishing his set.

"You're funny, for a big nigga," she said. "Very funny."

Sleazy laughed.

"Thank you. I think." He took a sip from the glass of Hennessy he had left on the table. "Meanwhile, all my boys are sweating me about you."

"Really?" she said, her eyes on the man at the other table. Sleazy followed her gaze.

"You want me to check this cat?" he asked in a harsh tone.

"No," she said, laughing. "Stop tripping. You're messing up my flow."

"Alright," he said. "But I suggest you let me clear these punks before you start kicking stank at 'em."

"Be quiet, Sleazy. I'm just having fun."

The man took a sip of his drink. She could still see the twinkle in his eye.

"Alright, mami," Sleazy said, "listen to me. Here's how this works: I'll introduce you to someone that's a friend of one of my friends, but again, no fucking my friends."

"Why is that?" asked Reesy.

"Because, if the fool tries to do you dirt, I don't want to have to beat down somebody I'm cool with. I'd rather squash a muthafucka I don't know. That way there's no complications. Got it?"

"Got it."

His two-way chimed. Sleazy read it and typed back a response, talking as he typed.

"If the guy's a friend of a friend, well, my friend can vouch for him without me knowing the cat directly."

"I see you've got this whole thing worked out."

Sleazy laughed as he drank his Hennessy.

"You don't understand, mami. With me, broads are either for bedding or bidding bye-bye. Anybody else is either my mom, sister, aunt, cousin, or grandma. I'm not used to having chicks as friends. This might be a real first for me."

"Me too," she said. "Every guy I've been friends with ended up in my bed. Except for one, but he was gay. My choreographer back in New York."

"Then this is a monumental moment for both of us," Sleazy said. "Let's toast to the trying of new things."

"That's for real," she replied. "Those three balls of fur at my house are proof of that."

He held his glass aloft. Reesy raised hers. The two of them clinked.

"You need to let me train 'em," Sleazy said around his drink.

"Ha," she laughed. "When can you start?"

"We can do it tomorrow. I'm a dog man. I know all the tricks of the canine trade."

"I'm sure you do."

Reesy leaned back in her seat and sipped her drink. This big dapper monster of a man had her back. It was almost funny. She glanced around the club at all the different men, then gazed over at him. It felt good not to have the pressure of a romantic relationship.

This was cool, she thought, giving the sexy brother across the room another peep. Perhaps the wedding disaster wasn't the end of the world after all. It seemed like L.A. might have a few surprises up its sleeve.

Sleazy came over the next morning to help Reesy with the dogs. His claims about being an expert dog trainer turned out to be true. In less than two hours he had taught them all how to sit using both spoken and nonspoken commands. They lined up in perfect unison, like miniature members of the Nation of Islam. All they were missing were the little bow ties and the FOI hats.

"The one thing you have to remember is that you're the alpha dog."

"What does that mean?" she asked.

"It means a pack of dogs always has to have a leader. Three dogs qualifies as a pack." He laughed. "I still can't believe you have three dogs," he said. "Just add water in this bitch and you've got a kennel."

"Alright, alright, so I have three dogs. So let's get past that already. How do I make them know I'm the alpha?"

"They already know it. You're bigger than them. You give them food. You control the environment. You just have to know it. When they get out of hand, talk to them like there'll be repercussions. If you're good, you won't even have to yell. They'll know you mean business even if you speak in a whisper."

She watched the dogs as they sat like little soldiers.

"Okay. I got it," she said as she looked at them. "From now on I'm the alpha dog."

The dogs gazed up at her, ready to do her bidding.

Sleazy had brought over wee-wee pads to help housebreak them. He installed a doggie door so they could go out whenever they needed to use the bathroom. It took him ten minutes to coax them through the hole, past the plastic flap. After that, the puppies couldn't seem to get enough of coming in and going out. As long as the garden gate that gave her access from the backyard to her car was locked, the dogs were free to run and play.

"So what you getting into tonight?" Reesy asked.

"A party," he said. He juggled Harlem in one hand as he sat on the couch. Peanut was in his lap, fascinated by his ever-beeping two-way.

"Oooh, that sounds like fun. What kind of party? Where?"

"No, ma'am," Sleazy said. "You're not coming to this. It's not your kind of scene. It's probably gonna get buck wild up in there, and I don't want to be responsible for introducing you to that type of thing."

Reesy was in the kitchen making pastrami sandwiches. She walked over to the doorway and watched him.

Sleazy had no idea of her background as an exotic dancer and she planned to keep it that way. She found it amusing that he had categorized her as the polar opposite—a Pollyanna that needed to be sheltered from everything that wasn't fit for polite society.

"So what is it, some kind of sex party?"

"Well, it's just a party party. At least, that's how it'll start off. But my girls Chloe and Zoe be gettin' kinda freaky. Some porn stars might roll by, you never know. It's a pretty thugged-out, hoeish kinda scene, but, you know, sometimes that's who I be."

"Ew," she said.

"Ew is right."

"Is Rhiannon going?"

"Hell, naw," Sleazy said. "That's like taking sand to the beach, baby. I don't need her breathing over my shoulder while I'm try-ing to wax me some neezy."

"What's neezy?"

"New ass."

"You're stupid."

Reesy went back into the kitchen to finish the sandwiches.

"So how do you know I might not wanna check it out?"

Sleazy picked up Dante and put him on the couch.

"Because it's not for you. That's all there is to it. End of dis-cussion."

Dandre was sitting by the water's edge, watching the sun go down. He was drinking Courvoisier straight from the bottle. He'd been there awhile and now the tide was coming in. His sweat bottoms were soaked and there was a sharp chill in the air. He seemed oblivious to both.

It had been more than twenty-four hours since Reesy had hung up on him. He kept replaying their conversation over in his head. What did she mean about seeing him with that woman? Did she know about Rejeana coming to his house?

There was no way she could have. She would have con-fronted him before now. He wondered if Rick had said some-thing to Misty. He didn't think his best friend would be that casual about something so grave. He hoped not. It could destroy his chances altogether.

The part about him trying to replace their baby with dogs had hit him like a foot to the gut. Bruce Lee's foot.

"Why can't I get this right?" he asked, his arms raised, the bottle extended. "How come everything I try to do with her keeps turning out wrong?"

Random beachgoers and lingering lovers walked by, wondering at the drunken nut sitting in the middle of the advancing surf.

Zoe had given him the bottle of liquor.

"Here, cuz," she'd said just a couple of hours earlier. "You look like you could use a good kick."

He hadn't eaten and his head was light. He stood, brushing sand from the backs of his legs. He grabbed the bottle and walked over toward the house.

"I'm going to bed," he said.

There was no point in going out, he figured. He had come to L.A. to get his woman back, and so far, his plan was failing him. Better to sleep it off and restrategize in the morning.

"Tomorrow's another day," he said, taking a swig from the bottle. "Yup. Tomorrow's another fucked-up day."

"He's out, girl," Zoe whispered to Chloe.

They both stood over Dandre, watching him sleep. He was curled in a fetal position on the bed. The empty bottle of Courvoisier was lying on the floor.

"Good lookin'-out, Z," Chloe said. "He's done for the rest of the night."

She high-fived her sister.

"And you know what happens when Big Brother's not watching," Zoe said.

The two girls stared at each other and grinned.

"Par-taaaaaaaaaaaaaaaaaaaay," they both squealed.

They grabbed each other's arms and danced a jig around the room.

\* \* \*

By midnight, the beach house in Hermosa was so rowdy, any attempt at quality control had long been abandoned by either of the twins. People were doing coke, smoking chronic, and popping not just X, but some Y and Z.

The sounds and smells of things carnal were everywhere, as threesomes formed and fractured off like small galaxies in a universe of sex. The hot tub was bubbling with nastiness, the scene of some girl-on-girl action that one of the fellas—a pathetic would-be-entrepreneur sort—filmed for his own version of *Girls Gone Dumb*.

Sleazy watched from inside the house, then turned around, scoping for any new action that might have arrived unnoticed. He spotted a petite girl in the corner. She was no more than five feet with long black shining hair, bowed legs, and slanted eyes.

"Oh shit," he said under his breath. "She's Asian and a midget. I done hit the jackpot." He made his way over to the girl, already chalking it up as a victory and future anecdote to share with the boys.

Chloe and Zoe were both on the couch with Ebay, who was trying to get his weed together.

"Wait," he said. "Let me roll another blunt."

Chloe dropped between his legs and grabbed his joint.

"Not before you let me smoke this first."

Dandre was deep into a dream. He and Reesy were together again—in love, in bed, into it—the way they used to be when things were good.

Reesy was on top of him, her hands on his chest, riding him with an urgency that seemed equal to his.

"I've missed you," he whispered. "I've missed you so much."

"I missed you too, baby," she said.

"Is it still mine?" he asked. "Do you still want to give it to me?"

"Why are you asking what you already know?" Reesy answered. "I'm always gonna give this to you. I'm never gonna give it to anyone else."

He flipped her over and pinned her against the bed, pounding her hard with profound desperation. She thrashed beneath him, calling out his name. He thrust harder, the cold feel of her tongue against his balls driving him . . .

Dandre shifted in the dream, still thrusting, wondering how he could be inside Reesy but still feel her tongue down below. He opened his eyes.

He was thrusting, but it wasn't into the woman he loved. It was a dark chocolate thing with scant brows, hazel eyes, and big silicone breasts. His mouth was on one of them. Her expression was savage as she bucked around.

Someone else was between his legs, licking his balls. He looked back in terror at yet another woman, this one blonde with breasts so large and artificial in appearance, they threatened to become airborne and float her away. She had a tongue like Gene Simmons, and it was no longer on Dandre's nuts. Now it was making its way up the crack of his behind.

Dandre screamed—a sound not unlike Dante's—and tried to dislodge himself from the girl below him. He kicked the balloon blonde away with his heel. An Asian girl stood to the right of the bed, an enormous black strap-on attached to her waist. She was preparing to mount the blonde, but Dandre's bitch-scream had canceled it all.

The shrieking could be heard downstairs, over the bumping sounds of the newest Tupac. Chloe raised her head from between Ebay's legs. She glanced over at her sister, who was sitting on Ebay's face.

"The Tonies," they said.

Both women abandoned a startled Ebay and made for the stairs.

The guy who had been filming the hot tub scene followed them.

166

\*   \*   \*

Dandre was huddled in a corner of the room, covering himself with a sheet. The Tonies—Tonita Green, Toni Cole, and Tonishi Wang—were doing each other on the bed. All three women were porn stars, but Dandre had never seen them before. He glanced at himself under the sheet. He was wearing a condom. While that was a partial relief, he was still terrified at the thought of what might have already occurred while he was asleep. He was sluggish, the dregs of way too much Courvoisier still polluting his system.

Zoe and Chloe appeared in the room, the camera guy right behind them. At the sight of the minicam, Dandre became hysterical.

He lunged at the guy and snatched the thing, smashing it against the floor again and again. Springs, metal, screws, and plastic ricocheted away as the man tried to get his equipment back. Dandre shoved him off as he removed the tape and tore it apart, ripping, tearing, pulling at the reel.

"Get out," Zoe and Chloe said to the Tonies and the guy. "Go. And tell everyone downstairs to get out too."

"Awww, Z," said Tonishi, "this is wack."

"Just go," Zoe said. "We'll catch you later in the week in the Hills."

Dandre kept tearing at the tape, the thought of Reesy seeing it enraging him. His breath was heavy and he was dripping sweat. He looked up, glaring at the twins.

They stood before him like naughty schoolkids and, except for the absence of clothes, that's what they felt like.

Dandre's eyes were red, wet, clouded with anger.

"I think he's crying," Chloe whispered without moving her lips.

"I think he's still drunk," Zoe answered in a similar fashion. "He might not remember this tomorrow."

"Oh, I'll remember it," he said. "I'll never forget what the two of you did." He wrapped the loose tape in a bundle and shredded it again. "You've got two days."

"Two days for what?" asked Chloe.

"To be outta here. That's all I'm giving you, then you're on your ass."

The naked twins flailed their hands, their eyes filled with fear.

"But, Dandre, how can you do this? We don't have anyplace else to go."

"I don't care," he said, getting up. He went into the bathroom. "I want you out. I asked you to respect me and you didn't. So don't expect me to have any respect for you."

He slammed the bathroom door. They heard the shower come on.

Zoe and Chloe stared at each other, the tattooed tongues on their asses licking at the air.

# Scenes from a Psychic

"I know this lady in Chicago. She's really good. You should call her."

It was a day later, and they were at Painted, a salon on Robertson in Beverly Hills. Reesy was having a margarita pedicure, complete with limes, tequila, the whole nine.

She found herself spending quite a bit of time with both Rhiannon and Sleazy, though not together. Rhiannon knew a little about the Dandre issue. Not much, just that it had been a bad scene for Reesy.

"I believe you still love him," she said.

"Of course I do, but that doesn't mean I want to get with him again."

Reesy wasn't sure how truthful she was being. Dandre was now haunting her dreams. That had happened once before, when she was trying to win him back after the Helmut debacle. Every night, like clockwork, she'd have a nightmare about him having unbridled sex with some beautiful celebrity.

This time, her dreams were different. There were no crazed sexfests. Now her sleep was filled with peaceful, loving images of her and Dandre holding hands and walking along the shore in Martha's Vineyard, strolling down Ocean Drive in South Beach, sharing a pretzel on Sixth Avenue in Manhattan. In one of the dreams, they were in bed and he was rubbing her very pregnant belly.

Each morning when she awoke, the yearning was stronger, no matter what she threw herself into to shake it off. When she opened her eyes the first thing she saw was always the dogs, staring into her face, walking reminders of the strong connection that remained between her and Dandre.

Then she would think about seeing him and that woman on his doorstep, and her confusion would begin all over again.

Rhiannon brought the subject up almost as much as Misty did. At odd moments, like now.

Reesy sat in the chair reading two books at the same time, one of which Rhiannon had raved about. Something by that Dickey guy—*Friends and Lovers*. She was surprised to discover Rhiannon was right. The book was juicy, well layered, with lots of killer sex. Shelby and Tyrel's yo-yo love affair made her *vida loca* seem calm.

She alternated between that and Junot Diaz's *Drown*, a collection of short stories about life and love set against the backdrop of New York and New Jersey that she connected with at once. Dickey and Diaz were as different as skates and scallions, but both were entertaining. She made a mental note to get her hands on as many books as she could by authors of color. Things had changed, she realized, and she had lots of catching up to do.

"You really should call this woman," Rhiannon said again.

"What are you talking about?"

"This lady, Miss Flora. She's a prophet. She's really good."

"You mean she's a psychic," said Reesy.

"Same difference."

"Not really."

The attendant poured a pitcher of ice water over Reesy's feet. Her margarita pedicure was on the rocks. She clenched her shoulders until the chill passed through.

"I'm not into that kind of stuff anyway," she said.

Rhiannon was getting a fill. She held her hands in a dainty position, like dog paws, as she rambled on about the talents of Miss Flora, the psychic prophet.

"She really is very good. She knows her gift comes from God, so she gives Him all the credit. I've never seen anybody as accurate as her.

"I think we should call her. She knows me pretty well. She'll read you for free if I ask her to. Most people have to pay her a fee, and trust me, they're pretty happy to do it."

"Of course," Reesy said, switching over from Dickey to Diaz.

She glanced up just as Malik Yoba, the actor, sauntered in with two very tall, L.A.-perfect women who, Reesy thought, if they weren't models, were doing a great impersonation of them.

"Rhiannon, girl, what's up?" he said, stooping and kissing her on the cheek. "Long time, long time. You look good, girl."

Rhiannon gave him a casual smile.

"You too. How long you been back on the left coast?"

"You know how I do it. Back and forth. I've got a place in the Valley."

"Right, right."

Reesy watched in silence, impressed at both Malik's in-the-flesh good looks and accessible demeanor and Rhiannon's relaxed, almost cavalier response. Considering the fact that she was a walking Ms. Potatohead of assembled pieces, she was pretty smooth, very together.

Malik walked over to an attendant who had been expecting his arrival. The two would-be supermodels sat off to the side and waited. Both were talking into headsets.

"By the way, Rhi," Malik said. "Thanks for that hookup with that woman in Chicago. She was good. She told me about a big gig I had coming, and I'll be damned if she wasn't right on the money. I've been keeping in touch with her. I've never had anybody read me that well and be that accurate."

Rhiannon raised her brow at Reesy.

"You talking about Miss Flora?" Rhiannon asked.

"Yeah, man. I've met my share of people who make crazy claims and talk mad smack, but she's good. I've put a few of my friends on to her."

"Yeah," Rhiannon said. "I've been trying to do that too."

Reesy turned her attention back to Junot Diaz and his crazy Dominican world.

Reesy and Dandre were riding horses on the beach. It was raining, but neither of them cared. She laughed as her horse galloped ahead. She looked back over her shoulder but he had already caught up. His horse raced alongside hers in perfect step.

"You can't outrun me," he said with a smile.

"But I had you for a minute." She grinned. "You had to fight to catch up."

Reesy sat up in bed with a jolt. Her heart was thumping as she stared into the darkness. She glanced over at the clock. It was early. Just 10:08 P.M. That meant more hours of sleep. And in that sleep was the threat that more dreams of Dandre might come.

She reached for the phone and dialed.

"Hello?" came the perky voice.

"Alright," Reesy said without preface. "Call her. I can't take it anymore."

"Let us pray first," Miss Flora said.

They were on a three-way call. Reesy was in her bedroom at home. Harlem and Peanut were at the foot of the bed. She no longer bothered putting them in the pen. The dogs had followed Peanut's lead and were now sleeping with her.

Rhiannon was at home in Lawndale. She had patched the calls together. Flora was in the Windy City, deep in a windy prayer about wanting to please God and do His work. Reesy listened to the long and vehement plea. She was sitting in the dark, fingering her ring, an unconscious habit. Flora shifted the focus to her.

"Are you pregnant?"

Aha, Reesy thought. Already this woman was wrong. She knew all these so-called seers were crackpots.

"Nope," Reesy said in a smug tone. "I don't have any children."

"Well, I see a little girl very strongly. Have you had an abortion?"

Flora's voice was heavy, each breath a labor. Reesy was astounded.

That was a lucky guess, she thought. Just because the woman asked about an abortion didn't mean she knew anything about her miscarriage.

"There'll be other children," Miss Flora continued. "Boys."

Now Reesy knew the woman was lying.

"You have so much energy," Flora said with a chuckle. "My goodness, you just never sit still. I'm glad you gave up that other kind of dancing you used to do. There's a higher calling for your talent and skills."

Reesy dropped the phone.

"Hello?" Flora said. "Hello?"

"What other dancing?" Rhiannon asked.

"She knows," the woman said.

Rhiannon assumed she meant the Broadway stuff. She had no knowledge of Reesy's exotic past.

Reesy fumbled around for the cordless phone. Now the game had changed.

She flicked the light on.

"I'm here," she said after a moment. "Sorry. One of my dogs made me accidentally—"

"Ummmhmmm," said Miss Flora.

Reesy was uncomfortable. This wasn't funny anymore. She felt like the woman could see clear from Chicago into her Manhattan Beach bedroom. She was afraid to lie for fear of being called out.

"Acting has been good for you," Miss Flora continued, "but you won't do a lot. You've already had your time on the stage. That was really just something you needed to get out of your system."

Reesy bit her nails. Harlem licked her ankles. She shook her foot to make the dog stop.

"Hmmm," Miss Flora said, her voice sounding troubled. "You've got issues with your parents. They're very controlling people. Lots of money and power."

Rhiannon wondered if this was true. Reesy seemed like the typical struggling Hollywood actress/dancer.

"There's a lot of change going on with them right now," Flora said. "Your father's very tense. He's picking up some old bad habits. And your mother's doing interesting things."

"Aah . . ." Reesy said with surprise, then stopped herself.

"You'll marry soon," said Flora. "It's going to seem very sudden, very abrupt." She cleared her throat. "Excuse me," she said, sounding like she was taking a sip of water.

"For me to do that, it must be someone I'm sure about," Reesy said.

"Oh yes," Flora said in a conspiratorial tone. "You won't have any doubt that this is the man you want to be with."

Rhiannon made some sort of unidentifiable noise that Reesy knew was meant for her.

"And, oh," Miss Flora said, "he is very sexual. He definitely knows how to come with it."

She laughed, which surprised Reesy. She'd gone from being serious, somber, and spiritual to talking about throwing down in bed. Reesy was confused.

"Don't get it twisted," Miss Flora said, like she could see the look on her face. "I'm gonna be real when I talk to you. I'm not gonna dress anything up. I'm just telling you what I see."

Reesy stared at the wall in front of her. This was all too bizarre. She still wasn't quite sure if she believed.

"The two of you are good together, but you have a lot of unclear energy that you need to work through. You have a hard time trusting men."

Reesy's head was so light, she thought it was going to pop off. No one, not even Misty, knew how deep her trust issues went with men. She was always the tough, ballsy girl who manipulated men, but like her mother, she was really scared. Everybody assumed she was teeming with self-esteem in that area. While it was true she was confident, it was because she remained at arm's length. One bad experience in college had made sure of that.

"There's a film producer. Very sexual, very exciting. You and him have strong chemistry. You ever heard of instant attraction? That's what the two of you have."

Reesy's mouth was open, but nothing came out. She assumed the woman had been speaking of Dandre, but now she was confused. The thought that her sudden marriage might be with someone else troubled her. She hadn't fully let go of her love for Dandre. She wasn't sure if she ever could.

Rhiannon was making noises again, this time a bunch of them.

"Is that your phone?" Flora asked.

"My bad," said Rhiannon.

Flora was quiet, then laughed again.

Harlem had climbed onto Reesy's lap and was licking her face. Reesy shoved her away. Harlem leapt back upon her and started licking again. Reesy got out of the bed and began to pace.

"He loves the water. He lives close to it. That's where he likes to go to think."

Reesy forced her phone to click.

"I'm sorry," she said. "Could you two hang on?"

"Sure," Miss Flora said with what sounded like a smirk.

Reesy clicked over long enough to make it seem like she'd had a call come in. After a few seconds, she clicked back. Rhiannon and Flora were talking.

"This is a lot for her," Flora was saying, "but she needs to pay attention or she's gonna mess around and sink herself."

"I'm back."

"I know you heard what I said," replied Flora. "Just be aware."

Reesy was silent.

"You've got a little time," Flora said. "You'll see for yourself. You'll be meeting a lot of new people, some of whom will be very loyal friends. Be careful of people claiming to be something they're not. They won't have your best interests at heart."

"Thank you, Miss Flora. Thank you, Rhiannon. I'm gonna have to take this call on the other line. I really appreciate you talking to me tonight."

"Sure," Flora said in that tone again. "God loves you. Just remember that in the middle of everything else. He's always with you through everything. You're one of His own."

"Yes, ma'am," Reesy said.

"Pay attention to your parents. They're going to be turning to you for a lot of emotional support real soon."

"I gotta go. Thanks again."

She clicked the phone off and jumped back into bed, bringing her knees up to her chest. The beating of her heart was relentless. Her brow was damp.

That was some crazy shit, she thought. Crazy, straight crazy.

Rhiannon must have told her some stuff about me, she decided. That had to be it. There was no way that woman could be that much on the money.

She looked at the cordless phone sitting on the edge of the bed. It felt like a spy. She stretched her leg toward it and kicked it off. The phone went flying into the hallway. Harlem and Peanut leapt off the bed and rushed after it.

Reesy looked at the time. 10:47 P.M.

Damn, she thought. It was too late to call Misty. Besides the three-hour time difference, she was pregnant and needed her sleep.

Sleep. Now she had to go back to sleep. Reesy grabbed a book from her bedside and began to read. Anything to avoid her dreams.

An hour later, the book was lying on her face and she and Dandre were Rollerblading on Venice Beach.

"Oh, I'm sure she was right," Misty said the next morning. "A lot of those psychics are very accurate."

"Shit," Reesy muttered.

Misty was at her Manhattan office, looking over paperwork.

"I just don't believe we were meant to hear that kind of stuff," she said. "Every person isn't capable of handling it. Take you, for instance. You think too much. All that information's gonna drive you crazy. You'll apply it to everything and it's gonna end up disrupting your natural flow."

"What natural flow?"

"You know what I mean. You won't be able to go about your business for wondering if it's a part of the bigger plan this woman talked about."

Reesy nibbled at her fingers.

"Me and Dandre are over anyway, so it doesn't matter what that psychic said."

"I thought she was a prophet."

"Whatever."

Dante, Harlem, and Peanut scampered around between her legs as she walked into the kitchen.

"Hey, have you ever heard of Eric Jerome Dickey?" Reesy asked.

"Yeah. He's good."

"How come you never told me about him?"

"I didn't think you liked reading that much."

"Oh."

She opened the fridge. The dogs sat on the kitchen floor, lined up in a perfect row, watching her.

"These creatures are nuts," she said. "I think they're little robots with cameras in them."

"At least they keep you company."

Misty signed a stack of paperwork. She made a strange noise.

"Did you just burp?" Reesy asked.

"Yeah, girl. That's all I do, burp and fart. I hate everything, including my ob/gyn. It's this African guy a friend at my salon referred me to. She said he was good. The first time I went to him, he asked me if I was experiencing any pain in my pussy."

Reesy laughed.

"Stop it. He didn't say 'pussy.'"

"Just as sure as I've got one, I swear he said it."

"And you're still going to him?"

"Yeah," Misty said. She belched again. "I really hate this. I was not trying to have any kids right now.

"Did Rick tie your legs open and force himself in?"

Misty heard the tone in Reesy's voice. She'd forgotten about her friend's recent loss.

"I'm sorry, Reesy. I don't mean to sound so harsh. It's not that I don't feel blessed to be having this baby—"

"But you are and you don't even realize it."

Misty released a deep breath.

"I know, honey. I just wasn't ready. The timing sucks."

"Well, be grateful that you have the chance."

The two women were silent. Reesy could hear Misty signing documents. She handed each dog a piece of cheese. They chewed in silence and waited for more.

"Things are gonna be okay, Reesy," Misty said. "You'll be pregnant again. That psychic lady said you were gonna have boys."

"Oh, now you want to quote her. I thought you didn't believe in them."

"That's not what I said. In fact, that's the opposite of what I said."

They were both quiet again. The dogs waited, watching as Reesy kept the cheese for herself.

"I just finished reading a really good book," Misty said in a happier tone. "It's about this couple that breaks up because the husband cheated with his wife's best friend. But they get back together because they have really strong faith in God. It's called *Temptation*. You should read it."

"Why?" Reesy said with irritation. "You already told me the ending, so what's the point?"

She hung up the phone. The dogs clamored over her for another hunk of cheese.

# Men Overboard

Tyrone was in the family room of the Snowden mansion, sitting in his favorite leather chair. His feet, clad in supple leather slippers, were crossed at the ankles on an ottoman. He smoked a cigarette as he watched Dan Rather.

Tyrene was outside by the dock, staring off into the early evening. Twinkling yachts drifted by through the intracoastal waterway of Las Olas, an exclusive area of Fort Lauderdale sandwiched between downtown and the beach. Their own multimillion-dollar yacht was parked just to the left of her. They hadn't taken it out since their return from New York, which was unusual for a couple known for their love of entertaining. Anushka, the cook, was inside preparing dinner, but Tyrene didn't want to be anywhere near her husband's smoke.

Tyrone could see her in his peripheral vision, but her self-imposed segregation didn't bother him. He was going to have his cigarette. He only had a few a day, he reasoned. It wasn't like the habit was full-blown.

The main line to the house rang once, just once. Tyrone glanced at the phone on the table beside him, waiting to see if it would ring again. It didn't.

Within seconds, Tyrene sauntered in, past him, on her way upstairs.

"How long, Anushka?" she yelled toward the kitchen.

"Fifteen minutes, ma'am," came the reply.

"Very well, then," Tyrene said, and disappeared into her office on the second floor.

Tyrone sat in his chair, fuming. This ritual of the one ring and Tyrene disappearing upstairs had been happening since their return and, despite his apparent coolness, he was bothered by it. He looked over at the phone beside him. Line one was lit.

I don't know what kind of game she's up to, he thought, but whatever it is, if she thinks I'm stupid, she's out of her mind.

Rick sat in the car in the Rite Aid parking lot.

He and Misty had run out of condoms and he needed to get more or there would be no sex happening in the Hodges household. She was adamant about no babies right away, but he wasn't convinced that was a plan they were going to adhere to. He knew his wife. She was a nurturer by nature. There was no way, he thought, that she would be unhappy once she learned she was pregnant. Everything would change and it would be for the better. He didn't want to be like Dandre, fighting for the chance at a future with the woman he loved.

Rick realized how blessed he was to have Misty. Now he wanted to cement the stability of his relationship with her and he knew having a child would do it. Misty would know it too, once she was pregnant. He knew what he was doing was deceptive, but it wasn't malicious. He loved his wife and he wanted a family. It would be good for the both of them.

He opened the box of lubricated Ultra Pleasure Trojans and emptied the attached packets of condoms into his lap. He pulled out the car ashtray and removed the tiny safety pin he kept there. He looked around to his left and right. The parking lot was filled with people rushing into and out of the store. It was too cold for anyone to be lingering and looking around, trying to check out what he was doing.

He began puncturing the packets one by one. The holes weren't conspicuous, just big enough to let the swimmers out. Misty would never see the outer packets to know they'd been pierced. He kept the condoms in the nightstand on his side of the bed. When it was time for loving, his ritual was to reach over at the opportune moment, grab one, and slip it on. Holes and all. He was always sure to pull out fast and rush off to the bathroom to discard the condom before she could notice any trace of a leak.

"Why do you do that?" she'd asked him one night. "You never used to run to the bathroom as soon as we finished."

"Because I know how paranoid you are," Rick had said. "I don't want any chance of a mistake."

He'd balled up the empty condom packet and thrown it in the bathroom wastebasket. He'd figured she'd never inspect them. Why would she? She was too busy for such foolishness, and there was nothing evident in his behavior to spark suspicion.

Rick had been doing this for more than three months. He was aware of all the nuances of Misty's cycle. He had gone online to learn about menstrual flow and ovulation, initial signs of pregnancy, basal body temperatures, darkening areola, anything that would indicate his success in hitting his wife's maternal bull's-eye. He read message boards for expectant mothers and women trying to get pregnant. He knew the abbreviations— *AF* for "Aunt Flow," *ttc* for "trying to conceive," *dpo* for "days past ovulation," and *hcg* for the hormone that increased once a woman was pregnant. He sometimes posted questions under a feminine name. He was deep into the world of babydom, often surfing the sites online at work.

Misty's periods were always prompt—every twenty-eight days—and he believed he'd become masterful at charting her susceptibility to conception. He kept his eye on her, checking her body for change. Each month he saw her reach for a tampon, his heart sank.

He nailed her at every turn because he was a self-professed horndog to begin with, but he was careful to save the best of the best for that brief window of time when she was ovulating. He'd hold off for a few days before to ensure his seed was rich and plentiful and then—once he figured her eggs were dropping—he came at her three and four times a day. He did her in the office, in the foyer at home, in the car by the side of the road. It always seemed spontaneous, as though he was overwhelmed with an urge of love that couldn't be denied. That was true. It was that very love that drove his zeal. Misty submitted each time, no matter how tired or harried.

It had been more than three weeks since she'd ovulated, but there were no tampon wrappers in the trash and there seemed to be no sign of Aunt Flow anywhere.

"It's stress," Misty said. "Sometimes my period gets thrown off when I'm too overwhelmed. All that stuff with Reesy, everything at work . . ."

"Sure," Rick replied.

There was still hope, he thought. The message boards said that when a cycle got thrown off, ovulation could happen at any time.

He kept poking holes in the packets.

He wanted to make sure he was ready when those little eggs fell.

"I'm coming there," Hill said. "I want to see you."

"Don't be ridiculous," replied Tyrene. "You can't come here."

She was in her office wearing a headset, pacing in front of her picture window.

"No one will know I'm there. I can stay at a hotel downtown."

Tyrene walked back and forth.

"You know you want me," he said. "Imagine me spanking that old yellow ass."

She grinned.

"You're so nasty. You're filthy."

"You love it."

"You can't come here," she said again.

"Then you're coming to Washington."

Tyrene stopped pacing and sat at her desk, both palms pressed flat against the leather pad.

"Can't do that. I've got too many things to attend to here and I have no business that calls me that way."

"Look, woman—I'm going to see you, one way or another. Either here or there. But I'm going to see you."

Tyrone stepped into his wife's office. She was looking down at her desk with a big, wide grin. Her voice was low and seductive. It wasn't a voice appropriate for clients. It wasn't a voice appropriate for anyone but him.

He didn't alert her to his presence. He just stood in the doorway, his chest feeling tight and constricted as he watched her entertaining whomever it was.

She glanced up, as if she felt his presence. Tyrone thought he could see her pupils dilate.

"I'll see about handling that," she said into the headset in an abrupt and diplomatic tone. "Right now my calendar's pretty full. Let me see what my husband thinks. Good day."

She pressed a button, terminating the call.

"See what your husband thinks about what?" asked Tyrone.

"I don't know," she said, adjusting papers on her desk. "Another benefit. The mayor wants to know if we'll host some affair or other on our boat to help somebody or other raise some money for something."

"Some affair, huh? You don't remember what the affair is?" He sat down at one of the chairs in front of her desk. "Perhaps I'll call the mayor back and find out exactly what it is."

"No need to do that. I'll call him tomorrow." She stood, glancing at her watch. "I've got a meeting with some people over at the library, and then I'm having dinner with Cheri, Dale, and Trish. I should be home around ten-ish."

Tyrone got up and waited for her to walk around the desk. When she passed him, he grabbed her shoulders and held her at arm's length. He peered into her face.

"You alright, Tyrene?" he asked, hoping she would confess, own up, admit to antics unbecoming a wife, something. Even though things had been contentious between the two of them of late and he found that he didn't like her very much, he still loved her. They'd been through too much, in his opinion, to be unraveling to the state they were in now. She had promised him once that no man would ever come between them; that they would be inseparable for life.

"We've done too much, seen too much, and lied too much to ever leave each other," she'd said as they lay in bed some twenty-five years before. They'd been laughing at the time. Reesy was young then, but even by that time they'd experienced many things together, a lot of which couldn't be discussed in the light of day.

He didn't know what she was doing now, but whatever it was, she was doing it without him, and that was the rub that he couldn't tolerate. That was the fly in the ointment that, in addition to his worries about his daughter's affairs, had kept him in a state of unrest.

"Are you alright?" he repeated.

"No, Tyrone, I'm not alright." She looked him in the face with bold assertion. "I haven't been alright since Teresa's disaster, and I've been even worse since you started up with those disgusting cigarettes again."

"I'll stop the cigarettes," he said.

"Then stop them, and stop them now."

She shook herself from the grip of his strong hands on her shoulders and went over to her jacket, hanging on a hook by the door. She slipped into it, staring at him as she did so. He stared back at her.

"I want every cigarette gone from every place you may have hidden one by the time I get home tonight. If you say you're going to stop, then I hope you mean it." She picked up her purse from the leather couch by the door.

She glanced over at him. His stare was penetrating, so much that it jarred her. Like he was judging her. He didn't know, she reminded herself. She knew that. There was no way Tyrone could know anything about her and Hill. Unless that Misty Fine had told her business. Misty Fine wouldn't tell her business. Tyrene wondered if Misty Fine had blabbed her business and it had made its way back to Tyrone that fast. Her husband was cunning, but he wouldn't remain calm if he'd received news like that. He didn't know, she decided.

"Are you going to be gone long?" Tyrone asked.

"I'm having dinner with Cheri, Dale, and Trish." His expression was still intense. "Relax," she said. "Your behavior's been strange ever since we left New York. Teresa may have lost her child, but the rest of us are okay. You're not going to lose everybody."

"Really?" he said, searching for truth in her words.

"Really," she said without looking at him. "Not unless you alienate us first with your disgusting cigarettes. Fix it."

She turned on her heel and left.

Tyrone was quiet as he watched his wife go. He'd given her too many years of leniency, he decided. Too many years of thinking she was in charge. It was time for a wife-check.

He could sense that Tyrene was involved in something duplicitous. He'd seen the difference in her body in the hotel room. That Saturday night at the Parker Meridien, she'd had marks on her body, and they weren't from unintended injury because Tyrene would have been quick to complain. She'd done her best to mask them. They hadn't made love since before they went to New York. Tyrone thought at first that perhaps—in a fit of rage and vengeance—his wife had sought a stranger's arms during that trip. He couldn't imagine who. Then he believed she'd made the marks herself to provoke him for cursing at her in the hospital, or for his taking up cigarettes again.

But now there was something else going on, something untoward, and it didn't seem like something she was faking.

She'd never cheated on him, as far as he knew, and he'd never wandered from her since they'd settled down after their earlier years.

He knew his wife. He knew her well.

"But can you ever really know a person?" his friend Trini the ballplayer had asked. "I thought I knew Elise. I would have never expected her to be pulling the shit she's pulling right now."

"Tyrene's been on a slack leash for too long," Tyrone said to himself. "It's time for me to put her on a choke chain before she gets out of hand."

"Call the travel agent and book me on the first flight going to Fort Lauderdale in the morning."

Hill. was sitting in his office at his practice. He'd seen six patients and had two more scheduled before the day's end.

"But you have appointments tomorrow," said Bridgette, his nurse assistant.

"Reschedule them," he said.

"You've got that big lecture in two days."

"Is it in the afternoon?"

"Yes," she said, hesitating.

"Then book my return for that morning."

He was talking to Bridgette on the phone. Before he could make his next statement, she had hung up and was standing in the doorway of his office.

She was a tall, muscular woman with freckled skin and green eyes.

"What are you doing, Hill? This is the second time you've had me cancel appointments in the past two weeks."

Hill gazed up at her, taking her in. They'd had their moment of fun when she first came to work for him. She was twenty-eight then. That was four years ago, and now he considered her past the cutoff age. He still felt that way, which made his fascination with Tyrene all the more inexplicable to him.

"It's that Alyssa girl, isn't it?"

"What are you talking about, Bridgette?" he said, scribbling nonsensical notes into his personal schedule. "That was a phase and now it's over."

"Like us?"

Hill stopped scribbling.

"We'll never be over, Bridgette. I'd be lost without you."

"Yeah, right," she said with a laugh. "Well, if this is a woman—which I suspect it is—I hope she's worth it. A ticket to Florida this late in the day is going to cost you an ugly penny."

"You mean pretty."

"I know what I mean," she said, leaving his office. He watched the sway of her voluptuous bottom beneath the tight white nurse's pants. Nothing.

He knew without question that any other man would consider Bridgette a stunner. Still, he found her unsexy. What did the old bird have that made him want her so? he wondered.

He leaned back in his chair, smiling. That was the part he loved most, he realized. The mystery of it all was a challenge in itself.

"Where've you been? You said you'd be here over an hour ago."

"I stopped to look at the Larchmont property on my way home," Rick said.

"Oh."

It was just eight o'clock, but Misty was in the bathroom doing something to her face. She had taken a shower and was ready for bed. Rick was quiet as he opened the nightstand on his side of the bed and put in the packets of condoms. He walked back into the kitchen and put the box and plastic bag in the trash.

When she came out of the bathroom, he was already in bed.

"You're not going to shower?" she asked.

"Nah. I'll get one in the morning."

"Oh," Misty said with a yawn. "You didn't want any dinner? I put everything in containers in the fridge. I can fix you something if you like."

She climbed in beside him. He opened his arms to welcome her in.

"That's okay, baby," Rick said. "I grabbed a pastrami sandwich before I left the city." He massaged her shoulders. "You look beat."

"I am," she said, closing her eyes, slipping into sleep. "Mmmm . . . that feels so good. Thank you, honey. I'm exhausted."

Rick kept rubbing her shoulders, pressing into the small of her back, rubbing away the knots.

Misty rolled over so that she was lying facedown. Rick began to work on her entire back. She drifted off to sleep.

Misty was already deep into a dream when she felt her husband pushing against her.

"Huh? Honey? Wha . . .?"

Rick had gone from massaging her back to kissing the backs of her thighs. He turned her on her side, spooning her. He reached his arms around to her front, fondling her breasts.

"Honey," she whispered, her voice thick with grogginess. "Baby, what are you doing?"

"I want you," he said, his voice low as he nuzzled her back. He felt her nipples harden. He kissed the nape of her neck and massaged her breasts again.

"Baby," she said. "You know I can't resist you."

"I know."

"But I'm tired."

"Me too," he said, "but I can't help myself."

Misty turned toward him, giving in to his touch. He reached for the nightstand drawer and pulled out a condom. He tore off the wrapper with one hand and pulled the rubber on.

He pushed her back with a gentle nudge and leaned over her, kissing her neck.

"I love you baby," he said.

"I know, honey. I love you too."


"I need to tap a phone."

"Of course," said the olive-skinned man behind the counter. "Just tell me what you want specifically. We've got it. It's all a matter of what you're looking to spend."

The Spy Stop on Commercial Boulevard sold all manner of tricky gadgetry, from Israeli pepper spray to Tasers to a black box that, when hooked up to the TV, would render everyone onscreen naked. At least, that's what the owner said. Given the $2,000 plus price tag, Tyrone was inclined to believe him.

The man showed him a series of devices—some simple, some complex—that hooked up to a standard household phone line.

"I need something for her phone at work as well."

The man scratched his chin, somewhat uncomfortable.

"Well, sir . . . I don't know. That's different. It's a place of business and it can get a little—"

"Trini told me I could trust you. He says he's come to you before and you always deliver."

Tyrone's dinner meeting with Trini the other day had been for the purpose of discussing this very thing.

"You know Trini?" the man said, his trepidation lifting. "Miami Dolphins Trini?"

"Yes, I do. He's a very good friend."

"And an excellent customer."

Tyrone examined the items the man had on the counter.

"I want the best, most nondetectable equipment you have. Price isn't an issue."

"Well," the man said, "if you really want to track her beyond just using the phone, I have GPS equipment."

Tyrone's brow raised.

"Like what I've got in my car?"

"Yes. A global positioning system."

"Good Lord. Is it detectable?"

"Not if you put it in the right place. The only thing better is putting a chip in her neck." The man glanced around. "Of course, you know—"

"It's illegal," Tyrone said. "As is ninety percent of what's in this store, I'm sure."

The olive-skinned man smiled.

"We prefer not to use that word, per se."

"I'm not worried about that. I can handle that part," said Tyrone. "I just need to make sure everything's installed before she gets home tonight."

"If she's not home, how can you put the equipment on her car?"

"She'll be in after ten. Can you have someone help me do it after that? Maybe around midnight?"

"Of course. But that'll cost you extra."

Tyrone rubbed his beard. He reached into his jacket pocket and pulled out a stack of money.

"I see Trini told you the smartest way to pay," the man said as he eyed the cash.

"Give me the best of everything you got," said Tyrone. "The phone stuff and the GPS. I'm going to need you to show me how everything works so I can track everything without her being suspicious. You think you can do that?"

"Absolutely, sir. Of course." The man hesitated. "I'm assuming the woman you're talking about is your wife."

"You assumed right," Tyrone said.

It was after 3 A.M. when Tyrone got into bed. Tyrene had been asleep for hours, full of lobster and Dom. She and her friends had celebrated a birthday at Tyrene's favorite hideaway restaurant, Fifteen Street Fisheries, just off the causeway.

She stuck her head in Tyrone's home office when she got in. There was a stack of legal briefs on the desk before him.

"You get rid of all those cigarettes?" she asked.

Tyrone glanced up, away from the manual for the phone-tapping equipment. It had already been installed in the house and on Tyrene's phone at the office. Now he was studying the instructions, which he had buried between the covers of the legal brief he was holding.

He figured he'd give her time—a couple of hours—to get showered and in bed. He could tell by the way she was leaning on the door frame that she would be out even sooner.

"The cigarettes are gone," he said.

"Good. I don't expect to see them again." She rubbed her eyes. "I don't know what possessed you to start up that vulgar habit again anyway." She yawned. "So nasty. So unbecoming."

"Really?" His tone was dry.

"Really," she said in response. She blinked at him, clearing her eyes. "Whose case is that?"

"It's the Hernandez appeal."

"Oh."

Tyrone sat the file in his lap. His wife stood in the doorway, watching him.

"I'm going to bed," she said after a moment. "You coming up soon?"

"Not for a while," he said. "There's a loophole in this thing somewhere, and I'm going to do my best to find it."

"Well, you do that, Superman," said Tyrene. "Good night."

"Good night."

Hill was at home, packing a bag.

Bridgette had given him the information for his e-ticket and the reservations for his hotel had been made. He would be staying at Pier 66 in Fort Lauderdale. It was a beautiful hotel just off the Seventeenth Street Causeway, which sat right on the intracoastal. He had stayed there many years before and loved the place, in particular the revolving restaurant at the top of the hotel.

He wondered how Tyrene would react once she learned he was there.

He wondered how he would react when he saw her again.

Hill sat on the edge of the bed. His dick grew hard just thinking about it.

It didn't take long for Hill's bag to come around on the baggage carousel. He grabbed it and walked over to the Avis counter. He wouldn't call her until he got to the hotel, he decided.

It was raining as he maneuvered his way from the airport to U.S. 1. The air was humid and warm. The sound of thunder crackled in the distance.

Hill smiled. He loved making love when it rained. He'd get Tyrene to the room, order up room service, and the two of them would while away the afternoon under electric gray skies.

He couldn't wait. He picked up his cell phone and dialed.

"You're where?" she said.

"Driving to Pier 66. Meet me there in forty-five minutes. I should be checked in by then."

Tyrene was in her office, pacing.

"How dare you come here," she said. "I didn't tell you that you could come here."

"Do you want me to go?" Hill asked. "I can just turn the car around right now and go straight to the airport. I'll be on the next flight out if that's what you really want."

Tyrene stopped in front of the office window, tapping her right foot as she looked out over the rain-splattered downtown area below. She gazed in the direction of the beach. She imagined Hill as he drove toward the hotel.

"Hello?" he said. "Are you there?"

"I'm here."

"So do you want me to go back home?"

"No," she said, her voice low.

"I didn't think so," said Hill. "Now, have that tight ass in my hotel room in forty-five minutes. I got something for you."

"Oh yeah?" Tyrene said with a seductive grin. "Is it as big as a bread box?"

"Bigger," he said. "And if you give it a good polish, I just might let it bust in your eye."

"You're disgusting," she said with a laugh.

"You love it."

"I'll leave here in ten minutes."

"Whatever," Hill said. "Just make sure you bring that ass over here before I have to come get it."

Tyrene hung up the phone.

"Fuckfuckfuck," she said. "Fuckshitdamn. Fuckfuckfuck."

Tyrone had broken the crystal water pitcher.

He'd thrown it across the room in a Brett Favre move that smashed the thing to bejeezus and sent three paralegals flying into his office.

"Mr. Snowden," said one of them as she stood in the doorway. "Is everything okay? What's going on in here?"

Legendary accounts of Tyrone's temper had lingered over the years, of isolated incidents that included him ripping a door off a hinge bare-handed and busting up an expensive mahogany credenza with a baseball bat. But those things were history. Aside from the occasional harried tone, he was even-tempered, in particular with his staff.

"Shut my fucking door," he barked.

The woman closed it posthaste and departed, the other two paralegals taking off with her. They listened outside for a moment. They could hear glass breaking and things being trashed. It sounded like wild animals had been loosed inside. Something hit the door with a thwock and the women scattered.

Tyrone was wearing a listening device and had been tracking his wife's calls all morning. He heard the conversation between her and the man, some stranger his wife seemed far too familiar with. The man had even called back with his room number—1102.

"I'll kill him," he said, his breath bordering on steam. "I'll kill the both of them."

Tyrone racked his mind about who the guy could be. The voice sounded like that of someone he'd spoken to before, but he couldn't connect it with any particular person. He wondered if it was someone they used to know years back. Or maybe it was a client or a city official.

"I need to talk to my daughter," he said.

Perhaps Teresa's voice would calm him, he thought. He needed something, either real or divine, to intercede on Tyrene's behalf; otherwise she was a dead woman.

He picked up the receiver of his office phone and dialed Reesy's cell. It went straight to voice mail after the first ring. He didn't leave a message.

Perhaps she's at home, he thought, forgetting about her trip to the Poconos. He dialed the number.

It was disconnected. Tyrone stared at the phone, then began smashing the receiver against the side of his desk.

Tyrene was on top of Hill, gazing into his eyes as he gripped her waist.

"You made me fly to this pussy," he said. "I've never gone anywhere for ass. It always comes to me."

He flipped her over and pushed her face into the pillows. He rammed himself hard inside her.

"Oh my goodness," she said, her voice muffled. "Oh, oh, oh."

He smacked her backside with the strong force of his palm. It made a stinging sound that echoed through the room.

"Don't leave a print," Tyrene said, turning her face so he could understand her words. "There's no way I'll be able to explain it."

He smacked her ass again and she let out a scream.

"Don't tell me what to do."

He thrust harder, jamming her head and neck up against the wall.

"Damn you, George Hilliard," she said. "Damn you and all this good-ass dick."

It was almost ten A.M., but Misty and Rick were still at home.

"Tell them we won't be in," Rick said into the phone.

"Is everything okay?" his assistant, Mary, asked.

"Yeah," he said. "We're both just a little under the weather."

"Of course," she said with a smile. "You must have a case of still-newlywed flu."

"See you tomorrow," he said and hung up.

Misty was in the bathroom vomiting. She'd been in there for more than twenty minutes and he hadn't been able to do anything to help.

"Are you pregnant?"

"No, I'm not pregnant," she screamed. "I wish you would just stop asking me that." She was crying.

Rick stood over his wife, watching her hang on to the rim of the toilet.

"Want me to go get a pregnancy test?"

"Could you just leave me alone, Rick? Could you do that? Just give me five minutes, okay? Something I ate last night didn't sit right."

"Fine," he said. "I'm going to run out for a minute. You want some breakfast?"

She had her head down on her forearm as she leaned against the bowl.

"Nothing, please. I just need to be alone."

"Alright, babe," he said. "I'll be right back."

\*   \*   \*

When Tyrone opened his office door, a small crowd was gathered around it. His all-African-American staff parted like a brown sea to let him pass. No one would make eye contact with him or dared to utter a sound.

He was holding some sort of contraption that looked like a radar. He banged the elevator button with his fist. The doors opened at once. Everyone was staring at him as the doors shut, but Tyrone only had eyes for the thing in his hand. It beeped as he gazed down at the thing. A little while before, it had relayed to him the location of his wife in her car, headed toward her foul tryst.

One of the attorneys stuck his head in Tyrone's office.

"Shit," he said.

The others gathered around the doorway.

The desk was destroyed and legal documents were everywhere. In addition to the pitcher, all the other crystal was broken. The armoire that held the TV where he watched the news was facedown on the carpet. Shards of wiring and scattered glass hinted that the TV was history.

"What do you think is wrong?" someone asked.

"I dunno," said the guy. "I guess the Hernandez case is out of control."

"Suck it hard," he said.

She did. She took him all the way inside her mouth, the way she used to do Tyrone years before. Hill's penis had a provocative shape and thickness. He even tasted virile. Every time she thought she was close to being satiated by him, he would do something else bordering on brutal—pull her hair, push her hard against the wall—that excited her to the challenge of yet another round.

She was almost out of the bathroom before she had the urge to hurl again. She dropped to her knees and leaned over the wastebasket. She had a series of dry heaves, but nothing came up.

"I can't take this," she said, her eyes squinched tight.

She opened them as she tried to stand. She was looking into the heart of the wastebasket. There were at least seven condom wrappers balled up inside.

"No wonder," she said. "I can't breathe for him fucking me every chance he gets."

She reached in and grabbed one of the offending things. She sat on the floor holding it. She could see the pinholes in it, but it took a second for the image to register. She smoothed the packet out. More pinholes. She reached in for another. Pinholes. Another wrapper revealed even more.

Misty rushed from the floor, her stomach lurching with her, and raced out of the bathroom to Rick's side of the bed. She opened the nightstand.

All the condoms had visible holes poked in them.

Emotions—too many to make sense—overcame her at once. She sat on the side of the bed and began to cry.

Rick walked into the bedroom holding a First Response pregnancy kit. Misty was sitting on the bed staring at him.

His nightstand drawer was open and all the punctured condoms were hanging out.

"What are you going to do?"

"I don't know, man, I don't know. I've got my gun. I think I'm going to kill them," he said.

Trini was on 826—the Palmetto Expressway—headed toward Hialeah. After hearing Tyrone's comment, he got off at the last exit in Miami Lakes before the Big Curve, went under the overpass, then got back on 826, headed the other way.

"Stop, Tyrone. Don't do it. I'm coming to where you are right now."

"It's too late, Trini," Tyrone said to the hands-free phone, his voice thick with anger as tears of disbelief streaked down his face. "I have to do it. I can't tolerate this situation. I've given my whole life to this woman and this is what she does in return? Hell, no." He slammed the steering wheel. "The bitch has to die."

"Pull over," said Trini.

"They're in room 1102 at Pier 66. If you see it on the news, you'll know it's me."

"Tyrone, man, c'mon now, stop." Trini hit the gas as he tried to calm his friend. He maneuvered his way toward I-95, hoping to avoid the lunch rush. It was just 11:20. He could still miss the bulk of the traffic. He wondered if he should take the turnpike and pick up 595, then realized that might be worse.

"Pull over and take a deep breath, Tyrone. Remember what you told me? You said I could lose my entire career, my whole future, my kids, everything, over some stupid shit my wife was doing. You said it wasn't worth it. You wouldn't let me be stupid. I can't let you be stupid either, man. You're my role model, c'mon."

Tyrone banged the steering wheel with the heel of his right hand. He was on Federal Highway headed for the Seventeenth Street Causeway and Pier 66. Drivers in passing cars stared in surprise at the giant of a man pounding the wheel of his Mercedes.

Trini was still talking when Tyrone went into the New River Tunnel. The call grew staticky, then dropped.

"Oh shit," Trini said. He hit "redial," but Tyrone wouldn't answer. Trini was in the fast lane, pressing hard to get to the Golden Glades Interchange, where several major thoroughfares—441, I-95, the Florida Turnpike, and 826—all converged. He zipped around cars as he knifed his Mercedes SL forward.

She was lying in his arms, hungry, waiting for room service. Her body was a study in blacks and blues.

"There's no way I can explain this to my husband," she said. "How in the world am I going to hide this from Tyrone?"

"So leave him," Hill said.

Tyrene raised up and looked at Hill.

"Oh, you're a foolish one. Do you think I'd leave my husband just for some dick? We've been together since I was a teenager."

"Then why are you in my arms right now?" he said.

She rested her head against his shoulder.

"I don't know. I guess I'm going through some sort of a midlife crisis. Women have them too, you know. One of my girlfriends has had a lover for the past five years, and she's older than I am." She stared off, her voice growing soft. "Her husband runs the biggest PR firm in the city, and he doesn't have the slightest clue that he's got her dick-on-the-side on the payroll."

The two lay in silence as Hill stroked her hair. He gazed up at the ceiling, angry at himself. This crass bitch, he thought. He could very well be in love with her, and there she was talking about what was happening between them being just an emotional blip. He was the dick-on-the-side in this scenario. He'd been an entrée his entire life, and she was reducing him to an extraneous side dish. Baked potato, fries, or mashed. Didn't matter, as long as it was a starch.

"So I guess that would make Tyrone the steak," Hill said.

"What are you talking about?" said Tyrene with a yawn. "Speaking of steak, where's our food?"

He looked into her eyes.

"So what would you think if I was in love with you?"

Tyrene laughed.

"Don't be ridiculous," she said. "You don't love me and I don't love you. This is chaos, confusion. Both of us are going through a phase." She stretched. "You'll be back to white girls in no time and I'll be but a memory. A good one, a damn good one, but a memory nonetheless."

"I am in love with you." He was serious. Tyrene scrunched her face up as she studied him.

"Look, Hill," she began, "I don't know anything about you. All those women. That girl you brought to the wedding. How do I know you haven't given me some kind of disease?" She shook her head. "I can't believe I've been so reckless with this."

"Raise up," said Hill.

"What?"

"I said lift that big yellow head of yours."

Tyrene sat up in the bed. Hill slid from beneath the covers and walked over to his garment bag. She watched his strong, lean body as he reached inside. He was beautiful from both the front and the back, with taut, intricate muscles that rippled when he moved. He's a god, she thought. Tyrone was but lumps of fatted meat compared to what was bending over on the other side of the room.

Hill pulled out some papers, walked back to the bed, and handed them to her.

"What's this?" She examined the papers, but couldn't make them out. "Hand me those glasses inside my purse," she said.

"Good grief." He reached inside her bag and retrieved them. "You aren't just an old bird. You're a blind one too. Haven't you ever heard of Lasik surgery?" he said.

"Haven't you ever heard of 'shut up'?" she replied as she put the glasses on.

She shook the papers once so that they were straight, a habit that came from years of handling legal documents. She read in silence, then glanced up at him, peering over the tops of the frames.

"So you carry the results of your AIDS test everywhere you go?"

"No," he said, getting back in the bed. "But I wanted you to see them. You're a shrewd, lawyerly bitch, and I knew this would come up sooner or later. I'm a doctor, you know. I always make sure my health is up to par." He raised his arms and leaned his head back into his palms. "If anything, I'm at risk messing around with you. You could be the town whore, for all I know."

Tyrene threw the papers at him.

"Why, you son of a bitch," she said with a snarl, taking off the glasses and sitting them beside the bed.

"Get to work, you prune," Hill replied as he shoved her head into his crotch.

"What were you thinking? Were you thinking at all?"

Misty was on the other side of the bed now. She tried to get away from him, but he was in front of her, kneeling.

"I'm sorry," he said. "I don't know . . . I guess I wasn't."

"This wasn't what we agreed to," she said. "We said we would wait. We said we'd spend some time with each other first. I can't believe you've been going behind my back all along, doing something as horrible as this." She held up one of the pierced condom packets. Rick looked away in embarrassment.

"What's wrong with me?" she said. "Why do I keep hooking up with the wrong man?"

"Baby," he said, "that's not true. I'm not the wrong man. You love me and I love you. We never agreed that we would wait to have children. We just talked about it, but you decided things for me. That's not right either."

"But going behind my back is? The right man wouldn't do that."

"No," he said. "That was wrong and I'm sorry."

"You're only sorry that you got caught," Misty said, her eyes red. "If I'd never found out, I'd just be pregnant thinking it was some kind of accident. Or, stupid me, that maybe nature stepped in because this was 'supposed' to happen."

"Are you pregnant?" he asked, his voice hesitant. "Is that why you were throwing up?"

She slapped him, Tyrene-style.

"Yeah, Rick," she said. "I'm pregnant. You got what you wanted. I guess that's just the way this marriage is gonna be, huh?" She dropped her head in her hands. "You get what you want whenever you want it. Fuck what I want. I just get to follow along."

\* \* \*

Tyrone didn't answer his cell phone after he lost the connection with Trini. He raced onward to the hotel, his mind riddled with images of his wife doing all the things she'd done to him in their more than forty years together. Reason told him there was no way she could fit all her clever little tricks into one afternoon, but he imagined her doing so.

Tyrene was a gifted freak with a genuine talent for the art of lovemaking, and he'd help groom her to be that way. She had a voracious appetite—sometimes too vast for him—but she never gave any intimation of straying.

They went through a brief period in the late eighties where they contemplated swinging again, but nothing ever came of it. After one trip to a place called Deenie's Hideaway in unincorporated Deerfield Beach—a den where guests could either watch or participate in sex with strangers—they changed their minds. Tyrone spotted a high-ranking official from the Broward County mayor's office. The person didn't see him. The last thing Tyrone knew he and his wife needed was for someone to have something on them and be able to leverage away a piece of their hard-won position within the tricounty social strata. Deenie's Hideaway was never discussed again.

Tyrone's eyes were as blurry as the windshield in front of him. He turned the wipers on, and while that worked for the glass, it couldn't get his eyes to clear.

He tried Reesy's cell phone again. She didn't answer. Everything was coming down on him at once. He was concerned that her home phone was disconnected. He wondered if it had something to do with her avoiding Dandre.

He'd investigate that situation after handling her mother, he decided. He was at the intersection of Federal and Davie Boulevard. The gun was on the seat beside him. He'd been angry before, but had never known the kind of rage he was experiencing now. The light lingered a little too long. He ran it, rushing on to get to Pier 66.

\*  \*  \*

He pulled up to the front of the hotel with a screech and stepped out of the car.

"Excuse me, sir. Excuse me."

It was the valet, chasing after him with a ticket stub.

"Thanks."

He ran into the hotel past startled guests and employees rushing to get out of his way, making a straight path for the bank of elevators.

There was a knock at the door.

"Finally, some food," Tyrene said, getting out of bed and slipping into a robe. "It took them long enough to bring their asses here."

The second knock was even harsher.

"Good grief," Hill said. "We're coming, hold on."

Tyrene went to the door and opened it.

Trini stood a few doors away, watching what was transpiring at room 1102.

He heard the elevator doors opening behind him.

"Why are you just standing there?" boomed Tyrone as he stepped out.

Trini threw his arm around the big man's chest as he tried to rush past. Trini was a lineman and was used to tackling. He was prepared to take Tyrone down in the hallway if he had to.

The door opened at 1102 and the waiter pushed the emptied cart back into the hallway. He glanced toward them, then shoved the cart in the opposite direction.

Trini shoved Tyrone back toward the elevator before the doors could close. When the doors shut, Trini opened Tyrone's suit jacket. The gun was sticking inside the waist of his pants. Trini took it.

"How'd you beat me here?" Tyrone asked.

"I did 120 on I-95. It's by the grace of God I didn't get a ticket and made it here before you."

"It's by the grace of God I didn't kill that bitch," Tyrone said.

"We're taking that equipment back."

"What equipment?"

"Everything you bought from the Spy Stop. You're the wrong person for this kind of stuff. It's going to be difficult enough keeping you from killing her with just the little bit of info you have right now."

"She's dead, Trini," he said. "I'm telling you, the little yellow bitch is dead."

"You're yellow too, Tyrone, so stop throwing stones. You and your wife need to talk soon and get to the truth. Before everything you've got—your firm, your nice big boat, your mansion, and the rest of your life—goes straight to shit."

# Toyz 'N Da Hood

"The 405 sucks."

"Welcome to L.A.," Sleazy said. "The fact that it's raining only makes it worse."

Reesy was stuck in gridlock just past the Mulholland and Skirball exit. She was antsy as she talked on her cell phone, excited about getting to her first real audition. Rowena had told her it was open casting, which was good, because she hadn't done any head shots yet.

"So where is it?" he asked.

"Stop making me think," she said. "I'm already keyed up. What are you doing up so early anyway?"

It was just 9:15. Reesy had made a mental note to call her parents later that day and tell them about her relocation. It hadn't been two weeks, but she figured it would be better to let them know before they happened upon her disconnected phone.

"I've gotta help my friends Chloe and Zoe move," Sleazy said.

"Chloe and Zoe?" Reesy said, stressing over the inching traffic. "You and your women, I swear."

"Yeah," Sleazy said. "Those girls are wild. They're the ones that had the party the other night."

"And now they're moving? What was it, a farewell bash?"

She blared her horn.

"Hey, hey, mami," Sleazy said. "We don't do that here. You'll get a ticket. Or shot. Relax."

"I can't relax. I'm gonna miss this audition."

"You'll be fine."

"Whatever. So your friends had a farewell party last night?"

"Well," Sleazy said, "it wasn't intended to be. Apparently the beach house they live in belongs to their cousin. He popped into town outta nowhere the other day and told them they couldn't throw any more wild parties. Well, these slicksters got him drunk and had a party anyway, so he's throwing them out."

"That's different," Reesy said, nudging her car forward. "I'm surprised a guy wouldn't be down for the kind of party you said it was going to be. Porn stars and all that. I thought that was every man's dream. He must be older."

"Nah. This Dandre cat is young. Can't be more than thirty-three, thirty-four. Good-looking guy, the kind chicks sweat and shit. I was surprised he wasn't down for some action."

Reesy stared at the bumper of the car in front of her. Everything around her seemed to stand still. She didn't speak. She couldn't.

"Yo, mami, you there?" Sleazy asked. "Did I lose you?" He could still hear feedback from cars going by, so he wasn't sure if the call had dropped. "Mami? Reesy? Hey, you still on the line?"

"Their cousin's name is Dandre?" she said.

"Yeah. I'm pretty sure that was his name."

She nibbled at the nail on her left forefinger.

"That's my ex," she said. "I can't believe your friends are related to my ex."

"Oh shit," said Sleazy. "Gitdafugout."

"So you've seen him."

"Well . . . yeah," he said, his voice riddled with disbelief.

She was already anxious. Now her nerves kicked into high gear.

"Maybe we should talk about this after you finish your audition," Sleazy said. "I don't want you going in there with your cap all twisted."

"I'm fine," she lied. "Just tell me what you saw."

Sleazy let out a deep breath.

"I don't know, mami. He seemed like a nice guy. He definitely wasn't trying to be down with any of the extra shit that's been happening in the house. Zoe and Chloe said he used to be into that kind of thing. I know if it was me, I would have been on everything in the room with titties. That's exactly what I was doing, as a matter of fact."

Sleazy decided he wouldn't tell her about the incident with the Tonies. According to the twins, Dandre hadn't been down for it and that was the main reason they were being kicked out.

"You might wanna rethink things," he said. "I don't think this cat is one of us."

The traffic began to move. Despite Sleazy's words of encouragement, Reesy's nerves were frantic as she maneuvered Black between lanes. She was still unable to process this less-than-six-degrees-of-absurdity moment.

"What do you mean by 'one of us'?" she asked.

"Pimptastic. Dickalicious. A part of the chosen few. He might have been once, but his card's been pulled. Or handed in. Damn. Now that's some tragic shit. That would make you a player slayer."

"Well, he's not getting another chance, if that's what you're suggesting. We're over."

"Just like that?"

"Yeah. Just like that."

"Meanwhile," Sleazy said, "he's sitting over there in that fabulous beach house all folded up on himself. You crushed that nigga like a cookie. That's cold, mami."

She drove in silence, looking for the 101 Freeway. A sign said it was a couple of miles ahead.

"Can I ask you a personal question?" Sleazy ventured.

"I don't know. Depends on what it is. Dammit, drive," she snapped at the driver ahead of her.

"It's pretty much a yes-or-no question."

"So go then."

"Did your boy cheat on you? Is that why you broke out?"

Reesy steered Black into the far right lane, squeezing in between cars that were trying either to get off onto Ventura Boulevard or merge onto the 101.

"Hello?" Sleazy said. "Hello? Hello?" She didn't respond. "Ree-see, is you wit' me?" he sang.

She merged onto the 101 in the direction of Ventura.

"Did he cheat on you?" he asked again.

She still didn't answer.

"Okay," he said, taking her silence for a no. "If that wasn't the problem, why'd you break out? Make this shit make sense to me."

"The problem was everybody saw pictures of him in a three-some on the day we were supposed to be married. Is that problem enough?"

Sleazy was wandering around his apartment in a robe. The remark made him sit on the couch.

"Damn," he said, his voice low. "He had a threesome the day you were supposed to get married?"

"No," she said. "Everybody in the church saw pictures of the threesome."

"So when did the threesome happen, at the bachelor party?"

"No. They were supposedly old, but anything's possible."

She exited on Reseda and took a right, speeding down the street.

Sleazy leaned back on the couch, considering what she had said.

"So you basically left him because you felt you were publicly embarrassed?"

"That, and other things."

"But nothing to do with believing he didn't love you, right?"

"No." The ring glinted at her as she gripped the wheel.

"I don't know, mami. This seems kinda murky. Some vindictive trick probably handed those pictures out at the wedding."

"Actually, it was a woman dressed in all black and a veil."

"See? There you go. I mean, c'mon. If a guy used to be a big-time player and suddenly hung up his hat because he found the One, well, discarded chicks don't take that too well. They like having the last say. Sort of like, if they can't be happy, then nobody's gonna be happy, especially the woman the man chooses."

"He should have had that under control," she said, glancing at the directions she had written on a notepad. "The repercussions were bad. Really bad."

"How can he control someone outside himself?" Sleazy said. "He couldn't stop you from leaving, could he? So why would he be able to tell some bitter bitch what to do? Who knows? It could be somebody he hadn't messed with in years and the woman just never got over him."

"I doubt it."

She didn't mention the woman's recent appearance on Dandre's doorstep.

"Trust me, I'm a man and I'm a player."

"Why would you brag about that?" she said, turning right onto Victory. "I'll never understand why grown-ass men consider it a badge of honor that they play with people's feelings."

"Don't hate, mami," said Sleazy. "These girls know what they're getting into. It's a game. They should stop deluding themselves. Women know a player when they see one. If they decide to participate, then what happens is on them."

Reesy was quiet as she searched for the address.

"I've seen some evil women in my day." Sleazy put his feet on the table in front of him. "They're all honey, sugar, daisies, and shit as long as they've got your attention, but the minute you move on, it's a crapshoot what can happen. I've had women scale buildings and break into my place, hold me at gunpoint, you name it. A SWAT team was called in to stop this one girl. She was strapped with explosives. The shit was sick."

"Why does it sound to me like you really love all this drama?"

Sleazy smiled.

"I dunno, mami. Maybe it's because in a twisted way I do."

"I gotta go."

"Good luck," he said. "Don't end up on no scratchy casting couch."

Reesy pulled into the strip mall, thinking she was late. She was surprised to see hordes of women of all shapes and sizes spilling out of the front door of one of the businesses. She'd heard of open castings, but she didn't expect this.

So what, she thought as she got out of Black. She knew how to handle competition, so that didn't scare her. What was a concern was the throng. Reesy hated waiting, and she didn't know what to expect with this process. The audition for *Black Barry's Pie* hadn't been as hectic as this. But that was for off-Broadway. This was Hollywood and the chance to be on film.

Two hours later, it was her turn.

She walked into a stale, empty room. Three people were sitting at a table facing her, one woman and two men. Another man was operating a minicam on a tripod.

The woman was small and brown with small eyes and a small Afro. The guy to the left of her was just as small with the same features. Reesy assumed they were brother and sister.

The other person was the real surprise. It was the guy from the club the night she went out with Sleazy. The cutie who'd been giving her the eye from across the room.

"Teresa Snowden?" he asked, glancing up from the sheet in

front of him. There was a glint of recognition in his eye, but his face revealed nothing.

His voice was bottom—a deep, dense, syrupy thing that oozed over her and made her feel sticky. Good sticky, not bad.

"Yes."

"What's your favorite food?" he asked.

"What?"

"Your favorite food? What is it?"

He leaned forward, his eyes piercing through her. The hairs on Reesy's body rose beneath the heat of his gaze. She wondered if he was kidding, then remembered the audition experience of *Black Barry's Pie*. It too had been deceptive. What she thought was going on had not been the reality of the moment.

Go with the flow, she thought. She figured he'd done this to everyone. She was going to show them that she was a sport.

"Fried chicken."

"Show me."

"What?"

"Act like some fried chicken," he said.

Reesy's eyes lingered on his. The rich black pupils twinkled and danced. She looked at the brother/sister act beside him. They sat with pens poised, pads positioned, ready to capture the moment. The man with the minicam zoomed in on her.

Without further prompting, she dropped to the floor and rolled herself from side to side. She was wearing a tight black turtleneck, a short black skirt, and black boots. She didn't care if they could see her panties and peeper beneath the skirt. It wasn't like her peeper hadn't been peeped before. She rolled and rolled and rolled and rolled.

She jumped up and shook herself off, throwing the best her fluid body had to offer into the act. She dropped to the floor again and made sizzling noises, writhing like a frenzied inchworm.

The brother/sister act couldn't contain their laughter. The cameraman wore a broad grin, trying to catch it all on tape. The cutie watched with an unreadable face—except for his eyes. They danced with delight, impressed by Reesy's enthusiasm and vigor.

She stood and brushed her skirt down. She swept the dust from her clothes.

The brother/sister act and the cameraman applauded.

"That was good," said the cutie with his nouveau–Barry White timbre. "I'm assuming you floured yourself, then hopped in the pan."

Reesy smiled.

"Clever," he said. "Very clever."

"Thank you."

Their eyes lingered. He pressed his lips together as if he was thinking. He rubbed his trimmed beard and jotted some notes on his pad.

"Is that it?" Reesy asked, preparing to go.

"No," said the cutie. His mouth widened into a fabulous smile. "Now show us a biscuit."


She was back on the 405 South just passing Wilshire when her cell phone rang. It was an 818 number.

"Hello?"

"Well, hello," the deep voice said.

Reesy's skin tingled.

"Hi."

"Hi there."

Neither of them spoke for about five seconds, then they both began to babble at once.

"That was different."

"You're good."

They laughed. Hers was a provocative sound. His was a thick gumbo that gurgled and stirred her pot.

"So we're breaking for the day," he said. "I'm about to grab some lunch. Are you still in the Valley?"

"I'm not too far," replied Reesy.

"You like Cuban food?"

"I love it," she said.

"So why don't you meet me at Versailles in Encino. It's right on Ventura."

"I don't know where Encino is," she said. "I'm new here."

"Really? From where?"

"New York."

"I'm from BK," he said.

"Really?"

"Really. I'm a Brooklyn son."

She smiled. That explained some of his sexy vibe.

"If I tell you how to get to the restaurant, can you meet me for lunch?"

"Is this a callback?" she asked.

"Oh yes," he answered in that malt liquor–smooth voice. "Most definitely. This is definitely a callback."

He was already at the table when Reesy arrived. He stood when she walked over. He was tall, about six feet three inches of beautiful meat. He smiled as he watched her. His teeth were dazzling.

Damn, she thought.

He held a chair out for her. She sat down and he took the seat across from her.

"Thanks for coming," he said.

"Thanks for calling. Today was my first Hollywood audition and now I'm having my first Hollywood callback," Reesy said.

"That's pretty rare in this town. It calls for a toast." He signaled for the waiter.

Reesy glanced around.

"Where are your partners?"

"They're off checking out a location we're considering. They're associate producers. I'm the big chief."

"The big chief?" she asked.

He laughed.

"I wrote the script, and I'm the director and executive producer."

"I guess that's pretty big," she said.

"Yeah. Troy and Ray just sat in on the initial auditions, but I'm handling all the callbacks myself."

"I'm assuming Troy's the girl."

"No," he said. "The girl is Ray."

The waiter was at their table.

"We'd like to order a drink," said the big chief.

"Just water for me," Reesy said.

"We can't toast with water." He looked at the waiter. "Bring us a couple of mojitos, please. We'll be ready to order when you bring back the drinks."

"Of course." The waiter nodded and left.

"Didn't I see you the other night at the comedy club?" Reesy asked.

"I don't know," he said with a mischievous smile.

"Right."

"Yeah," he admitted. "I was there. Imagine how surprised I was when I saw you walk into the audition."

"Good surprised?"

"Most definitely," he said.

"So I never got your name."

"It's James," he said, extending a massive right paw. "James Rivers."

She reached out her left hand to shake his. There was a tangible jolt of energy as flesh met flesh. He glanced down at the ring on her finger. It sat between them like a sentinel pit bull.

"Aha," said James. "So we're married."

"Not married."

"Engaged."

"Not engaged."

"Fakin' the funk."

"Too fat to get the ring off."

"I would never call you fat."

She pulled her hand away.

"So we were once engaged?"

"So what's up with the royal 'we'?"

"Touché," James said with a laugh.

The waiter arrived with the mojitos. "Are you ready to order?" he asked.

James looked at Reesy. "Perhaps you should check the menu. I always have the same thing."

"No," she said. "I know what I want. The pollo asado." It was her favorite Cuban dish.

"I'll have the roast pork," James told the waiter. The guy scribbled on his pad and went off. James raised his mojito. Reesy followed suit.

"To auspicious beginnings," he said with a sly smile.

"To hopefully booking my first movie."

They bumped glasses and sipped their drinks.

"So am I the first callback?" Reesy asked.

"You're the only callback."

Reesy sat her drink on the table.

"You're kidding," she said.

"Nope. I saw over two hundred girls today. You were the one. That fried chicken bit blew everyone away."

Reesy picked a lime from her drink and nibbled at it. Something about this didn't make sense. There was no way he could pick her just like that. She'd always heard that Hollywood was different, tough. Aside from the random idyllic fairy tale of overnight discovery, this kind of thing didn't happen.

"So are you saying I got the role?"

James nodded.

"Yes, you did. You're the leading lady."

"But I didn't even do any lines. You don't know if I'm flat, what kind of chemistry I might have when I read against somebody. Nothing. I don't get it. This doesn't seem right."

James leaned forward and grabbed her hands.

"Look, lady, the way you rolled on that floor—everyone in the room could see that you were willing to go out on a limb to throw yourself into a part. We watched the tape again after you left, before the next person was called in. You should have seen yourself." He shook his head as he laughed. "Hysterical. Sexy, fun, hysterical. Kind of like a black Lucille Ball, you know." He drank some mojito. "We were all digging it."

The waiter returned with two plates heaped with food. He placed the plate of roast chicken in front of Reesy. The aroma was intoxicating, rich with onions and garlic. There was rice and plantains and a small bowl of black beans. Within seconds, James was forking his roast pork, tearing at the succulent meat. He took a bite, juice dripping down his chin. He wiped it away with his hand, no napkin.

Reesy bowed her head and said quiet grace. James's fork froze, poised midway on a second arc to his mouth.

"Oh," he said. "Sorry."

She glanced up.

"Sorry for what?" she asked.

"Not waiting for you."

Reesy picked up her fork.

"Eat your food," she said. "Don't worry about me."

He didn't. He went at the plate like it was execution day and this was going to be his last meal. There was something feral about it.

James fucked the same way he ate his pork: with abandon and gusto, no moment of silent appreciation of the meal before him, no napkin. Juices dripping down his chin.

They were back in the stale, empty room where she had auditioned. It wasn't far from the restaurant, and Troy and Ray weren't expected back for a few more hours.

She wasn't quite sure how they ended up there. It had all

been a blur of emotions run amok, a whirlwind she didn't stop herself from being sucked into.

James had paid for lunch and walked her to Black. He asked her if she would take him back to the "office." Troy and Ray had dropped him off at the restaurant before they headed out on their location-scouting expedition.

"I let them take my car," he said.

James exuded sex and had a rapier wit, which, to Reesy, was always a sign of true intelligence. He had an immediate comeback for every quip she made, which challenged her. She appreciated a man who thought quick on his feet and in his seat.

James had asked her to stop at a 7-Eleven when they were on their way back so he could buy some bottled water. At least, that's what she thought he wanted to stop for. It turned out to be bottled water with a side order of condoms.

"I shouldn't be doing this," she said as she lay beside him, circa round three. "We're going to be working together. This is not a good start."

"One has nothing to do with the other," James replied. "I'm feeling you. You're feeling me. That was apparent the other night at the club."

Reesy realized his words were true. There had been an electricity between them from the very beginning. The pièce de résistance was that James was a superior lover. He was savage, adventurous, hyper, animalistic—like an adrenaline-high cheetah in the throes of a fresh kill.

His weaponry wasn't too bad either. It was thick, sturdy, a generous serving of solid meat that made her reach out and grasp it to see if it was real.

After Rhiannon's revelations about physical alterations being a common occurrence in L.A., Reesy didn't consider anything beyond inspection anymore.

It had been many months since she had seen new dick. For a time, when Reesy and Dandre were happy and planning their life together, she believed the days of foreign dick were done. She was pleased about it. Dandre was a total package and everything about him—to her—equated hitting the jackpot. He was the consummate lover, confidant, and friend. He was beautiful, soothing to her eyes and to her spirit.

And his dick was a fabulous testament to perfection. The standard. It was museum-worthy.

Seeing James's wood had excited her, but, in an odd way, she found herself comparing it to Dandre's.

She stared it in its one eye and studied the girth of the head. It didn't seem symmetrical, like there'd been a flaw in the mold in which it was cast. She sat on the thing, wondering at the way it sort of just pushed in without ceremony, nothing like how Dandre's introduced itself with more of a natural glide. She bucked on it, but it didn't hit the corners the way she liked.

She realized how Goldilocks must have felt, trying out those three bear beds. As pretty as James's dick was, and despite his talent at putting it down, something about the way he fit just wasn't quite right.

Now that the urgency of the sex had subsided, something discomfiting—a strange sense of sadness—was tiptoeing its way across her brain.

She glanced down at the penis hanging limp and spent on James's thigh.

Her eyes flitted across her left hand. The ring glinted at her. She twisted the thing, trying to turn it around.

Her finger was too thick. The ring wouldn't budge.

The ride back to Manhattan Beach seemed longer than her trip cross-country. It was too much time alone, too much time to think. She blasted the radio to drown out her thoughts, but her brain was aflutter.

It had been a while since she'd done anything as reckless as her moment with James. Reesy had done casual sex before.

That wasn't the problem. But what the incident did, more than anything, was make her realize how much she still cared for Dandre.

"I don't want to love you, you fuck," she said to the windshield wipers as they flashed back and forth. "Not after what you did to me. Not after what you did to my life."

She thought about Sleazy's words and his insistence that what had happened at the wedding may have been out of Dandre's control. That didn't matter to her. Holding on to her resentment was easier than wrapping her brain around the concept of letting him into her heart again.

Sex with James wasn't premeditated, although she had an intuitive feeling that by going back to meet him for lunch, something more than discussing her getting a role in the film was going to occur.

It was supposed to be closure, an act that would shut the door on her and Dandre and the loss of the baby. Opening her life—and her legs—to new L.A. experiences.

Everything is still too fresh, she thought. That explained why she was feeling so sad. It was like trying to work out after not hitting the gym for months. Her dating muscles were atrophied. Her emotional reflexes were shot. She was determined to fix that.

"I'll just keep at it," she said.

Soon enough, she reasoned, being with someone else would seem easy, and her love for Dandre would begin to fade away.

Pier Avenue was right in the heart of Hermosa Beach. It was a street teeming with retail stores, restaurants, and bars. There was always a crowd of people strolling, shopping, passing through on their way to the beach, or enjoying good food, good drink, and good times with friends.

Dandre sat in a pub with a tall glass of Guinness. It was his third. He nibbled on a chicken wing as he tried to kill time.

He didn't want to be at the house when Zoe and Chloe left. They had cried through the night, appearing in front of him with their eyes swollen, faces puffy, that morning.

He was not going to be swayed. He knew the girls had money. They hadn't paid rent in five years but were always working. They could get another place if they wanted. Their dramatic display didn't change the fact that they both had disrespected not just his request, but his person as well.

He sat in the booth, contemplating whether he should tell Reesy about the incident with the three women, and about Rejeana coming to his house. He wanted both things out in the open so they could never haunt him again, like those atrocious pictures.

Dandre was determined not to let anything else come between him and Reesy, once he got her back.

"I'm going to tell her," he said into his drink.

"I wouldn't do that if I was you."

Sleazy slid into the booth beside him.

Dandre glanced up at him, alarmed by his appearance. This was one of those friends of the twins. Another L.A. party hound who was a part of his cousins' slumming crowd.

"What's up, man?" Dandre said, not hiding his annoyance. "What are you doing here? The twins are back at the house. They're moving today."

"I know," Sleazy said. "I'm helping them."

"Then why are you here? I hope they didn't send you over here to help plead their case, because it's pointless. Don't waste your breath."

Sleazy grabbed a chicken wing and bit into it. Dandre slid away from him, deeper into the back of the booth.

"Sure," he said. "Help yourself."

"Thanks," said Sleazy. "I will."

He grabbed another. He signaled a waiter, pointing at Dandre's Guinness and holding up two fingers. The waiter nodded.

"So you can go back and tell Chloe and Zoe your trip over here was useless. I know they told you I was here."

"Yeah, they told me where you were, but that's not why I'm here," Sleazy said. "I think I might be able to help you with something you need."

Dandre nodded, as if he got it. This was an L.A. hustle, he figured. This guy was about to tell him about some kind of hookup. Everybody on the come-up had some kind of scam that they tried to put their friends onto. This guy must have thought Dandre was down for that kind of thing. He already knew Dandre and his dad owned the beach house. He must have figured they had money to burn.

"No thanks," he said, "I don't need anything."

Sleazy licked buffalo sauce from his fingers. His two-way beeped. He read the thing, then put it on "silent" so they wouldn't be interrupted. The waiter sat two beers on the table.

"Thanks, man," Sleazy said to the waiter. He took a swig, licking foam from his top lip. "So you don't need any help with Reesy?" he said as he stared into the glass of beer.

Dandre started, his brow furrowed, his eyes dark. He'd seen Sleazy at his beach house, in the midst of major freaking.

"What do you know about Reesy?" Dandre asked. "How do you know who the hell she is?"

Sleazy got another wing.

"This thing is huge, more like a turkey wing than chicken. These fucking hormone-injected Frankenfoods are gonna kill us all."

Dandre grabbed him by the wrist, tight. Sleazy glanced over at him.

"Don't worry," he said. "I'll order some more."

Dandre didn't release his grip on the big man's wrist. Sleazy let the chicken wing drop.

"Tell me how the hell you know my girl."

"Your ex-girl," he said. "The wedding is off."

"Look, man." Dandre's voice was raised as he grabbed Sleazy by the collar. The bartender heard the commotion and gestured to the waiter.

"Chill, man, chill," Sleazy said. "Relax. I'm on your side. That woman still loves you. I just came here to help."

Dandre searched his face for a hint of truth. He saw it. He let go of Sleazy and leaned back.

The waiter came over to them.

"Everything alright over here?"

"Everything's fine," Sleazy said with a smile. "We would like some more chicken wings, though. Extra sauce on the side, if that's not a problem."

"Sure," replied the waiter with a skeptical tone.

"Thanks, man."

The waiter glanced over at Dandre, who was staring off into space.

"He's alright," said Sleazy. "We're just having man talk. No big deal."

The waiter left.

Dandre turned to Sleazy, his voice a deep growl.

"Tell me how you know her. Tell me how you know our business."

Sleazy opened his mouth, but Dandre cut him off.

"Then tell me how you know my cousins. I've seen you at the house. Were you a part of that whole situation where I got set up with those girls the other night? Was that all a part of sabotaging me with Reesy?"

"Hey, hey, hey," Sleazy said around his drink. "I met Reesy a few days ago through a friend of mine. A chick named Rhiannon."

"Reesy doesn't know a lot of people out here. I've never heard her mention this person before. I would remember a name like that."

"She met Rhiannon at the gym. We all had lunch together in Santa Monica. Reesy and I really hit it off."

Dandre's shoulders squared.

"Not like that, man," Sleazy said, raising his hand. "Relax, brother, relax. Damn." He put his hand on Dandre's shoulder. "The girl loves you. No matter what she says, she's got you all up under her skin. She's still got her ring on. Knowing how women are, that's saying a lot."

Dandre released a deep breath and grabbed his beer. He drank and drank and drank. It was a long gulp that resulted in a near-empty glass.

"So what do you want? I'm assuming you want something from me in exchange for something to do with her." He stared at Sleazy. "I'm right, aren't I?"

The waiter put down a fresh plate of chicken wings and a stack of napkins. He cut his eyes at them, still wary about their earlier exchange.

"I don't want shit from you," Sleazy said once the waiter was gone. He poured the extra sauce over the wings. "Reesy's good people. I could tell that from the second I met her. She thinks she's tough and all that, and she is, but L.A. is crazy. It'll eat her alive or turn her into something that nobody who used to know her will ever recognize. I mean, look at the twins."

Dandre cleared his throat.

"They know how to take care of themselves," Sleazy said. "But they're a part of the ugly underbelly now. Those girls are really out there."

"What ugly underbelly?"

"L.A. This place is like the bowels of hell."

"Right," Dandre said. "I need to get Reesy out of here."

"Well, see, that's the funny thing about this town. If you've got someone here that you love and believe in, it's a reciprocal thing, and y'all are building a life together, this place can be heaven." He rolled a wing around to get some of the extra sauce. "But if you're single and on the prowl, or if you're single and just don't know what kind of people are out there waiting in the shadows, you can kiss your soul good-bye. This place will crush the shit out of it."

He bit into the bird. Dandre gazed at the table, wondering where Reesy was and if she was safe. Sleazy's words were making him uneasy.

"Yeah, man," said Sleazy, "your cousins are first-class diggers, straight chickens, you know what I'm saying? Cold-blooded. I've seen those girls take men for their money in ways you wouldn't believe. They're generous with it, I gotta give 'em that." He sucked on a chicken bone. "Whenever they score, they set it out for everybody with a big-ass party. Still, it's crazy. Z and C are my friends, and I'm not saying anything to you that I wouldn't say to their face, but I pity the man that ever falls for either one of 'em."

Dandre nodded. He knew how his cousins got down, and there was nothing he could do about it. They were long past the point of return.

"So are they really your cousins?" asked Sleazy.

"Distant," Dandre murmured, still gazing ahead.

"Well, your girl ain't out there like that," Sleazy said. "At least, not just yet. That's what I think I liked about her when I first met her. She's, what, in her early thirties?"

"Yeah." Dandre reached for a wing.

"See," continued Sleazy, "by that age, broads are kinda bitter, jumpy, always expecting the worst because they've been raked over the coals enough to be pissed the fuck off about it."

"True, true." Dandre bit into the wing, sauce dripping onto his plate. Sleazy handed him some napkins.

"Thanks, man."

"No problem. So your girl, even though she's thirty-something . . . I don't know. She's still not tainted. You know what I mean?"

Dandre shook his head. He knew Reesy wasn't tainted, but he also knew she wasn't pure. When she was an exotic dancer, she saw some crazy things. She had shared with him sordid stories of her days at the Magic City in Atlanta; he knew about her almost being raped when she used to dance in New York at that skanky club, the One Trick Pony. This was all before her off-Broadway days. His woman had seen the underbelly and had navigated within it well. That he knew for certain, whether Sleazy was aware of it or not.

"I'm not saying she's Snow White," Sleazy said, sensing the layers of Dandre's silence. "I can tell she's been around the block."

Dandre chuckled.

"I don't mean that with disrespect." Sleazy picked up a wing. "I know she's experienced is what I'm trying to say."

"That, she is," Dandre replied.

"But the thing with Reesy . . . the thing that really catches your attention . . ."

The wing was raised en route to his mouth, but then Sleazy lapsed into a semi-reverie describing the merits of Dandre's girl. He held the meat aloft as he spoke.

"The thing about her is . . . her eyes. There's something about the way she looks at you."

"Yeah, I know. Her eyes are huge. It's like she's looking right through you."

"Yeah, but no. That's not what I'm talking about." He bit into the chicken, talking with it in his mouth. "It's the way her eyes dance. They've still got a light in them, you know? Like she hasn't seen the worst life has to offer yet. Like she really hasn't even seen much of anything bad. I know she has. Shit, what happened at your wedding alone was enough to make a mutha-fucka an overnight psychotic."

Dandre's skin bristled at his words. He wished he could wipe that incident from not just his memory, but from the mind of everyone who was there that day.

"But your girl didn't go dark. Sure, she's angry about some shit. Sure, it hurt her pretty bad. But she's still got that light in her eyes, you know what I mean? Like she's still got hope in human beings. It makes you want to protect her. It makes you want to be her friend."

"You sure you're not feeling her?" Dandre asked. "You're not just coming here to case the competition, pretending to be down with me but really just sizing me up?"

Sleazy laughed.

"Not hardly," he said. "You can tell when another man is checking for your girl. It's a vibe they give off. I know for a fact you're not getting that vibe from me."

"True. I'm not."

Sleazy nodded as he drank the last of his beer. He signaled to the waiter for two more.

"What's your name, man?" Dandre asked. "I'm sitting here telling you all my business and I don't even know your name."

"Sleazy," he said. "Just call me Sleazy."

Dandre laughed as he chugged his beer.

"C'mon, player. What's your real name?"

Sleazy picked up a bone from the plate in front of him. There were still a few remnants of meat clinging to it. He chawed at it. Dandre pressed him.

"C'mon, now. I know when your mama pushed you out the womb, she didn't look at the doctor and say, 'I think I'll call him Sleazy.'"

"Actually, that's kinda what happened, 'cept it was more like my dad pulling one of them Kunta Kinte stunts. Going out beneath the shining moonlight, holding me up to the heavens. 'Behold, the only thing sleazier than me.'"

Dandre and Sleazy both laughed. The suspicious waiter gave them a furtive glance as he passed.

"What's your real name, man?" Dandre asked again. He reached for another wing.

Sleazy took a deep breath, held it for about five seconds, then released it.

"Leslie," he said in a voice so low, Dandre had to strain to hear it.

"Come again?"

Sleazy stared him in the eye. This time his tone was strong and clear.

"Leslie," he said. "Leslie Caron Grayson."

"Oh shit." Dandre laughed so hard that, when he inhaled, a piece of chicken was sucked back into his trachea. He had a coughing fit. Sleazy slapped him on the back with his big open palm. The errant piece of meat came flying up and out.

"Thanks," Dandre said, still coughing. "I appreciate it, Big Les."

"Yeah, right. Keep that shit to yourself."

"What, Leslie? I think it's befitting a pimp like yourself."

"Fuck you, man. At least I'm not bitch enough to give a girl a houseful of puppies."

Dandre made a startled move.

"What next," asked Sleazy, "gumdrops and bunnies?"

He and Dandre faced off, their expressions tense. After a few pregnant seconds, both men broke out laughing.

"So here's the plan," Sleazy said. "I'll stay close to her. I talk to her all the time. I'll keep putting in the good word and see what I can do to get the two of you reconnected."

"I appreciate it, man," Dandre said. "I don't want to get her back through anything calculated and underhanded. I'd feel funny about that."

"That's not what we're doing."

"Okay. I mean, I appreciate you being a negotiator for us and letting me know that she's okay."

"That's all I'm talking about," Sleazy said.

"Hey, let me ask you something."

"What's that?"

"How'd you know who I was? The twins don't know Reesy. They've never even met her."

The two men were walking down the Strand, back toward the beach house. The rain was no longer falling, although the sky was still gray.

"I mentioned your name to Reesy this morning. She was on her way to an audition and asked me what I was getting into. I told her I had to help the twins move because their cousin Dandre was tripping because they were throwing all kinds of wild parties. When I said 'Dandre,' she got all quiet, and that's when she told me who you were."

Dandre's stomach felt tricky, like he might be sick.

"Does she know about that scene with those chicks upstairs?"

"The Tonies? Nah. I didn't say anything to her about that. After she told me about the thing with the pictures, I figured I'd keep that situation to myself."

"Thank God," said Dandre.

"I told her you probably had nothing to do with the chick that passed those pictures out. That maybe she was just a disgruntled broad from your past." Sleazy paused. "Is that true?"

"It's exactly the truth."

"Good, because I care about Reesy. I don't want to see her get played. If some punk is responsible for making that light go out in her eyes and I hear anything about it, I'll break him in half."

"That won't be necessary," Dandre said.

"It better not be. I told her that she couldn't fuck with any of my boys because if they did her dirt, I'd feel funny having to beat 'em down. But you and I just met. The shit ain't cemented yet. I'll still kick your ass if you try to fuck her over."

The two men stopped walking and squared off. They stared at each other in silence.

"She wants to mess with one of your boys?" Dandre asked after a moment.

"Nah," Sleazy said. He pulled two cigars out of his shirt

pocket. He offered one to Dandre, but he refused. The two resumed walking. Sleazy snipped the end of his cigar, then stuck the stogie in his mouth.

"You sure she's not open to other men?"

"Hell, naw," Sleazy replied, talking around the cigar. "She's just selling wolf tickets. That girl ain't thinking 'bout nobody but you."

Reesy had returned home at three to find the dogs sitting in the kitchen, which was the only area of the house she allowed them while she was away. The puppies had grown bored, and yet again, a destructive mob mentality had taken hold. This time they gnawed the lower cabinets where she kept the pots and pans, and left tiny teeth marks dotting the painted wood.

Once Dante's wailing subsided, she let them out of the kitchen, into the rest of the house. The dogs traipsed behind her, scampering between her legs as she headed to the bathroom to shower.

She decided she would call her parents and tell them about the move, but there wasn't an answer at the house, and neither one of them was in the office. She didn't try their cell phones. She figured she would call again later that night, perhaps around nine, which would be midnight their time. Better to tell them when they're sleepy, she thought, rather than hit them with the news when they were at their most coherent and judgmental.

After showering, she lay down for a nap. The phone rang five minutes after her head hit the pillow. She looked at the caller-ID box. It was Misty.

"Hey, girl," Reesy said in a tired voice, lying back against the pillows. "You'll never guess what I did today."

She could hear choking and sobbing. It wasn't unfamiliar. Reesy knew the unmistakable sound of Misty upset.

"What's wrong, honey?" she asked, sitting up. "Misty . . . tell me what's wrong."

She could hear her friend struggling to talk, but the words kept running into phlegmy clots of interference.

"What happened? Is it the baby? Talk to me, please."

"R-r-r-r-r . . ."

"What?"

"R-r-r-r-r-r-r . . ."

"I don't understand what that means. Are you okay? The baby's okay, isn't it? Please tell me you didn't change your mind."

Reesy could hear her fumbling with the phone as she blew her nose. Misty took a few deep breaths and attempted to speak again.

"Rick," was all she managed to get out.

"Yeah? Rick. Okay. Is Rick alright? Does he know about the baby? Did you tell him?"

Misty's breath came in heaves and she began to cry again.

"P-p-p-pins. H-h-h-holes. H-h-holes in the c-c-condoms."

"I'm sorry, sweetie," Reesy said. "I don't understand."

Harlem jumped on the bed and ran toward her. Reesy gave her a gentle nudge with her foot. The dog was back within seconds. Reesy stood and walked toward the living room.

"H-h-h-he was p-p-punching holes in th-th-the condoms."

Misty's words finally connected and Reesy understood.

"What?" she screamed. "He was punching holes in the condoms? When? Today?"

"F-f-f-for months," Misty said.

"Is that why you're pregnant?" Reesy asked.

"Y-y-y-yes."

"Oh my gosh." Reesy sat on the couch. All three of the dogs jumped on the couch with her. She got up and went to the dining table. She didn't know what to say. She couldn't imagine Rick doing something like this.

"Are-are-are you still there?" asked Misty.

"I'm here," Reesy said, sitting at the table. She was in a stupor. "So he knows you're pregnant now, right? He knows his little plan worked."

"Yeah."

Peanut scratched at Reesy's right foot. Reesy ignored her and the puppy scratched harder. She rubbed the dog's chest with her big toe. The puppy made a contented moaning sound.

"So you're leaving him, right? This is some foul, lowlife shit."

"I-I-I-I . . ." Misty stammered.

"You're leaving him, right?"

"I-I-I-I . . ."

"Don't tell me you're not going to fucking leave him, Misty. What he did was wrong. There's no two ways about it. You can't rationalize anything right out of this."

"I c-c-c-can't just run away again."

"What do you mean by that?"

"I-I-I . . ." She tried to speak over the sobs. She breathed in and out three times to control her words. "I always run away," she said.

It was true. Misty had run from many bad love affairs and always landed somewhere worse. She went from Stefan the bed-wetter in Fort Lauderdale and ended up with Roman the lover in Atlanta, who, after months of spending every day with her—except for the weekends—disappeared and never called her again. He had gotten married during his absence, and Misty learned the news while she was peeing in the stall of a mall bathroom. She overheard Reesy talking to a friend who turned out to be the sister of the woman Roman had wed.

"I can't run away again," she said.

"Oh, great. So you just stay with a loser who'll sabotage your entire life."

Misty didn't respond. Reesy could tell she had gone too far.

"Sorry," she said. "He's not my husband. I can't speak for you. I'm just saying—"

"I know what you're saying." Misty's voice was clear now, strong. The sobbing had stopped. Reesy's protests had snapped her out of whining mode and put her on the defensive. "I'm not running away. He and I are going to deal with this."

233

"What's to deal with?" Reesy asked. "He's a liar and a cheat and now you're pregnant. How can you ever trust him again?"

"We've decided to go to therapy."

"Therapy?" Reesy spat. "What the fuck will therapy do?"

"I'm hanging up," Misty said.

"Wait . . . no . . . I'm sorry. Don't hang up."

"Then stop judging me and my situation."

"I'm not."

"Yes, you are."

"I'm sorry. I'm just protective, I guess." Reesy stopped scratching Peanut's chest. The dog pawed at her foot again. "Damn," she said, getting up and walking into the kitchen. "These fucking rats are getting on my nerves."

"It's time I learned to problem-solve," Misty said. "I don't want to run away from things again. I'm carrying his baby. We're married. I can't just call everything off and walk away."

"Right," Reesy said. She wasn't sure what she meant by the word as she said it.

She took a bag of cheese cubes out of the refrigerator and walked back down the hall, into the bedroom. The puppies followed her.

"So you're going to stay and work it out," she said.

"Yeah. I can't run anymore, Reesy. You need to understand how I feel about that. It was the first thing that I wanted to do, but something in me said it wouldn't solve anything."

"Whose idea was therapy?"

"Rick's," Misty said.

"Really?"

"Really. He knew he fucked up."

"I'll bet."

Misty let out an audible breath.

"Sorry," Reesy said.

She handed the dogs some cheese.

"One day you'll see that running from things isn't the answer,

Reesy. Has it made things better for you, now that you've moved to the other side of the world?"

Reesy started to say yes and tell her about James and the Amazing Technicolor Fuck. It would have been a lie. Things weren't better. In fact, they were more confusing now than ever. Being with him had made her more aware of Dandre. She couldn't admit that to Misty. They were supposed to be yin and yang. That's what they'd been forever. It was rare for them to agree. She saw no point in altering the balance of their universe.

There was a smear of cheese on her diamond. Without thinking, she reached for a tissue from the box beside the bed. She wiped the ring, careful not to do anything that could mar the perfection of the surface of the stone.

"Are things better for you?" Misty repeated. "Have you even dealt with your feelings about Dandre? Is he out of your system?"

"I don't want to talk about him," she said, tossing the tissue in the trash.

"Of course not," replied Misty. "You just want to pass judgment on me."

The dogs gazed up at Reesy.

"I'm the alpha dog," she said to them.

"What?"

"My friend Sleazy told me—"

"Who the heck is Sleazy?" Misty asked. "Please tell me you haven't started your pattern again."

Reesy's face squinched into a frown.

"And what pattern is that?"

"You know what you do."

"No, I don't. Please tell me."

Misty took a breath, measuring her words.

"You know. Sometimes you'll sleep with someone to get over something that bothers you."

Reesy had known what Misty was going to say, because it was real. If she lost a job, she gained a screw. When she and

Misty used to argue during the days they shared an apartment, she would go out and put her rage into sex with a relative stranger. It wasn't a regular thing, but it was the best way she knew to release what she was feeling.

She wondered if that was what she'd done today. She expected to be relieved after getting with James, less burdened, somehow. Instead, all she was left with was a heaping plate of fucker's remorse.

"You haven't done that, have you?" Misty asked.

"Why don't we get off me," Reesy said. "I didn't fuck Sleazy. He's a friend. He's like a big brother who watches over me."

"Well, just be careful. Anybody with a name like Sleazy can't be down for anything good."

Reesy didn't bother to counter her remark. She saw no point in defending someone Misty didn't even know.

"You're not crying anymore," she said. "I guess you got it out of your system."

"It's not out of my system. You just pissed me off enough to make me stop."

"Then my work here is done," she said with a smile.

"Yeah," said Misty. "I guess it is. Thanks for being there for me."

"Of course. You're my sister. I care about what happens to you."

"Ditto," she said as she blew her nose. "Be careful out there."

"I am," Reesy said.

"Okay, girl. I'll call you later."

Reesy clicked off the phone. She sat on the side of the bed, unable to move. The dogs stared up at her, still in their military positions.

"Julian was right," Reesy said to the three. "All men are muthafuckas."

Harlem yipped. She gave them some cheese.

\* \* \*

236

The phone rang at 6 P.M.

She'd been asleep since her conversation with Misty, dreaming of being on a boat with Dandre headed for Catalina. The dogs were on the bed beside her, deep into whatever it was that puppies dreamed of. The bag of cheese was empty. It had been looted by them as she dozed.

The caller-ID box displayed the words "unknown caller." She wondered if it was Dandre and almost didn't answer. Maybe it was Misty calling back from her cell.

"Hello?"

"So why don't you come over and hang out? Maybe we can watch a movie or something."

"Who's this?"

"How quickly we forget," said the deep voice.

"James."

"Well, I'll be damned. She didn't forget."

Reesy sat up in the bed and stretched. The puppies, one by one, did the same.

"What time is it?" she asked, looking around.

"Six o'clock," he said. "What you doing in bed?"

"I was tired," replied Reesy with a yawn.

"Then I guess that means I was effective."

"Hmph."

"So why don't you come over?" he said. "I'll cook us something to eat."

"Really?"

"Sure."

She imagined him standing in a sprawling kitchen in a fabulous house in the Hollywood Hills, chopping cilantro and onions, tossing them with shrimp into a sizzling wok. She figured him to be a good cook, considering the way he relished both eating and sex. James was a sensualist. It would only make sense that same zeal would translate into culinary skills.

"What are you going to cook?" she asked.

"Let me surprise you," he said. "You just show up."

Reesy stretched her legs, considering his offer. It was rainy and cold, but she wouldn't mind being around some company. She looked at the puppies. They'd be okay.

"Alright," said Reesy. "Give me your address."

She did Mapquest on the computer before she left. James had tried to give her directions, but she preferred the computerized method over everything else. It was foolproof.

She took the 105 to the 110, getting off a few exits before downtown.

She headed east. The neighborhood had a distinct inner-city feel to it.

This wasn't the Hollywood Hills. She knew that much for sure.

The directions led her to a weathered apartment building. Guys were hanging out front despite the rain. They watched her, eyeing Black as she pulled into a parking space.

Shit, she thought, where the fuck is this?

"'Zup," one of the guys said with a nod as he blocked the doorway.

"Hi," she said, respecting the rules of the street.

"Yo, that's a Boxster, right?" another one asked.

"Yeah," Reesy replied, stopping and making eye contact with him. She saw him check out her engagement ring.

"Dayum, baby," he said. "Somebody must be lovin' you right."

She smiled.

Reesy had learned a long time ago that men in groups could be like dangerous dogs. If they sensed fear, they preyed upon it, often reacting as a pack to take their victim down. If a person took them head-on, though, then respect was due. Reesy wasn't about to give off fear. The man stepped aside and let her pass.

"Hey," she asked, "what area is this?"

"This is Watts, baby," the guy replied.

"Thanks. I appreciate it."

Watts, she thought. She'd heard Fred Sanford talk about this place too. If she remembered right, it was riot-prone. Maybe that was a long time ago. She wasn't sure. What she was sure of was this wasn't the Hills.

She walked into the building. The hall was pissy and dirty. A stack of soiled diapers leaned beside the elevator. The sound of loud music could be heard coming from behind one of the doors on the first floor.

She pressed the elevator button several times. The doors creaked open and, after she got on and pushed the button for the fifth floor, the doors struggled shut. It was a small, claustrophobic box with an ammonia stench. She wondered if she had taken down the wrong directions. This couldn't be where James Rivers lived. He was a producer, and, from what she knew, this wasn't how Hollywood producers lived.

When the elevator doors opened, she walked down the hall to apartment 521. She gave the door a tentative knock. She could hear the sound of a TV. She knocked again.

The door opened. James stood there in all his fineness. He flashed his dazzling smile.

"You made it," he said, embracing her and guiding her in.

"Yeah," she said, looking around. The pungent scent of sage rushed over her.

"What's that you're cooking?"

"I made my specialty," James replied with a smile. "I'm sure you'll like it."

"What is it?"

"Sausages and rice."

The apartment was as spartan as any she had ever seen. There was a black leather couch, a sixty-inch high-definition TV, a DVD player, about fifty DVDs, a Sony PlayStation, a glass coffee table, a floor lamp, and an orange candle. There was no artwork of any kind.

"Sit down," he said. "Let me fix our plates."

Reesy sat on the couch. There was no dining table. She assumed they would eat while they watched TV.

*Pulp Fiction* was playing. The scene where Samuel L. Jackson and John Travolta had to clean smattered brains from a car. Reesy watched the screen. After a second, she didn't feel so hungry anymore.

James came in with two plates and set them on the coffee table in front of her. He went back into the kitchen.

Reesy stared at her dinner. It was a big piece of kielbasa, scored and browned, smothered with onions. Beside it was a mound of white rice with a small pat of butter melting in the middle.

She wondered if him feeding her sausage was some sort of ghetto mind trick—foreshadowing of what he planned on stuffing her with later. The food smelled good, but it was not the cilantro-shrimp stir-fry she had envisioned.

James returned with two Heinekens and sat beside her.

"You drink beer?" he asked as he put one before her.

"Yeah."

"Cool."

He began to eat at once. Reesy was startled at his abruptness even though she had experienced this with him before. She bowed her head and said silent grace. She knew this was a time when she would most need divine protection.

Samuel L. Jackson was on TV complaining about being on brain detail.

"Perhaps we want to fast-forward from the gore since we're eating, you think?" she said.

James glanced at her, his mouth full of food. He swallowed, licked his fingers, and picked up the remote. He stopped the movie and turned to *Entertainment Tonight*.

Reesy was just biting into her sausage when she noticed a leggy brown roach creeping across the opposite wall. She put down the sausage and took a long swig of beer.

James leaned over and kissed her on the cheek, leaving a greasy spot where his lips had been.

Reesy picked at the rice to make it seem like she was eating. Her ring seemed brighter than ever.

She wondered what Dandre was doing.

James had her pinned on the sofa with her legs wide open and raised in the air. She had managed to elude his meal but there was no avoiding what he wanted to eat.

His face was buried between her thighs. Reesy's eyes were closed and her mouth was open. James was good, very good, but her thoughts were not in Watts. They were far, far away, in a brownstone on the Upper West Side, in the bed of the man she'd almost married. He used to do her like this, only better. This time around, the fucker's remorse was settling in before the act had even started.

There was a thunderous knock at the door. A banging sound that startled them both.

"James," a woman's voice screamed. "James. Open this damn door right now. I know you're in there. If I have to use my key, muthafucka, it's on."

Reesy scuttled away from him. James's face bore an expression of clear panic.

"Who the hell is that?" asked Reesy.

"Sssh," James said. "Don't say anything."

The woman pounded the door again.

"I hear the TV, James. I know you're in there. I can smell that damn sausage."

"James," Reesy whispered. "Who is that?"

"It's Ray," he said.

"The woman from the audition? Your associate producer?"

"Yeah."

"Is she your girl?"

"Well," he said, "we kinda live together. I didn't know she was going to be back so soo—"

Reesy pushed him out of the way and pulled on her clothes. The pounding at the door continued.

"James," the woman screamed.

"How can I get out of here without any beef?"

"Act like you just came by to pick up a script," he said.

"You know I don't give a fuck about a script, right? After this, I don't want shit to do with you."

"Fine, whatever," he said. "Just play it off for now. Ray is crazy. I never know if she's packing heat."

He got up and fastened his jeans, then rushed the plates and empty beer bottles to the kitchen.

Ray banged at the door. Reesy heard her put a key in the door.

James grabbed a script from beside the TV. He handed it to Reesy. She was standing there looking at the script when Ray walked in.

"How come you didn't open the damn door?" she asked.

James frowned at her.

"Because," he said, "I was trying to explain to her about the character, and how we plan on doing this, once we get the funding."

"You don't have the money to make this yet?" Reesy said. She shook her head. "I don't believe this."

"Now look what you've done, Ray," he said. "You're scaring her off. We're never gonna get this shit made if you keep bugging out like this."

"I'm out," Reesy said as she walked past a stupefied Ray.

"I'm sorry, baby," she heard the girl say to James.

Reesy slammed the door behind her and prayed that Black was still outside in one piece.

\*   \*   \*

It was 9:45 as she navigated the 110 South. She figured now was a good time to call her parents and tell them she had moved. After the scene she had just left, she found herself needing the anchoring of her father's voice.

She dialed from her cell phone. The call was answered on the very first ring.

"Hello."

It was her mother. Wide awake and very alert at forty-five minutes past midnight.

"Hi, Tyrene."

"Daughter," Tyrene said with undisguised relief. "Where are you? Your number at home is disconnected, and you haven't been answering your cellular phone."

"When did you call my cell phone?" Reesy asked.

"Tonight. Several times. I didn't leave messages."

"Well, there you go. I had it turned off, so there's no way I'd know you called."

"Where are you? Why is your home phone disconnected? Do you need money?"

"I moved, Tyrene."

"Oh, I see. Well, as long as you're safe."

"What?" Reesy would have never predicted her mother's response.

"Listen, Teresa, I've got a bit of a concern. Do you think there's any way that you can come home for a few days?"

"Why? Is there something wrong?"

"Well, I don't want to alarm you, but I think your father's gone crazy. He destroyed his office at work today and he's been downstairs locked up in the library. I can hear him in there pacing back and forth. He won't speak to any of us. Not Anushka, not me. The only person he halfway deals with is that ballplayer Trini. Maybe you can come and talk some sense into him."

"What happened?"

"I don't know. I think he's cracking up. He hasn't been right since we came back from New York."

Reesy's brow furrowed. Why was everything so insane? she wondered. She glanced up at the sky. A full moon peeked from behind the clouds.

That explains it, she thought.

"I'll see if I can get a flight out tomorrow," Reesy said.

"Thank you, daughter. We really need your help."

She was just pulling up to her house when her cell phone rang.

"Hello?"

"What's up, mami? I've been waiting to hear back from you to find out how that audition went. So what happened?"

"I got the part," she said, "but I don't want it."

"Why?"

"Because," she said, "it was bogus. They don't even have the money to make it."

"That's how folks get down in L.A. every day. Everybody's a producer. Everybody's got a film. Most of them don't have any money."

"You've done this kind of thing to someone before, haven't you?"

"It's a good hustle," he said. "A nice way to get ass. I've fucked mad hoes by telling them I'm a producer."

Reesy was silent.

"Uh-oh, mami. Did one of 'em give you a callback?"

"Yeah." Her voice was just above a whisper.

"Did you do him?"

"Yeah."

"Damn," he said.

She was sitting in the driveway with the engine off and her head leaned back against the seat.

"He lives in a broke-down apartment in Watts and I don't think he has a car." She paused. "I'm scared of this place. The rules are crazy."

"There are no rules," said Sleazy. "Perhaps you should think about giving your boy another chance."

"Where'd that come from?"

"I'm just saying. The odds of finding a good one out here are slimmer than slim. From what you said this morning, it sounds like what happened with y'all can be fixed."

"Well, that's not happening any time soon, if ever."

"Why is that?" he asked.

"Because," she said, "I'm going home to Florida tomorrow. Hey, do you think I can get you to watch the dogs?"

"Sure, mami."

"Great. I'll leave a key under the mat and let my landlord know that you'll be coming by."

"Okay."

"Just remember, Sleazy—don't let them out the front door or out of the yard without a leash. And if you give them access through the doggie door, make sure the garden gate that leads to the backyard is closed so they can't get out."

"I know, mami, I know."

"I know you know. I'm just making sure." She got out of the car. "They've got puppy chow, but I'll leave some money so you can get them some chicken."

"Chicken?"

"Yeah. They like those roasted hens they have at Ralph's. Be sure to give them the bones."

"Sure."

"And make sure they have lots of ice water, and get some cheese cubes. They love those things."

"Damn," Sleazy said. "Those little fuckers eat better than me."

"She's going to Fort Lauderdale."

"When?" Dandre asked.

"Tomorrow. Apparently there's some kind of drama with her

folks. She said she's going to see if she can leave first thing on whatever airline has a flight open."

Sleazy and Dandre were at the beach house. The twins had been packed up and moved out. There was nary a trace of them left.

Sleazy was on the couch. Dandre was pacing as he nursed a drink.

"Did she say how long she'd be gone?"

"No, she didn't."

Dandre kept pacing. He sipped his scotch.

"Mind if I light up?" Sleazy asked.

"Nah, man, do your thing."

Sleazy clipped his stogie and fired it. He took a few puffs, then exhaled the pungent smoke into the air. His two-way beeped. He grabbed it off the coffee table and checked it, typed something back, then put it down.

"I'm going down there," Dandre said.

Sleazy took another puff, then reached for his drink on the coffee table.

"How are you going to explain that?" he asked. "She's going to think you're stalking her. You've gotta handle this carefully. There's a fine line between loving somebody and freaking them the fuck out."

"I haven't approached her yet. The most I've done is put puppies on her doorstep. I haven't even been stressing her with calls. I know where she lives, but I haven't shown up on her unannounced."

He sat in one of the leather armchairs.

"So how are you going to explain it?" Sleazy asked.

"I'll figure that out when I get there. I know where her folks live. She and I were just there a couple of months ago."

Sleazy shrugged. "Do what you gotta do, man." His two-way went off again. He picked it up.

Dandre nodded and finished his drink. He watched the big

246

guy typing on the tiny box. He was relieved that wasn't his life anymore. Phone tag, two-ways, wild parties—the perpetual quest for the next piece of ass. He'd had his fill of that life. Watching Sleazy made his need to reconnect with Reesy seem even more urgent.

"So how'd she say her audition went?"

Sleazy puffed his cigar and shrugged again.

"She said it was wack. I don't think she's too keen on the way they do things out here."

Sleazy continued to puff his cigar. He blew smoke rings in between sipping his drink.

He was still surprised about Reesy's encounter with the producer, but he figured he'd keep it to himself. As far as Reesy and Dandre knew, they were both 0-and-0. Even though each had had sex with a stranger since his or her arrival in town, neither party was happy about it.

Don't ask, don't tell, Sleazy thought. That seemed to be the best route for him to go.

# Where My Dogs At

Hill was sitting in first class, headed back to D.C.

It was morning, just after ten, but he was already drinking the heavy stuff. He needed it. The scotch was necessary to help chase away what he was feeling for Tyrene.

They had spoken by phone before he left. He'd uttered the *L* word again.

"Would you stop it," she said, sitting in her office. "This is just an affair."

"I don't have affairs," had been his reply. "I've never been with a married woman. I've never had to."

"Then get over it. It's just sex."

"So you don't love me at all?" he asked.

"I don't know, Hill, I don't know. I like you a lot. I don't know what I feel. There's chaos in my house right now. My husband is on the rampage. He won't even speak to me. He didn't come into the office today. I'm only here for a few minutes, then I'm going back home."

"Do you think he knows about us?"

"He can't. I've done nothing to give him any indication that this is going on." She paused. "Was going on."

"What does that mean?"

"I have to go. I'll talk to you later this afternoon. On second thought, maybe not today. My daughter's on her way here."

"From California?"

"California? No. She was in the Poconos."

"Oh," Hill replied, confused. "Dandre said she moved to California. He went out there to get her to come back."

Tyrene exhaled a heavy breath, remembering Reesy's disconnected phone. She grabbed her forehead and closed her eyes.

"I can't take this," she said. "Everything in my life is falling apart."

I can't take it either, Hill thought as he sipped his drink. Something had to break in this dangerous liaison. He and Tyrene were volatile together, but good. He liked the powder-keg way they interacted. As for her relationship with her husband, it seemed to Hill that all she did was complain about Tyrone and his ways.

He reminded himself that they had been together for years. Perhaps that counted for something.

He wasn't sure. Outside of his late wife, the longest he had been with someone was four months, so his points of reference weren't very reliable.

"You did what?"

Dandre walked through terminal one at LAX, headed for the gate for his Southwest flight to Fort Lauderdale. According to Sleazy, Reesy had taken the prior flight. He wanted to make sure he didn't bump into her until they were in Fort Lauderdale.

He was talking on his cell as he looked for the gate.

"What made you do some mess like this? What were you thinking? You couldn't have been thinking."

"I was scared, man," Rick said. "I didn't want to lose her."

"Well, this seems like a surefire way to do it."

He got in line to get his boarding pass. Even though he had arrived an hour and twenty minutes before the scheduled departure, the line for boarding passes was already long.

"Why didn't you talk to me about this first?"

"I don't know," answered Rick. "I got so caught up in it that I really couldn't talk to anybody. I mean, I know it was wrong, but I felt like I was doing it for us."

"You were playing God is what you were doing." He dropped his carry-on bag at his side. "So now what?"

"Now I'm praying she doesn't leave me."

"Is that what she said?"

"At first. She said a bunch of things. We're going to go see somebody."

"For what? An abortion?"

"No," Rick said. "To talk about it. To talk about why I did this."

"A therapist?"

"Yeah."

"Whose idea was it to go?"

"Mine."

"At least you've got one functioning brain cell still left in your head."

"I'll do anything to save our marriage." Rick's voice was tinged with subdued panic. "I can't lose her. I don't want to end up like you and . . ."

Dandre pressed his lips together. Rick sat in silence on his end of the phone.

"See, Rick," Dandre said, his voice low and even, "the difference between you and me is, I've done nothing stupid since I've been with Reesy. I haven't sought trouble. If anything, trouble found me."

The older woman in line in front of him angled her head so that she could hear better.

"Let me ask you this, though. Did you say anything to Misty about Rejeana coming by my house?"

"Nah, man," Rick said. "I'd never tell her about that. And you shouldn't tell Reesy about it either. It's best to just keep it to yourself."

"You haven't learned anything, have you?" Dandre said. "I'm not going to lie to Reesy. Deception won't get us anywhere."

Rick didn't respond.

"I haven't done anything behind her back to ensure she'll stay," Dandre said. "I just wanted to make sure she was aware of my presence. And I've been tenacious. It's important to me to know that if she comes back, it's because she wants to be there, not because I rigged some situation that trapped her into it."

The woman turned at him and smiled.

"That's nice, young man."

Dandre gave her a courteous nod.

"I'm sorry, man," Rick said. "I didn't mean that the way it—"

"I know. But don't look at my situation as a disaster, because I don't. I just see it as a bump in the road. Take a lesson from it. If anything, be steadfast. Make Misty believe you realize what you did was stupid. Stop acting like you own her. She's not your property, man. You can't just play with her life like that."

The Southwest ticketing agents had arrived at the counter. The line began to move. Dandre picked up his bag.

"Just keep the faith, Rick. Everything ain't always as bad as it seems. Tomorrow's another day."

"What?"

Dandre laughed.

"I can't believe I just said that shit."

Reesy sat on the plane, staring out the window, tracing the outlines of the clouds with her finger.

The puppies had lain on the bed, groggy, watching her throw things into a bag. She'd put them in the kitchen but left the doggie door closed.

"Uncle Sleazy will be here soon to see you," she'd said. "He'll let you out. Be nice. I'll be back in a while."

It was still dark when she'd left the house. Dante let loose with his bitch scream when he heard Black's engine warming up. She'd cringed as she backed out of the driveway. The sound of the dog's cries ricocheted through the entire neighborhood.

She thought about Tyrone and Tyrene as she gazed out at the aquamarine sky. Her parents' relationship was tearing at the seams, perhaps already shredded to bits. It was evident the last time she spoke to the two of them together. Maybe what happened in New York had sent everyone reeling in directions for the worse.

She remembered Miss Flora's words: "Pay attention to your parents. They're going to be turning to you for a lot of emotional support real soon."

"I'll be damned if that woman wasn't right," she said to the window. The seat next to her was empty. The man in the row in front of her glanced at her between the seat.

She wondered if the other things Flora had said would prove true. She'd mentioned marriage and more children. Boys.

The ring on her finger glimmered in the sun.

Reesy imagined what it would be like having a family of her own. With Dandre. It was the first time she had allowed herself the luxury of thinking of being with him again. She missed him, she admitted in silence. She missed the way he held her, the way he listened, the way he made her laugh, the way he loved. She couldn't picture a better partner than him. They had seemed so perfect.

But then, she'd thought the same of Tyrone and Tyrene.

The image of Dandre in those pictures flashed across her mind. She squeezed her eyes closed.

No, she thought. No way. She couldn't leave herself vulnerable to that type of thing again. Romantic relationships were disastrous. They always fell apart. Her parents were proof. Misty was proof. Just when it seemed like things were safe, there Rick was, poking holes in their trust.

"You have a hard time trusting men," Miss Flora had said.

Once again, the woman was right.

\*   \*   \*

Tyrone sat in his leather armchair in the library. He was on his thirtieth cigarette. They were the only things keeping him from killing somebody.

Trini had taken the gun, and he had gotten all the equipment from him and returned it to the Spy Stop.

At least, Trini thought he had it all.

Tyrone still had the tap on Tyrene's phone at the office. He knew that it was Hill who had been with his wife. He'd heard their conversation when Hill was headed to the airport on his way back to Washington.

Tyrone was in a daze at he sat in the chair.

He heard the doorbell ring. Anushka would get it. It rang again.

He reached for another Newport and fired it up.


"Is Tyrone home? I see his car's here."

It was Cheri Pearson, the next-door neighbor.

Kaye and Cheri Pearson were a fun-loving, charismatic, successful couple—prominent fixtures in South Florida's social circuit. Kaye was the promoter of the Fort Lauderdale Boat Show, an annual high-profile extravaganza that featured numerous celebrities, glitterati, and an assortment of spectacular water vessels. The Snowdens' yacht was featured every year.

Cheri was a shrewd, pretty, vivacious blonde who had become a good friend to Tyrene, which was a feat in itself. She was the one white woman Tyrene allowed herself to trust. The two got together at least once a week for lunch or dinner at an area restaurant, or for a night spent chatting in one or the other's home.

"He's in, ma'am," Anushka said, "but he's unavailable at the moment."

"Okay. I just wanted to see if he and Tyrene were interested in attending—"

Tyrene's car pulled into the driveway.

"Never mind, Anushka," she said. "I'll just ask Tyrene. She's who I really needed to speak to anyway."

"Yes, ma'am."

Anushka disappeared inside, relieved not to be charged with having to speak to Tyrone.

Tyrene got out of the car and rushed over to Cheri.

"Have you seen him?" she asked in a harried tone, grabbing the surprised woman by the arm. "Did he snap at you too?"

Cheri gave her an comprehending stare.

"Did I see who, Tyrene? What are you talking about?"

"Oh Lord. I don't know what to do. I'm afraid to go in there."

"What's wrong?" Cheri asked. "Is there a problem with Tyrone?"

Tyrene was still holding on to Cheri's arm as she led her away from the house, down to the end of the driveway.

"He's been on edge since the thing with Teresa," she said, "but he's been a raving lunatic since yesterday afternoon."

"Do you think he's having a nervous breakdown?" Cheri asked. "She is your only child. Maybe her wedding plans falling through and losing the baby hit him as hard as it did her. He was so excited about it. Kaye said he'd never seen a father so proud."

"I don't know what it is," Tyrene said, shaking her yellow dome. "All I know is it's too much for me, Cheri. I've got so much on my head already."

She pulled her close and whispered, "I've been having an affair."

Cheri gasped. "Tyrene."

"I know, I know. I don't know how it happened. It started in New York. The guy doesn't live here, but he came into town yesterday to see me."

"Do you think that's what's wrong with Tyrone?" Cheri asked.

"No," Tyrene said with a wave of her hand. "He's completely clueless when it comes to that. Tyrone would never expect that of me. I didn't even expect it of me. I think he takes for granted that nobody else would want his feisty wife."

Cheri exhaled an enormous breath. This was a heavy burden for her.

"I don't know, Tyrene," she said. "Men are very intuitive when it comes to that kind of thing."

"Maybe, but not him. He's drifting. I can tell. He's smoking again and his behavior's erratic. I don't know what to do. I asked Reesy to come home."

"Are you going to tell her about the affair?"

"Of course not. I can't. Besides, there's no reason for it to come up." She nibbled at the tip of her well-manicured nail. "I think I'm going to cut it off."

"I think you should," Cheri said.

Tyrene studied the younger woman's face. Cheri seemed wise and centered, much wiser than she felt in that moment.

"So what should I do?" Tyrene asked.

"Just talk to him, Tyrene. He's your husband, after all. No matter whatever happens between you two, you've known him for years, probably longer and better than anybody else. Talk to him. He probably just needs a big hug and some reassurance."

Cheri held Tyrene's hands in hers. Tyrene's eyes were teary. Cheri pulled her into an encouraging embrace.

"It'll be okay," she said. "I'm right next door if you need anything. All you have to do is call me, okay?"

"Okay," Tyrene said, wiping a tear from her cheek.

Tyrone took a long drag of his cigarette as he watched the two women from the library window.

She's probably bragging to the neighbors, he thought. "Everybody knows she's making a fool of me."

Reesy took a cab to the house. She didn't bother to rent a car. She figured she could always use one of her parents' four vehicles.

She paid the driver and rushed to the door. She rang the bell, then used her key.

Tyrene was standing in the foyer when she came in.

"Daughter," she said, throwing her arms around Reesy as if they were the best of friends.

What manner of madness is this? Reesy thought.

She knocked on the door of the library.

"It's me, Daddy," she said.

She heard the lock click open. She let herself in.

The place was a nicotine fog. Reesy began coughing the instant she walked in.

"Tyrone," she said. "What are you doing? Are you trying to kill yourself?"

"Perhaps."

She went to him and threw her arms around his thick waist. While she had never been close to either of her parents, Reesy was always more empathetic to her father.

"Can we get some fresh air in here at least?" she asked. "This is awful. You can't do this to yourself."

She opened the French doors that led outside. The Florida humidity met the cigarette stench and made the room even more dank and miserable.

Tyrone sat in his leather chair. Reesy came over and sat at his feet. She leaned against his knee.

He put his hand on her head.

"I'm leaving your mother."

"What?" she cried as she pushed herself up from the floor. "Why? What happened? Tyrone, are you serious?"

"Sit down, or I'm not going to be able to get this out."

Reesy set back on the floor with reluctance.

It was a while before her father spoke again. He lit up another cigarette first. Reesy thought about stopping him, but from what she could see of the butts in the ashtray, she was already about thirty-five cigarettes too late.

"She's been cheating on me," he managed to say. "Right up under my nose, after all these years, she's been making a cuckold of me. Can you believe that, Teresa?"

Reesy's head was reeling. A cuckold? Her father was speaking in Elizabethan terms. Her mother must be right, she decided. He was losing his mind for sure. She wondered if he'd been drinking as much as he was smoking.

"Daddy, Tyrene's not cheating on you. Why would she? You give her everything she needs. She'll never find another man that lets her boss him the way you do."

Her attempt at being lighthearted failed. Tyrone erupted in a fit of tears, horrifying his daughter. She stood and ran behind the chair, throwing her arms around his neck.

"Tyrone, oh, don't do this. I can't take it. I've never, ever seen you cry."

The big man got up from the chair and marched around the room, trying to shake the tears off. He coughed and convulsed and sobbed in an awkward dance that made Reesy want to go clock her mother for bringing her father to such a state.

"You don't understand," he said. "The reason I locked myself up in here is to keep from killing her. If I stop smoking these cigarettes, she's a dead woman. It's the only thing that's keeping me calm. That's why I know I have to leave her. I can't stay. If I do, I'll end up in jail for the rest of my life. Or I'll just kill us both and put everybody out of their misery."

Reesy was shaking, unable to believe what she was hearing. Tyrone talking of killing Tyrene was too much. Although her mother could be pretty annoying, Reesy didn't believe she deserved to die.

"Tyrone, please. I really don't think Tyrene's been unfaithful. A lot has happened since the day I was supposed to get married."

She sat in his leather chair, watching him pace.

"Everybody's been going through changes. You took things a little hard. You were the only person who didn't vent that day. Maybe now it's just starting to come out."

Tyrone puffed and pulled on the cigarette with urgent apprehension.

"C'mon, Daddy, this is Tyrene you're talking about. Be realistic. This is probably all just some passion of the mind."

"Passion of the mind?" Tyrone bellowed. He pounded his fist on the library desk. A vase bounced off and shattered on the floor. "Passion of the mind? I'll tell you about a passion of the mind. I have proof. How's that for a passion of the mind?"

He stared down at her, his nostrils flaring with rage. Reesy was crying as she looked up at him. Tyrone almost said the words, but through his haze of wrath, he saw the dread of expectation in her eyes. He stopped himself.

He realized his daughter had experienced enough recent pain, and although things with him were a maelstrom of chaos, he had to protect her. He couldn't burden her further by telling her about the despicable father of the despicable man she almost married.

"I'm sorry, baby," he said, dropping to his knees before her. "I'm sorry, I'm sorry, I'm sorry. I'm so sorry."

He reached out, enfolding her in his arms.

"It's best that I leave," he said. "I don't want to hurt anybody. If your mother wants to be with someone else, I'm not going to hang around and watch her make a fool of me. I've done everything for her. I'm not going to stand for this."

He let go of her and stood. Reesy reeked of the smell of his cigarettes. He walked to the door.

"Where are you going?" she asked. "Are you at least planning to talk to Tyrene?"

"Can't do that," Tyrone said, clearing his throat. "We have nothing further to say. I'll send for my things later. Sela."

He opened the library door.

"Daddy?" she said, feeling once again like his little girl.

Tyrone didn't look back.

Dandre rented a car at the Avis counter and made his way toward the beach. The route to the Snowdens' house from the airport was not complicated. U.S. 1 South to Seventeenth Street Causeway, a right, then head in the direction of the beach. He didn't remember the exact name of the street they lived on, but he knew it by sight. He figured Reesy should be there by now. Whatever was going down with her parents, he wanted to be by her side to help.

Sleazy pulled up to the back house. He could hear the dogs as he got out of the car.

"Yeah, yeah, you little slap-happy rats. You know I'm coming with grub, don't you?"

He grabbed the bags from the car and walked to the front door. He lifted the mat and got the key, put it into the lock, and went inside.

Dante's wailing drowned out the minor yips from Harlem and Peanut.

"Goodness," he said.

He opened the kitchen door. They burst past him, almost knocking him over.

"Come back in here," he said. "I've got your food."

They raced back into the kitchen, leaping at the bags.

"Sit," he said, "or you're not getting anything."

The dogs lined up in a perfect row.

"Nice."

He took out one of the roasted hens and began tearing pieces off it to put in their bowl. He ate some first.

"Shit," he said to the dogs. "This is pretty damn good."

He shredded half of the chicken and put it into the bowl. He mixed the bones in and set it on the floor.

The puppies waited for his command.

"Good," he said. "I see I trained you well."

They didn't move as they eyed him and eyed the food.

"Go," he said.

They mobbed the bowl of chicken.

He watched them for a moment, then went over and uncovered the doggie door. He pulled at the doorknob to get out, but the side door was swollen shut again. He put his foot against it and pulled. It flew open under the pressure of his weight. He banged his back against the counter behind him.

He headed into the backyard. His two-way beeped. He removed it from the holster and checked. It was a promoter he worked with who booked comedy shows around the country. The message was urgent.

His cell phone was in the car. He looked at the side door that led to the kitchen, but didn't feel like struggling with it again. He went up the garden path to the gate that led to where the car was parked. He unlocked it and left it ajar as he got his cell phone. He sat in the driver's seat with the door open.

"Yo, T, what's up? It's Sleazy."

He listened as T told him about a major gig in Chicago that was paying ten grand if the man who was backing the event could speak with Sleazy, just to establish a comfort level. The job had boiled down to him and another comedian.

"I'm pushing for you," T said.

"Good lookin'-out, bro. I appreciate it."

"He's with me right now and we need to make a decision in the next five minutes about what we're going to do. He's already talked to the other dude, but I told him you're better at working a crowd."

Sleazy nodded as he listened.

"Cool."

"So I just need to know if you're down to do it, then I'll put him on the phone so he can get a feel for you."

The dogs ran past Sleazy as he said yes. It took a second for him to register what he'd just seen. He jumped out of the car, calling after them.

"Hey. Hey. Heyyyyyyyyyyyy."

"Who you talking to?" T asked.

"Oh . . . my . . . God," Sleazy said, watching the pack of dogs haul fur down the driveway, hit the sidewalk, take a right, then disappear.

"They're headed for Sepulveda. T, man, shit. Shit, shit, shit. I gotta go. I'm about to be in some deep-ass trouble."

He clicked the phone off and stuffed it in his pocket as he ran toward the street in search of the pups.

Tyrone's Mercedes passed Dandre's rental car, but neither man noticed the other. Dandre slowed as he neared the house. He pulled into the driveway and got out of the car.

"What do you mean, you couldn't stop him?" Tyrene asked. "You were supposed to help. At least he was still living here. Did you tell him to leave? That didn't enter his mind until you went in there to talk to him."

"Are you having an affair?"

Reesy studied her mother's face for a sign of something that would make everything make sense. Tyrene's cheek twitched.

"What did you ask me?"

"Are you having an affair?"

Misty must have gotten to her, Tyrene decided. Well, she thought, I'll just deny, deny, deny.

"No, I'm not."

"Daddy says you are. He says he has proof."

Tyrene's heart skipped.

"He told you that?" she asked, her voice shaky. "Oh Lord," she said, looking around, as if expecting to be arrested. "So he knows. He knows about me and Hill."

Before Reesy could react to the sucker punch of her mother's words, her cell phone rang. She looked at the number. It was Sleazy. She had to take the call.

She held a finger up for her mother to wait. She pressed the "talk" button. "Hello."

Tyrene saw her chance and took off in a mad dash upstairs. She locked herself in the master bedroom.

The doorbell rang at the same time. Reesy walked to it as she talked on the phone.

"Reesy." The voice on the phone was several octaves higher than its natural pitch.

"What's up, Sleazy?" Reesy said. "Can I call you back? I'm kind of in a moment."

She opened the front door. Dandre was standing on the step. Sleazy spoke before she had a chance to react.

"I lost your dogs," he said in a panic.

"What?" she screamed, staring into Dandre's eyes.

"I'll call you back." Sleazy sounded as hysterical as she felt. "I'm trying to find them now."

He hung up without saying good-bye. Reesy stood on the doorstep, unable to speak. She was overwhelmed with too many emotions at once. She was trembling. Dandre could tell something awful had just transpired. He reached out for her. She fell into his arms and began to sob.

It took him more than twenty minutes to calm Reesy down.

They were on the couch in the family room. Anushka had prepared dinner and put it in the fridge. She made tea before she left. It was sitting on the coffee table in front of them.

Reesy couldn't drink it. She was much too upset.

She cried for her father, out there driving around somewhere, feeling betrayed by a woman he had trusted for most of his life. She cried for her mother for not being woman enough to admit she was as wrong as he was. She cried for the puppies as she imagined them lost and helpless, wandering up and down the streets. Or worse.

She cried for herself, in Dandre's arms, relieved to see him, but confused and frightened. She wanted to be happy, but she was feeling too many things to be able to separate that emotion from the rest. She wanted to be angry at him for showing up at her home—how did he know she was there?—but she wasn't. She needed him. She needed the strength of his arms to shield her from all the pandemonium whirling around her.

Her cell phone rang. It was Sleazy. She handed the phone to Dandre. She was much too shaky to try to speak.

"Hello."

"Hey . . ." Sleazy started, confused. "Is this . . . is this Dandre?"

"Yeah, man. What's up with the dogs?"

"I got 'em," Sleazy said, his breath coming fast. "They were halfway to Hermosa, but I caught up with 'em. Some people pulled over and helped me."

"Thank God," Dandre said.

Reesy glanced up at him, her eyes drenched.

"Are they okay?" she asked.

"They're fine," he said.

She collapsed onto his chest and cried fresh tears of relief.

Thirty minutes later and she was still in his arms.

Dandre held her without any pressure. She rested her head against his chest, her arms around his waist. Neither said a word about being with each other. Tyrene was still upstairs, locked in her room.

"Our parents are fucking," Reesy said into his chest.

"What?"

She didn't look up.

"Tyrene and your father have been having an affair."

He put his finger under her chin and lifted her face. Her eyes met his.

"Are you shitting me?"

"No."

"Is that what's going on here?"

"Apparently."

He leaned back against the couch.

"Oh my God," he said under his breath.

"Exactly," Reesy said under hers.

Tyrene was in her bedroom, facedown on the bed, crying. Her life was over, as far as she knew it. She didn't think she could show her face in town again.

She forced herself to sit up. She walked to the sink in the vanity area and turned on the faucet. She splashed cold water on her face, then looked up at herself in the mirror.

"Buck up, woman," she said. "When the going gets tough . . ."

Her eyes were red and puffy and her face was flushed. She was in great shape, but the fact remained that she was almost sixty. She wondered what had come over her to make her behave the way she had. It was too late for her to be destroying everything she had worked so hard to build.

"Who'll want me?" she asked her reflection. "I don't know how to be alone."

Her reflection seemed to answer her back.

Tyrene took a few deep breaths, then walked over to the phone. She dialed the number and prayed for an answer.

"Hello?"

"Hi," she said.

There was a pause.

"I didn't think you were going to call."

"Well, I did. Do you still want me?" she asked.

"Of course."

"Then I'm coming tonight," was all she said.

Reesy and Dandre were still holding each other when Tyrene came down the stairs with a bag. She walked into the family room. She gasped when she saw Dandre.

"What are you doing here?" she asked.

"I came to make sure Reesy was okay," he said.

He waited for her to attack him, but she didn't. Tyrene wasn't in a position to throw stones at anyone, and all three of them knew it.

"Where are you going with that bag?" Reesy asked. "Have you talked to Tyrone? Are you going to him?"

"I'm going to Washington," Tyrene said in a calm tone.

"What?" Reesy said, standing. "Are you out of your mind?" She walked over to her mother. "You're not leaving here. This is insane. You and Tyrone have both gone mad."

"I'm leaving, Teresa. Your father left me, so I'm going too."

Dandre's head was in his hands. He wondered what his father was thinking. Hill hadn't mentioned a word of this to him.

"What about the firm?" asked Reesy. "The two of you just can't abandon everything."

"Don't worry," she said. "We'll sort that out. I'll talk to the partners. Everything will be fine." Tyrene was amazed by her own composure.

"So you're going . . . just like that."

"Yes. I'll be back in a few days."

"Well, I won't be here," Reesy replied. "This is madness. I'm going back to California."

"Yes," Tyrene said, her lips pursed together. "Thank you for letting me know you had moved."

"Thank you for letting me know you were an adulteress," Reesy said.

Tyrene slapped her.

Reesy slapped her back.

Dandre rushed over and stood between the two women.

"This isn't solving anything," he said. "You both are upset. Why don't we all just calm down."

The doorbell rang.

"That's my car," Tyrene said. She went to the coat closet and slipped on her mink. She picked up her bag and stood with her hand on the doorknob.

"You know where to reach me," she said.

Reesy turned her back to Tyrene so she wouldn't have to watch her leave.

"Well then," said Tyrene.

She opened the door and walked out. It was cool outside, but some of the Florida humidity still managed to seep in.

Reesy and Dandre were back on the couch. She was leaning into the crook of his arm.

"You should eat something," he said.

"I can't."

He rubbed her head, his fingers dancing through her short-cropped curls.

"It'll be okay, Reesy," he said. "I don't know how, but everything is going to be okay."

"How do you know that? Everything is fucked up. Rick and Misty, Tyrone and Tyrene, me and—"

He put his finger on her lips.

"We're not fucked up. We just had a situation. Nothing about how I feel has changed. Nothing."

"What about that woman? I saw her at your house."

"What woman?" he asked, nervous. He didn't want to confess anything if it wasn't necessary. "What are you talking about?"

Reesy pushed away from him.

"See what I'm saying? You still can't be honest with me, so what's the point."

He pulled her back. He took a deep breath and looked her in the eye.

"Rejeana came to my house after you got out of the hospital."

"Who's Rejeana?"

"Nobody. Well, I mean, not that she's a nobody, she's just nobody to me. She's a girl I used to mess around with back in the day. I hadn't seen her in a couple of years."

Reesy shook her head, trying to figure out a way to get her emotions to disengage.

"I was wrong," Dandre said, sensing her withdrawal. "I didn't handle that situation right when I broke things off, and it never did sit well with her. Rejeana was always dramatic and I knew that about her, but I strung her along anyway. I kept her around knowing I didn't have any intentions of ever getting with her."

Reesy stared at him, wondering why she was having such a hard time hitting the emotional ejector switch.

"I was a different man then. I'm not too proud of some of the things I did."

She blinked back any tears that threatened to erupt, relieved to know that there was no way they could ever go on.

"I was right," she said. "See, you and me, we can't work. Nothing lasts, nothing works. People lie. People hurt each other. Tyrone and Tyrene have been together for decades and look at them."

"We're not Tyrone and Tyrene."

"And Misty and Rick. He was punching holes in the condoms."

"And they're seeing a therapist to work things out."

Reesy shook her head.

"It can't work, Dandre," she said, moving away. "It doesn't matter how much I love you. It doesn't matter how much you love me."

"But you do love me," he replied, pulling her close, his voice a whisper. "Everything else can be worked out."

"No. It can't. There's no such thing as a perfect relationship. I thought my parents had it, and I was wrong."

He turned so that his whole body was facing her.

"Is that what you wanted? Perfection from me? Because I can't give you that," he said. "I would never try to."

Her eyes filled up.

"All I can do is love you, Reesy. Be there for you, be your friend when you need me, and even when you don't realize you need me. But I'm not perfect. I'm just a man."

"I can't trust you," she said.

"You can try. And you can be there for me when I'm feeling weak. I don't want anybody else, but the world is rough. People are always trying to break couples down. We have to fight for our relationship, not just walk out on it."

She listened, searching his eyes for game.

"I don't want to do what Tyrone and Tyrene just did," he said. "I can't just walk away. I want to know that you'll come after me if I do. That's what you did before. And when you left me, I came after you. That's how you fight for each other. You don't just quit."

He was right. The time that he'd found her naked with Helmut, he did run away. But she was persistent and did everything she could to make him believe that she cared, even when it was too painful for him to listen.

She took a deep breath, turning over his words.

"Reesy, listen to me," he said. He reached out and touched her hair. "We don't have to be perfect people. We can't be. I mean, maybe what we need to learn out of all this is the fact that we're imperfect to begin with, and we work from there."

He outlined her face with his finger. She leaned into his palm.

"You're still wearing your ring," he said.

"Yeah," Reesy replied in a soft voice. She held up her finger. "I can't get it off."

"It's never coming off. It's not supposed to."

He leaned forward and kissed her, his lips gentle and light against hers.

"I didn't get a chance to say how much I love what you've done to your hair. It's beautiful. You're beautiful." He grabbed the back of her head and pulled her mouth to his.

She didn't resist when he pressed her down into the couch. He kissed her eyes, her nose, the point of her chin. His lips trailed down the curve of her neck to the tops of her breasts.

"I love you," he said.

"I love you too."

# PART 4

---

*Redux*

# Lord of the Ring

"So you sure you're ready to do this?" he asked.

They were back on Southwest, high in the sky, headed to their side of the world.

"I'm sure," she said. "But I'm scared. I'd be lying if I said I wasn't scared."

"Why don't we call your boy Sleazy," Dandre said.

Reesy looked at him with surprise.

"So you know we're friends."

"Yeah. He's a good guy. He was really looking out for you."

Reesy laughed.

"So now I get it. He's the one who told you about me going to Lauderdale." She shook her head. "That dirty dog. He never said a word."

"He told me if I fucked you over, he was gonna beat me down like a two-dollar crackhead. So I guess I had to do right by you."

"He said that?"

"Yup."

She lifted the armrest and leaned back against him.

"We should call him and tell him. I need to see if everything's okay with the dogs anyway."

"Raise up so I can get my wallet," he said.

She leaned forward. He took it from his back pocket, then pulled her back against his chest. He took a credit card from his wallet, then reached for the phone. He swiped the credit card through it.

"Here, baby," he said. "Dial the number, then hand it to me."

Reesy punched buttons and waited a while. She thought it was going to roll over to voice mail.

"Who dis?" Sleazy said after the third ring.

She handed Dandre the phone.

"What's up, man. It's Dandre."

"Hey, hey, what's crackalatin', nukka? I see you hooked up with your girl. I was surprised when you answered her phone."

"Yeah," Dandre said. "How the pups doing?"

"They're good, man. Those rats scared the shit outta me. I almost had an aneurysm when I thought I'd lost 'em."

"So did Reesy."

"I'm sure. Shit, I already got three kids. I don't need three more."

"You've got three kids?" Dandre said with a laugh.

"Yeah, man. But that's another story. Come check out my act and you'll hear all about it."

Reesy waited for Dandre to drop the bomb.

"So check this out," he said. "Speaking of acts, you think you could watch the dogs for a couple extra days?"

"Sure, man. Things must be working out for you two."

"Kinda." Dandre paused. "We're on our way to Vegas."

Sleazy was silent.

"Hello?" Dandre said. "Hello, hello?"

Reesy took the phone from him.

"Sleazy? Sleazy, are you there?"

"Are y'all doing what I think you are?" he asked in a whisper.

"Depends on what you think we're doing," Reesy said.

"Y'all are about to do the damn thang."

"And just what would the damn thang be, Sleaze? Be specific."

She glanced up at Dandre. He was smiling.

"You marrying this nigga?"

Dandre took the phone.

"Quit harassing my about-to-be wife."

"Damn," Sleazy said. "Kudos, man, kudos. Y'all are better than me. Congrats."

"Thank you. We'll give you a call once we've done the deed."

He put the phone back in its slot. Reesy stared at him with a twinkle in her eye. He wrapped his arms around her and held on tight.

"So what do you think our parents are doing?" she asked.

"Let's not think about them right now," he said. "They've had a lifetime of choices and actions and shit. This is our time. For one whole day, let's just think about us."

"We'll think about them tomorrow?"

"Yeah, tomorrow. Tomorrow's another day."

Reesy laughed.

He glanced out the window at the city in the desert.

"Vegas, baby," he said.

She leaned over and looked out.

"Yeah. Vegas, baby. Vegas."


When morning broke through the window of their spacious room at the Bellagio, Dandre was making love to his wife.

She looked up into her husband's face.

Tomorrow had finally come.

## About the Author

LOLITA FILES is the bestselling author of five novels: *Scenes from a Sistah, Getting to the Good Part, Blind Ambitions, Child of God,* and *Tastes Like Chicken.* She lives in Los Angeles, where she is currently developing projects for film and television.